THE PLUMBER OF
SOULS

THE PLUMBER OF

SOULS

MICHAEL GUINZBURG

CARROLL & GRAF PUBLISHERS
NEW YORK

PLUMBER OF SOULS

Carroll & Graf Publishers
An Imprint of Avalon Publishing Group Inc.
245 West 17th Street
New York, NY 10011

Library of Congress Cataloging-in-Publication Data is available.

ISBN: 0-7867-1323-2

Printed in the United States of America
Interior design by Jennifer Steffey
Distributed by Publishers Group West

TABLE OF CONTENTS

THE PLUMBER OF

SOULS

THE MILLIONTH PASSENGER

I AM NOT A HANDSOME MAN. I am not an ugly man. I am somewhere in the middle. When I was young my mother often told me, "You're no movie star, sonny, but then again you're no circus freak. You fall somewhere between Alain Delon and Jo-Jo the Dog-Faced Boy." Thank you very much, Mother, for that lasting vote of confidence. And then Mother would sigh, guzzle some wine, stare pensively into my eyes and sing me her blues: about her first love, her second love, her true love, about her first menstrual period, her father's roving hands, the butcher's gifts of pork chops and kisses, about making love to Uncle Claude in the barn. Her fears, her hopes, her bunions, her secret recipe for Andouillette: everything. Ambitions, disappointments, nightmares, fantasies. You name it, she told it. And afterwards, no matter how personal the revelation, she would feel no guilt. She would kiss me and hug me and whistle a happy tune, she would sleep peaceful and dreamless as a rock, her soul light as a mote of dust waltzing in the sunlight. I was better than a priest, she'd say, much, much better, for my eyes did not judge, they did not condemn before absolving the sin. My eyes absorbed all the pain.

1

Mine is a sad face, an open face, a face that looks as if it has been on the receiving end of much punishment and misery from the Fates. Yet it is a face without the least trace of bitterness. Innocence, sweetness, melancholy—but no bitterness. An uncomplaining face. A forgettable face. Yes, there is something about my face that inspires trust, and without even trying I am able to milk the deepest secrets from absolute strangers. A plumber of souls, that's what I am, a human enema. I flush emotional waste from the system.

To look at me is to trust me. Old ladies smile: the wrinkles smooth, the eyes twinkle, the heart goes light, and the years melt away. Granite-eyed gangsters go soft: the tough facade crumbles, the violence evaporates, the macho slinks off into the sunset. Hardhearted businessmen and disappointed housewives sign over their cares to my keeping. Yes, I am better than whiskey, more relaxing than Valium, I am a giant shot of truth serum that allows the honesty to flow like honey wine. Look at me—be it on a bus, on a train, on a plane—and you will suddenly feel a blessed blanket of fatigue draped over your shoulders, your legs will turn to jelly, your feet will stop stepping, you will pause . . . you will beg my pardon and ask if this seat is taken. I tell you, you will come to me. And I will look up from my paperback, my sweet, sad, almost-ugly face open and inviting, I guarantee you I will, and I will shake my head and say, "No, please sit," and you will sit. You will sigh and I will shut my book. I will smile and you will smile. Polite smiles: my smile will be comforting, your smile will be comfortable. You will feel warm and safe, relaxed, as if you've slipped into a fragrant bubble bath. . . . And then you will sigh again, a huge release, like a punctured bicycle tire gasping flat, and whether you want to or not you will tell me things, things you would not tell your spouse, your priest, your best friend, or your lover. You will look at me and you will think, "This is a man who would not hurt a fly, a man who has known much sadness, who has sung the blues so often in his life that if I sing him my blues, he will hear them, accept them, not judge me, he will shake his head in commiseration, and then he will forget my blues and go back to his blues. . . . Yes, I must tell this good, sad-faced man my story. . . ."

✠   ✠   ✠

"Is this seat taken?" asked the well-dressed man clutching a briefcase, on the night flight from Toulouse to Milan.

"No," I said, smiling. "Please sit."

"Thanks," said the man, sitting next to me and sighing like a laborer unburdening himself of a load of bricks. "My assigned seat is back there, but I prefer to sit near the exit on a plane."

"Most people do," I said, drawing him further into the warm web of my comfort zone. "But this plane is a fine plane. She is like a young strong pregnant mother eagle from a very good family. Flying is her joy, her job, her duty, her destiny, and we, the passengers, we are her eaglets-to-be, her little loved ones. She will protect us with all the skill and heart and pride in her being and she will not descend until we are safe. She will not lay us, so to speak, until we arrive at the feathered nest, which in this case is Milan."

The man laughed, an open, unforced laugh, already he was relaxing; and then he sighed again, smiled shyly, and said:

"I see you are reading a mystery."

"Yes," I said, shutting my book and smiling. "I have figured it out already."

"But you have only started reading."

I smiled and nodded and buckled my seat belt, shrugged as if to say, "These writers cannot surprise me." And it's true, writers do not surprise me. Not in their writing, not in their personal confidences. Why, once I met a writer on a train, an American in the film business, he was, and without any prompting he poured me a complicated story about his torrid love affair with a female spider monkey, love at first sight, it was, how he kidnapped her from the San Diego Zoo and installed her in his Beverly Hills home, dressed her in his wife's negligees, he couldn't help himself, how his wife left him, how the monkey watched daytime television and fell into a depression. . . . As Hollywood love stories go it was really relatively tame. . . . Ah, but I digress.

The well-dressed man clutched his briefcase, buckled his seat belt. His eyes wandered to the pretty stewardess as she bent over a passenger two rows up from us. His eyes drank in her ripe plump curves, legs and buttocks well-muscled from countless hours walking up and down the aisle, bending over. He sighed again, licked his lips nervously. I smiled at him. Relax, my friend, relax. Relax and tell me all.

"A drink?" asked the well-dressed man.

"Yes," I said. "That would be fine."

When the plane was airborne, and after our drinks arrived, served with a bend and a smile, when he had sipped and sighed and sipped and sighed and sighed and sipped and sighed some more, he told me his story:

4

Once upon a recent time, in a town that shall go nameless here, there lived a man and his wife and daughter. He was not a happy man, though on first glance one might have assumed he was. After all, he was a prominent member of the local community, a pillar as they say, a respected successful businessman of forty-seven years, the president of one of the nation's top producers of paté de foie gras. The man's name was Leon.

Yes, on the surface it seemed that Leon had everything a man could possibly want. He had a lovely thin wife whose name was Simone. He had a pert pretty daughter whose name was Marie-Laure. He had a Mercedes Benz, a Land Rover, and a Peugeot. He had health, wealth, the respect of his neighbors, the jealousy of his competitors, a fine home, a business which, despite the recent national trend toward vegetarianism and healthy eating, showed every indication of solidity, even growth, and to top it all off he had, installed in Milan, a young acrobatic mistress of South American extraction with stupendous breasts named Maritza. Oh yes, his doctor had warned him to drink less whiskey and more wine (aside from the health benefits, the doctor had pronounced that drinking wine was his patriotic duty), had said the blood pressure was a bit high, the weight a bit much, the prostate a bit swollen, nothing to worry about yet really, that he must take more exercise, "and I'm not talking about the horizontal variety, Leon, you old goat," but really, despite those minor tingles of mortality, everything, it would seem to a casual observer, was going like a happy script: Leon's life was perfect. Okay, there was that minor flare-up with Simone a year back after he'd met Maritza and asked for a divorce (which she'd laughingly refused), but since then they'd gotten along fine: he made sure to buy her jewelry and she made sure to spend his money. They even had occasional marital relations. Not the worst arrangement, really, after twenty years of the old ball and chain. Things were pretty damned okeydokey. What more could a man desire? What, indeed? A son, perhaps? A grandson? An heir? Hmmm. That's what a normal mind would think.

Enter David, on a motorcycle. David was twenty-two, fresh from a second-rate university, traveling around the region taking pictures of churches and church steeples for a book he hoped to have published in Milan.

David was tall. David was handsome. David had broad shoulders, thin hips, large green eyes and a sensuous, slightly cruel mouth. And David had a strange, almost communistic effect on the female of the species: when first setting eyes on him, women of all ages were suddenly struck by the overwhelming urge to give up their possessions, most notably their panties. He was that kind of handsome. And he knew it.

Add to all that the fact that David was an orphan who had grown up in a series of church orphanages, and voila: instant romantic figure. Attractive, mysterious, serious, dark, charming, dressed in black jeans and boots and a white T-shirt, possessed of a black motorcycle and obsessed with taking photographs of churches and church steeples (he had a briefcase full of pictures of churches and church steeples, and the fringed leather saddlebags on his motorcycle were fat with cameras and developing chemicals), David was welcomed with open arms and many hallelujahs at the parish of ——. They gave him the cottage out behind the rectory for as long as he wanted. The cottage by the apple orchard. The cottage where Cardinal —— had slept! The bed where the Cardinal had. . . . Ahh, he was a fine man, the late Cardinal was, a good friend of the Pope.

Yes, to Father Bernard and the nuns and to the good citizens of the sleepy little town of ——, David was a breath of fresh air, a poetic figure, an artist. Yes, an artist. And not just any artist, as Father Bernard explained to the nuns shortly after David had retired to the cottage that first night, his flat hard belly full of hot soup and cold mutton and his ears still ringing with heartfelt "God bless you's." Not your run-of-the-mill money-hungry young painter or writer or silly actor, types as common as dung beetles in these difficult times of fragile faith, no, David was an artist concerned with questions of the spirit. Witness: his interest in churches and church steeples. Most admirable in one so young, so young and poor, an orphan no less, one with only the clothes on his back, the motorcycle between his legs, the camera slung around his neck and the briefcase full of photographs of churches and church steeples. Yes, an artist, said Father Bernard, an artist and a poetic figure. And like any poetic figure worth his salt, Father Bernard decided, David needed a job.

So one fine sparkling day, when the air was so clear and fresh that even the dying in the local nursing homes were filled with hope, not long after David had arrived and impressed everyone with his politeness and good looks and his pictures of churches and church steeples, when he had become a familiar figure in town with his camera and his tight black jeans and his powerful black motorcycle, Father Bernard read in the classified section of the local paper that Leon's company required a photographer to help create a new catalog. So he called his parishioner Leon to recommend David, then sent David to meet Leon.

David drove his motorcycle into the farm compound. The motorcycle, like David's camera equipment, had been bought with money David earned taking pictures of university girls who dreamed of one day becoming fashion models.

David's eyes missed nothing: the three cars parked in front of the comfortable home, the many workers bustling about, the storehouse piled high with sacks of corn, the enclosed areas packed with thousands of geese, the shuttered barns jammed with penned geese being fattened for the kill, the slaughter-house and cookhouse and canning house and the large trucks being loaded with cases of paté de foie gras destined for the alimentary canals of gourmets the world over.

David's nose wrinkled with disgust at the smell of gooseshit. The night before it had rained heavily, and the odor of goose-shit and wet feathers was overpowering. The fat geese (so many of them!) were jammed into wire cages in the dim barns, teams of ten sitting in their own waste, squawking unhappily, fat and flightless, their thin legs folded underneath them like boiled spaghetti, their feathers caked with gooseshit, their livers swelling. Their angry eyes said it all: they were miserable. Trapped. Eating and shitting, eating and shitting, waiting for the inevitable. . . . The endless cycle of all damned flesh. Poor pitiful beasts, David thought. Castrated by circumstance, they've forgotten they are birds. I will never forget what I am, he said to himself with an inner smile, reaching into his pocket and feeling his pride and joy: a bird of prey.

In the office he opened his briefcase and showed Leon his pictures of churches and church steeples.

"I am especially fascinated by the steeples of churches," David explained with his earnest church-orphan charm as the goosemaster gobbled an afternoon snack of thinly sliced fresh foie gras, washing it down with a glass of local marc. "It's as if the church, the body of man, were stretching his arms into the sky, his fingers trying to grasp God's feet so that he can pull himself to heaven."

Leon grunted, barely looking at the pictures or acknowledging the ridiculous stream of crap flowing from the young fellow's handsome mouth. He was more interested in David's face. The animation, the seductiveness. Was I like that once? Yes, he is me twenty-five years ago. Yet to be bludgeoned by responsibility, yet to have his dreams dashed on the rocks of reality. He is young and full of fire. He'll find out the score soon enough, the hopeless idealist. The wandering orphan with his insipid pictures of churches and church steeples . . . an orphan, hmmm. No family? He's perfect!

"What are you doing for dinner tonight?" Leon asked.

"Nothing special. I usually eat with the nuns and priests and poor little orphans who remind me so much of myself at that age . . . or I grab a croque-monsieur at a place in town."

"Nonsense, my boy," Leon said. "Tonight you will eat with us. A good home-cooked meal. We'll strap the feed bag on you and put a little meat on your bones."

"Monsieur . . ."

"Call me Leon."

"Monsieur Leon."

"Just Leon."

"Okay, Leon. About the job . . . ?"

"Four thousand francs," said Leon, doubling the amount he'd been prepared to offer any other shutterbug. "And expenses. You start tomorrow. I'll tell you more about it at dinner. My wife will be very happy to meet you, and our daughter too, I'm sure."

✢　　✢　　✢

Said Leon to David as they drank a Pacherenc and wandered about the farm before dinner:

"You must make the geese look happy."

"I will make them look like the happiest geese in France."

"Good man! You see, this new catalog will be printed not only in Spanish and Italian and Russian, as it has for a few years now, but also in English. We are at present engaged in a holy war with Israel for the United States foie gras market, so it is very important that we please the Americans. They are completely obsessed with the idea of animal cruelty."

Near a little pond with lily pads they passed a farm worker walking ten geese on leashes. The fat geese stretched their weak, atrophied wings, waddled clumsily, stumbled into one another, snarling angrily like drunken football fans.

"I have started the geese on an exercise program, as you can see. You must take pictures of François walking the geese to show the Americans that the geese are treated well."

Leon gave a medium-hard kick to a goose who had waddled into his path. The goose achieved a three-foot flight, as close as it would ever get to the clouds.

David nodded. Make the geese look happy. Fat, happy geese. Being stuffed with grain, grain shoved down their throats until their livers swell to the size of goiters or a baby's head or a circus giant's shoe. That's some kind of happiness. Like Martine, the would-be model back in ——. She'd never make it. Her ass was too big, her nose too big, her breasts too big, her appetite for cheeseburgers and sex: too damn big. "Oh David! David!" Her breath stinking of McDonald's and fellatio. "More more more!"

David was sick of women, their needs, their neuroses, their insatiable needs and incomprehensible neuroses. How they liked to mother him, mother him after fucking him. Why did they insist on that? The mothering? David wanted to photograph them, for sure, fuck them once or twice, okay, then be done with them, move on to the next. He couldn't stand that mother-hen nesting business.

Simone, wife of Leon, was lovely. Just forty, she was trim and well-dressed. She shopped in the finest shops and pampered her body at the finest spas. To David she appeared fairly content, comfortable, but underneath the veneer of strained jolliness and gentrified sophistication, he could tell she was hungry, desperate. The gleam in her eye. A crotch-watcher, an ass-checker, stuck in this jerkwater town like a gazelle in quicksand, she did everything except drool. And the daughter, Marie-Laure: oh, yummy! Too short to be a model, but trim, with clean lines, flexible as a Ukrainian gymnast, with short blonde hair cut like a boy's, nubile, nineteen years old and ready to be licked, a human ice-cream cone, sweet and fresh and tasty, no harmful additives. What a cute little butt on her! Pure clean fun! And he could tell she liked him too. She'd barely said two words all evening, as if her tongue was stuck to the roof of her mouth with a thick glue of lust. Like her mother, she'd hardly touched her foie gras, only nibbled at her goose and asparagus, sipped politely at the wine, yet he kept catching her looking at him out of the corners of her dark-blue peepers, a little bit close together for true beauty, those eyes, but good for sneaking glances. And her nipples, stiff and proud as little soldiers on parade. Yes, this was going to be fun, loads of fun.

And when David, at fat, red-faced Leon's prompting, told mother and daughter about his life in church orphanages, his life among the nuns and priests, his university studies, his interest in photographing churches and church steeples, his theory that church steeples were the hands of man reaching for the feet of God, how he intended soon to publish a book of his pictures in Milan, about the lovely little cottage Father Bernard had given him for as long as he wanted—you know, the one behind the rectory, nestled in the trees where the apple orchard starts—he could see twin headlights of desire and decision gleam from both women's eyes. Yes, he thought, this will be a fun summer, a summer to remember.

And so it came to pass in the quiet little town of —— that even before the first goose was photographed, David had slept with both mother and daughter. He knew it was going to happen. They knew it was going to happen. Perhaps even Leon knew it was going to happen. . . . Perhaps Leon didn't care.

"No photos today," said Leon, the morning after that first dinner. "I just want you to get a feel for the geese, their lives, the life of the farm, the aura of class we impart to them."

"I understand," said David, stepping around a slick of fresh gooseshit.

"Don't be shy with the shit, my boy," Leon said, clapping a meaty hand to David's shoulder, stopping him. Leon leaned over and scooped the gooseshit up, rubbed it in his fingers, then shoved the grainy gray-green greasy stinking stuff beneath David's nose. "Smell it, boy! The finest gooseshit in France!"

"It certainly is fragrant," David said politely.

"I'll take it over Guerlain any day," said Leon with a hearty laugh, wiping his fingers on his pants. "The local horticultural society buys all our gooseshit at a very good price. They say, properly composted the roses thrive on it."

And so it went. David learned the goose business, the business of geese and gooseshit, how the goose didn't have to lay a golden egg to be worth its weight in gold. The goose was the golden egg, a real moneymaker. From paté to goosefeather parkas and pillows to Christmas goose dinners to gooseshit on roses. And David was smart enough to recognize a good thing when he saw it.

Only one thing bothered him: why was Leon doing this? He didn't need to write an encyclopedia about geese and gooseshit to take some crummy publicity shots, to make the bloated, miserable geese appear as joyous as jet-setters frolicking on the Côte D'Azur, instead of tortured martyrs to the foie gras—loving palates of the consumer world. That was the easy part, like making pictures of would-be models, lighting the shot just so, so that the mousy brown eyes seemed mysterious, the pimples were invisible, the fat-rippled thighs looked sleek and slim as a dancing nymph's. The fiction of

happy geese would be easy after some of the girls he'd photographed. No, it must be that Leon had a plan for him. Fat
disgusting Leon who picked his nose with his gooseshit fingers
had a plan for him. Yes, David thought that evening before
dinner, splashing in the bathtub where Cardinal ——— had
lathered his shriveled ecclesiastical balls for the last time, as
he happily scrubbed the stink of goose from his hard body,
blowing the goosey snot from his nose, the man is lonely. He
wants a son-in-law. The man wants a son, a grandson. An
heir! It must be something like that.

✢   ✢   ✢

Leon told Simone that, as planned, he had to fly to Milan that
night, a quick overnight trip to meet a Venezuelan buyer and a
Russian department store president.

"The nouveau riche in Venezuela are crazy for our foie gras.
Almost as crazy as the Russian Mafia. They say that a case of our
foie gras in Moscow buys an audience with Yeltsin. Can't disappoint the Venezuelans. Sorry dear."

"Yes, dear," said Simone. "We mustn't disappoint the
Venezuelans. Or Boris."

Ah, she looks happy, thought Leon, her breasts are perking.
She knows that a trip out of town means a new piece of jewelry for
her. A new bracelet and she'll come in buckets! I could write a
book: *The Middle-Aged Wife's Wrist As An Erogenous Zone*, a scientific study
of precious gems and spontaneous orgasm, by Leon ———.

The stupid fatman, thought Simone, he thinks I am happy
about his business. Let him go to his slut in Milan. He does not

know that my legs are weak with desire, that I spent the afternoon in a tub, bathing in rose-petals, that I douched myself with raspberry juice and honey and sparkling mineral water in preparation for his absence, that I have an itch that his stupid goose-loving hands cannot possibly scratch.

And she kissed him, perhaps more warmly than she had in months.

"Where is Marie-Laure?" asked Leon at the door.

"At the exercise spa," said her mother. "I think that young man you brought home last night has captured her interest. She said she wanted to get in shape."

"Good, good," said Leon with a hearty laugh. "I think he is a fine boy. Perfect, just perfect."

David, perfect David, ate his soup and bread with Father Bernard and the nuns and orphans.

He's a good boy, thought Father Bernard.

He's a good boy, thought all the older nuns.

He's a hot hunk of man-meat, thought young Sister Genevieve, her face blushing under her habit, staring into her soup. God forgive me, she mentally crossed herself. God forgive me, but he is so handsome, so good, so kind, so dynamic, so romantic, like Lord Byron or Rimbaud with his curly locks, like . . . God forgive me, like Michelangelo's David, he's so finely formed, so perfect, so perfect, but his thing, I have seen the bulge, my David's must be bigger than Michelangelo's David's, oh, God forgive me! Oh, God!

Sister Genevieve scraped her chair back and ran from the room, her face red as a ripe tomato with shame.

"Now I wonder what's wrong with her?" asked Father Bernard, polishing off his soup and stabbing a hunk of goose from a platter. The goose had been a gift from Leon, a thank-you goose for sending him David.

"Youth," said Sister Marguerite, the oldest nun of the bunch.

"Weak bladder," said ever-practical Sister Lavinia, born in Turin.

"Diarrhea," said little Michel, the nastiest-minded of the nine orphans then living at the church. And all the orphans giggled.

David coughed, suppressing his giggles behind his napkin. That little Michel, he thought, my kind of kid. But he knew why sweet little top-heavy Sister Genevieve with the tiny waist and gawking eyes had run. He recognized the look.

"A marvelous dinner," he said, smiling at Sister Marie-Paule. "You really must open a restaurant. That's the best soup I've had ever."

Sister Marie-Paule blushed. What a nice young man, she thought, and him so interested in churches and church steeples. Who says orphanages create criminals? Those dirty, greedy politicians who've ruined the economy, that's who. Why, the prime minister, the things he said about the poor orphans, he ought to have his mouth washed with laundry soap!

✣   ✣   ✣

David walked in the moonlight. The town was quiet, serene, perfumed by apples and flowers and only the slightest hint of goose-shit. Yes, it was a good town, a good place to cool my heels, thought David. The last town wasn't so good. The people were too nosy. I'll have to be more careful. Only twenty or thirty more photos and the book will be complete.

✛   ✛   ✛

Leon sat on the plane to Milan, drank some wine, ate some foie gras, enjoying the fine service. It was a good foie gras, not as good as his, mind you, but a very good foie gras. He had no illusions about foie gras. One top-quality foie gras was as good as another, just about. It was the packaging that counted. That and the myth. The myth of happy geese. No such thing actually, but a little lie greases the wheel. But that's life. It's a goose-eat-goose world, thank God. The geese had made him rich. And now David had arrived, like the answer to a prayer, only Leon never prayed, didn't buy the God business, though just to be on the safe side he went to church and confessed to Father Bernard and helped the orphanage out with gifts of cash and geese and goosefeather pillows. Yes, everything was going according to plan, like clockwork. And Maritza was waiting in Milan. No, check that, Maritza's breasts were waiting. . . . And all of it paid for by geese. The goose that laid the golden breasts. . . .

✛   ✛   ✛

Simone drove the Mercedes through the dark quiet town and parked in a lonely street, not far from the church. Not near, not far. She remembered from childhood the old gate in the fence behind the apple orchard. It was still there. What a delicious sense of anticipation she felt. I am coming to you, David, I am yours, my strong young buck with the proud shoulders like a basketball player on television. I am yours to hold and stroke, to whisper to, to love and hold and love until the first goose wakes. . . .

✤   ✤   ✤

In the town of —— most of the young people hung out at Tin-Tin's Love Shack. There was pinball, there was *foosball*, there were video games. There was music, there was drink, there was gay laughter and croque-monsieur. . . . Hey, there was David! There was Marie-Laure! There were David and Marie-Laure dancing. There were other girls watching with envy, other boys jealously watching the other girls watching. What does this guy have that we don't? What's this? David and Marie-Laure leaving, hand in hand? And out in the night, in the quiet still night in the quiet little town of ——, there was the sound of a black motorcycle singing the song of youth.

✤   ✤   ✤

Leon licked champagne from Maritza's stupendous breasts. Shlurp, shlurp, went his tongue.

"Leon," she said throatily, slathering his manhood with paté and nibbling, "I am just crazy for your foie gras."

"Tell me, my dear," said Leon between sandpaper-tongued slobbers, "have you any Venezuelan blood?"

✣ ✣ ✣

Naked and fragrantly fresh as a flower, Simone lay on the cool white sheets of the bed in the little cottage by the apple orchard. And not once did she think of the late Cardinal.

✣ ✣ ✣

On a hill above the little town of ——, under a moon which spoke of love and death and the mysteries of the universe, on top of a checkered tablecloth borrowed from the orphanage, David and Marie-Laure made the kind of love that young girls and old men and silly geese only dream of.

✣ ✣ ✣

And in his office, fueled by a decent cognac, picking bits of goose from his teeth with an ivory toothpick once owned by the late Cardinal ——, a gift to the Cardinal from His Holiness the Pope, Father Bernard ruminated on David's pictures of churches and church steeples. Something was missing from the pictures. What was it? What was it?

✣ ✣ ✣

And in her room on the top floor, Sister Genevieve ignored the sounds of orphans joking and farting and giggling and jerking off, hitting one another with goosefeather pillows, ignored the soupy snores of Sister Marie-Paule next door, ignored the Bible under her pillow, the cross around her neck, ignored it all and thought of David, perfect perfect David, out there somewhere, riding his black motorcycle through the black night, with his green eyes and sensuous lips and the dangerous bulge in his black jeans. . . .

✛   ✛   ✛

"What the hell are you doing here?" David asked the thin lovely goosemistress lying naked on his bed, her hair fanned out like peacock feathers on his pillow, the diamonds winking on her earlobes, the gold gleaming on her wrists.

"Darling, don't be that way."

David was only being that way to buy himself a few minutes. Three times with Marie-Laure and even he, a prime stud of twenty-two, didn't feel up to it again. . . .

Simone sat up in the bed. Yes, all the preparation had been worth it. She saw the magic bulge in the black jeans.

"I have brought you a rose petal," she said. "Like a mother kangaroo carrying a secret message in her pouch."

And she came to him, David thought, like dust to the hose of a vacuum cleaner.

"Lovely, oh, yes, oh oh oh oh oh . . ." Simone's moans drifted into the night, pollinating the apple trees.

✛   ✛   ✛

Satisfaction is a rare thing indeed. But the next day, all of our main characters in the little town of —— were satisfied, at least all of them who had indulged in the delicacies of the flesh.

David was satisfied that he'd had both mother and daughter in the same night. That he had given of himself equally to each. Three plus three equals some kind of record, some kind of superhuman effort. And he'd taken some very good shots of Simone, yes, very artistic, very very artistic. It would take a bit more sweet-talking with the daughter, a few more nights of triple delight, yet soon, soon, soon she would be his too. Captured on film, immortalized disposable flesh.

Simone was satisfied. Deeply, deeply satisfied. Satisfied to the point where she walked funny.

Marie-Laure was satisfied. He was not her first, no, but so far the best. She imagined that one night after making love on the checkered tablecloth that so resembled Yassir Arafat's headdress (the PLO leader must a good man to have along on a picnic, she thought, I wonder how many of those things he has in his closet?) they would jump on the motorcycle and speed out of town, tearing the soft fabric of the good citizens' dreams as they roared past, never stopping, never looking back.

Leon, back from Milan, watched the young stud photographer at work, making his smelly geese look pretty as fashion models, their shit-caked feathers stylish as Claude Montana frocks. Leon was satisfied, very satisfied. It was only a matter of days, perhaps weeks, before he would be with those breasts, I mean, with Maritza the voluptuous pretzel, full-time.

Only Father Bernard and Sister Genevieve were not satisfied. Sister Genevieve because she was haunted by guilt and lust and confusion about her vows; and Father Bernard because he was troubled, really and truly troubled by whatever it was that was missing from David's photos of churches and church steeples.

21

✛   ✛   ✛

Days passed. By the light of the sun David photographed geese and goose by-products. By the light of the moon and stars and even one afternoon with his camera along as chaperone, David made love to Marie-Laure. And in the wee hours of the morning, on the cool sheets in the little cottage where Cardinal —— had said his last prayer, he made love to Simone.

Leon took his trips. To Paris, to Madrid, to Geneva. To Amsterdam. To Lisbon. To Brussels and Barcelona and Bilbao. And of course to Milan. The new Europe was a wonderful world of moneymaking opportunity. The totality of the ancient Frankish Empire was wide open! He was like Charlemagne! Charlemagne Of The Geese! A man of wealth and taste and vision, and the airline treated him accordingly. And the acrobatic Maritza, she, too, treated him like a king. He was happy as he hadn't been for years.

✛   ✛   ✛

One hot day when even the flies seemed as lazy as government workers in August, as Father Bernard listened to a spiteful old woman's confession of poisoning her son's marriage—"his awful empty marriage, no love there I tell you!"—the priest realized with utter horror what was missing from David's photographs of churches and church steeples. Love. There was no love there. Technically perfect the pictures were, but empty of the one thing that mattered: love. It was as if David saw churches and church steeples as cold and monstrous and full of hate. If those were the hands of man, thought Father Bernard, shuddering in the hot, close confessional, then God help the feet of God. He was struck by the need to warn God to wear combat boots.

✠ ✠ ✠

Michel, the nastiest-minded orphan, small and dark with the face of sneaky ferret on a diet of crushed glass and rubbing alcohol, had decided that David was his hero. The previous afternoon he and David had shared a cigarette under an apple tree and David had told him many things, about life and death and gravity and applesauce. About how Isaac Newton had sat like this under an apple tree until an apple fell on his head; not only had old Isaac discovered gravity, but applesauce as well. Two for the price of one. About how he, David, had sat on the Ramblas in Barcelona and gotten so sick of beggars telling him their woeful tales and demanding coins that he took to giving them razor blades instead. "Let them cut their throats if they're so damn miserable." But what Michel remembered most was David's recipe for Nuns' Panties Soup: take the dirty panties of five nuns, boil them in chicken stock, add spices, a dash of wine, and voila: instant hilarity! And Michel had tried it out that night. He'd snuck into the nuns' rooms, filched their panties from their dirty laundry, then slipped them into Sister Marie-Paule's soup. And what hilarity there had been! The nuns screaming, the orphans laughing, Father Bernard fuming. When no one confessed, Father Bernard had whipped all the boys with his belt and sent them to bed without supper. But it had been worth it. He wanted to grow up to be just like David, handsome and mysterious, with black jeans, a black motorcycle, a camera with a big lens, and a head full of important knowledge and hilarious recipes.

He decided to tell David that he was his hero. So late that night, when the moon was hiding out like a criminal in a prison of clouds, he snuck out of the dormitory room, checking to make sure that his slobbering, snoring mates were slobbering and snoring for real, ran barefoot across the field to David's cottage, and peered through a slice of breeze-blown open window shade.

What he saw: David pinning the goosemaster's wife to the bed in the manner made famous by dogs. And it made him excited in a way that the circle jerks in the woods with Frank and George never had. He was paralyzed.

And when Simone had departed, happy, so very happy, sneaking away toward the old gate as quiet as a thief, her loins heavy with treasure, little Michel stayed and watched David smoke a cigarette and scratch himself through his shorts.

David felt the eyes. David always felt the eyes. He'd been sensitive to people looking at him from childhood. How Father Albert had looked at him and looked at him, devoured him with his eyes for two whole years before devouring him . . . and then the whippings afterward. . . .

"Come in, Michel," David said through the open window. "I see you there."

Michel came in.

"A cigarette?" David asked. Michel nodded. They both smoked. Crafty boy eyes staring at crafty young man eyes through clouds of smoke.

"So you saw Madame and me." It was not a question.

"I saw what I saw."

"You saw what was between her legs?"

"I saw."

"What did you think?"

Michel shrugged. David smiled, stubbed his cigarette out, took the cigarette from the boy's fingers, stubbed it out.

"I want to show you something," he said.

Michel, suddenly, was scared.

"Don't be scared. I want to show you how girls and boys differ."

"I know all that."

"I don't think so."

And David unlatched his briefcase and took a fat folder of photographs from within. And Michel was frightened, for the look in David's eyes was not kind. But Michel was excited, for these photographs were not of churches and church steeples.

"This is a girl," David said, pointing at a photograph. "And this." Michel's eyes bulged like a happy frog as David spread the pictures on the bed. "All these are girls."

The boy recognized Simone, he recognized Marie-Laure. The rest, a whole wide world of breasts and buttocks and hair and flesh, white teeth smiling the secrets of life into his soul.

"This dark down between their legs is soft and cuddly as goosefeathers, but the thing it hides has teeth sharp and cruel as a trap." David put his arm around the boy's thin shoulders. "You see, Michel," he said, stroking, "I take pictures of girls to one day show the world what they are." David held up a sheet of embossed paper, a letter from a publisher in Milan. "I have an Italian publisher interested. On one page will be pictures of churches and church steeples and on the opposite page will be pictures of girls. Girls as they truly are. Not perfect and made-up and looking like fairy-tale princesses. None of your airbrushed whipped-cream magazine dreamgirls, no. Girls as they really are. Girls are ugly, dirty things with filthy souls like the unscrubbed insides of toilet bowls. Not like men."

David opened his shorts and guided the paralyzed boy's hand within.

"Feel it? Like the steeple of a church, stretching to God."

And then he gently pulled the boy's pants off, pulled the boy's shirt over his trembling shoulders, caressed the soft goosebumped boyflesh, kissed him between the dirty shoulder blades, gently pried the clenched, belt-striped peach cheeks open.

"Girls are not beautiful like this."

"Please, David, don't. I'm scared."

"Hush, my darling. I am your first?"

The boy nodded, a tear plopped from his eye and dripped onto David's steeple.

"Bend over, sweetheart. It is my sacred duty to make you a man."

"Please, no."

"Ahh, orphanages ain't what they used to be."

And so the unsentimental education of Michel began, and for the first time since Sister Jacqueline discovered the late Cardinal —— dead in his bed, the apple trees heard screams of pain and sorrow.

⁜　　⁜　　⁜

Sister Genevieve dreamt of Mick Jagger on the cross, wearing a crown of thorns. And then it was David, not Mick, David with horns, not thorns, and snakes coming out his mouth. She awoke sweating, breathing hard, her heart pounding as if she'd run a marathon. She prayed.

✢　　✢　　✢

At breakfast, Leon winked at Simone.

"You're looking very well these days, my dear."

"A new exercise program, dear. Tightening my thighs."

"Good good. And your lips, so full, as if stung by bees."

"I read about it in an interview with an American actress. You kiss your own hand a hundred times every morning to make the lips plump, and then give oral pleasure to a wet baguette to make them supple."

"And who ever said the Americans were barbarians?"

✢　　✢　　✢

Father Bernard listened to Sister Genevieve's dream.

"I must ask David to leave," he said. "His influence on the children is unhealthy. I think it was he who was behind last night's . . . soup."

✢　　✢　　✢

And now our story goes into high gear. David had completed taking his photographs of geese, had developed them in the makeshift darkroom he'd set up in the cottage bathroom. He'd given them to Leon. Leon was ecstatic.

"We must celebrate! A big family dinner . . . son."

✠   ✠   ✠

Father Bernard was in a terrible mood. Angry. Quivering with anger. The nuns and orphans ate their soup in petrified silence. The table had three empty places. Michel and Frank had been sent to bed with a fresh whipping instead of supper. Father Bernard had found them in the woodshed earlier, performing unspeakable acts in the manner made famous by dogs. And David, damned David, who the nasty one on top confessed had taught him. . . . The motorcycle roared off.

"Where is David going?" asked Sister Lavinia.

"To Monsieur Leon's to say goodbye. I have asked David to leave. Tomorrow he will be just an unpleasant memory."

Cries of consternation rang out around the table from orphan and nun alike, but were quickly swallowed when they saw the look of Old Testament anger on the priest's face.

Sister Genevieve, so very young, jumped to her feet and ran from the room in tears, her full breasts bobbling like puppies wrestling in a sack.

"David is not good," said Father Bernard. He looked from face to face, daring them to argue.

No one met his eyes. Soup spoons clicked against soup bowls, orphans and nuns shlurped soup, and the motorcycle's song faded into the distance.

✤   ✤   ✤

The results of that evening's events in the quiet little town of ——
are well known to one and all who follow the news. But before the
well-dressed man next to me could tell them to me in his own honest
way, lessen his burden, he had another load to drop.

"Excuse me," he said, placing his tray upright and rising,
holding onto his briefcase like a life preserver. "I must use the
facilities."

I waited, thinking over what he had told me, how complete a
telling it had been, how honest. I was curious to see if the rest
would come out so cleanly.

"Where was I?" he asked upon returning to his seat and sig-
naling the stewardess for more drinks.

"Please, my dear, two more. And some foie gras."

He smiled warmly at her and offered her a rather large bill.
The girl smiled politely and refused the money.

"I couldn't possibly, sir. Against company policy, but thank
you for the thought."

When the drinks had come and he'd gobbled some foie gras
and stared at the stewardess's retreating legs and sighed and
sipped and sighed some more, he fell back into the story. He
could no sooner stop telling it than a man in a wheelchair can
stop dreaming of running.

✤   ✤   ✤

It seemed that when David arrived at the farm that night for the
big family dinner, he was greeted warmly by Leon and taken for
a walk, man to man.

"I have spoken with Marie-Laure," said the Charlemagne Of The Geese. "She will have you for a husband."

"Will she? What if I'm not game?"

"Think of it, David. Money, position, prestige and . . ."

"All the foie gras on God's green gooseshit earth? Thanks, but no thanks, Leon. You think I want to become like you?" David asked with a cruel sneer. "Fat, useless, caged by responsibility? Bored out of my skull until my dreams end up cooked and puréed and packed in a can? Thanks, but no thanks."

"You can have Simone too."

"You know about that?"

"I had my suspicions."

✢   ✢   ✢

Meanwhile, back at the cottage by the apple orchard, Sister Genevieve was lying face down on David's bed, her tears soaking the pillow, the pillow that smelled of David . . . and of something else. What was it? Not the dying-old-man smell of the late Cardinal, no. And this long hair? Too long to be David's. And this short blonde hair? Too short to be David's, too blonde.

Sister Genevieve rose with a start, a look of comprehension dawning on her tear-mapped face. And then she saw the briefcase, partially hidden under a chair.

She opened the case. And she found them. Hidden beneath the pictures of churches and church steeples. Pictures of women. Naked women. How many! How terrible! Lovely lustful women. Low creatures, beasts of Satan. There was

Simone ——, and there was her daughter, Marie-Laure. Smiling, leering, legs open, tongues wagging, plumping their breasts, touching themselves. David, how could you? I have loved you so purely, so cleanly! I have been planning on forsaking my vows for you, quitting the calling, buying some crotchless panties and a lace bra . . . and now this? This blasphemy to love?

With a rage in her heart and fresh tears in her eyes, Sister Genevieve left the cottage, ran through the apple orchard, exited the compound through the old gate, and walked swiftly down the road.

Like a neurotic penguin with breasts, thought a passing truck driver on his way to Angoulême.

✣   ✣   ✣

"We have a problem," said Leon to David and Simone and Marie-Laure as they sat to eat. "I have asked David to stay on as a member of the family with full family rights."

He gave a look full of lecherous meaning to his wife, and she leered back.

"And I do mean full, Simone; but David has refused the offer."

"I do not understand, David," said Marie-Laure. "I thought you loved me."

"I love no one," said David. "It's not in me to love, at least not in the way you want. Sorry, sweetheart."

"Just because you do not love," said Simone with a meaningful glance at her husband, "doesn't mean you cannot stay. I've managed twenty years without love quite well, thank you very much. Married to this stupid fat goose of a man. Stay, darling."

David looked at them. Leon and his wife and daughter all begging him to stay, and all he could do was laugh. Simone's eyebrows did push-ups and her nose flared theatrically, beseeching him.

"Sorry, sweetheart," he said. "No can do. I'm just not built that way."

His look encompassed both women.

"Sorry, sweethearts. Thanks for dinner . . . and for everything."

Leon rose from the table, excusing himself. Marie-Laure stared at her food, refusing to believe the implications of her mother's words and tone, of David's reply. Simone fixed David with burning eyes, offering him all she had. And David . . . David just laughed and cut into his goose dinner, placing a morsel in his cruel, handsome mouth and chewing between laughs.

In his study, Leon spun the dials of his safe, swung the heavy door open, and filled a briefcase with stacks of cash. It was a great deal of money, one hundred thousand francs, and when the case was full Leon closed it, took a loaded pistol from the safe and, leaving the safe open, returned to the dining room.

"This is for you, David," said Leon, handing him the cash-pregnant case.

David felt the weight.

"For me?"

"Actually, no," said Leon, taking the case back and pulling the pistol from his pocket. "I just needed your fingerprints on the case."

"Father," squealed Marie-Laure, rising. "Have you lost your tiny fucking mind?"

"Sit, girl," said Leon, leveling the pistol on her pretty blonde head. "It pains me, but this is the only way. You see, as your mother knows, I keep a mistress in Milan, and I must have her, not just once in a while, but always. Now, I've asked Simone for a friendly divorce, but she has refused. I had thought David might help me out, keep everyone happy, maybe even take some photos that might provide me with divorce material, allow me to bring my mistress closer to home, maybe even marry her, but this way is better, much better. Scandal-free tragedy."

Leon laughed, an ugly sound that would have scraped paint off a battleship, his face twisted with cunning and madness.

Simone and David and Marie-Laure watched him, stupefied.

"But I have photos," said David, not really believing the ludicrous situation he'd fallen into. "Of your wife."

"Yes," said Simone. "He has photos. Naked as the day I was born, as the night I was married, except for my jewelry. Lewd photos, Leon. Instant divorce. I won't fight it."

"Desperate lies," said Leon, almost sadly. "Too late. This is what I shall tell the police: David won my confidence, made love to my daughter and my wife, and when I refused my permission for him to marry Marie-Laure—after all, David, you are an orphan and I am a man of standing, the Charlemagne Of The Geese—you decided to get even. So you took my gun and forced me to empty my safe, you shot my wife and you shot my daughter and were about to shoot me when I jumped you and wrestled the gun away from you and shot you in the belly. And that's how it happened. It was a tragedy, a good old-fashioned classical tragedy."

But Leon was wrong. Had the next moments gone as planned, it might have been, as he predicted, a tragedy, but unbeknownst to him, floating out there in the cosmos were the elements of cheap melodrama.

The doorbell rang.

✥   ✥   ✥

Sister Genevieve had trudged through the fields and woods, unseen by the good citizens of the quiet little town of —— who were in their homes eating their dinners and watching television. She was angry as a goose, and somewhere along the way had picked up a piece of heavy branch from a fallen tree. Yes, David, I will smite thee, she thought, ringing the doorbell. With righteousness, I will smite thee. Thee and thy harlots.

✥   ✥   ✥

Leon kept the gun trained on the table while opening the door a crack. Who could that be? The workers were all at dinner.

The sight of a small, teary-eyed nun with a large club almost made him laugh.

Sister Genevieve, her brain addled with thoughts of God and betrayal and crotchless panties, her eyes full of tears, expecting Simone or Marie-Laure or David to answer the bell, kicked the door wide and swung the club mightily, smashing Leon's head. Leon fell, dropping the gun. Sister Genevieve walked calmly into the room, picked up the gun.

David and Simone and Marie-Laure were too surprised to move.

"Well, David," said the nun. "You have been unfaithful to me. What do you have to say for yourself, my love?"

David had nothing to say. Nothing. He hadn't even flirted with this one, had he? The bitch was bonkers. What was she talking about?

Marie-Laure was percolating with anger.

"Her too?" she cried at David. "You filthy scumsucking sack of shit!"

Simone just laughed. It was all too ridiculous. Her hated husband lying dead, his head caved in, this little mouse of a nun with the comically huge chest and the big gun, David just sitting there chewing goose, and Marie-Laure standing there cursing like a waterfront whore with hemorrhoids.

David spoke calmly.

"Give up the gun, Sister. Let's put an end to this insanity."

"You want the gun, my love?"

David nodded.

She pointed the gun at his chest, then quickly jerked it to Marie-Laure, shot her once in the head. Brains splattered the goose, a piece of skull landed in Simone's wine, and the nubile blonde did a graceful pirouette and crashed to the floor.

Simone wailed, ran to her daughter. The nun calmly stepped over to the mother, placed the gun against her well-coiffed head and pulled the trigger. . . .

It was a horrible mess. We do not need to go into the details. The police report contains the grisly details for the those with a prurient need for details.

Now, quickly (for the plane is not so very far from Milan): the nun was in shock. She couldn't speak. Her eyes were empty as a broken promise. David took the gun from her, but she wouldn't drop the heavy piece of wood. He thought it over in a flash. I must get out of here, I must. I'll be blamed. No one will believe she made this mess on her own. They'll say I put her up to it. I'll go down for conspiracy to commit murder. They'll lock me up in a cage like a goose and throw away the key. Gotta get out of here! Gotta make this crazy nun disappear!

He wiped the gun of prints with a napkin, placed it in Leon's hand, pressing Leon's fingertips so that his prints would be found. Returning the favor.

"Come on, Sister," he said, taking the briefcase and the nun's hand, dragging her out the door, sitting her on the motorcycle, getting on the bike himself, kick-starting it. "Let's get the fuck out of here."

It was quite a sight, the handsome young man in black jeans and boots and a white T-shirt, a briefcase on his lap, and the top-heavy nun holding a club, her arm around his waist, riding the black motorcycle fast out of the quiet little town of ———.

And they were gone no more than five minutes before Leon groaned.

✢   ✢   ✢

François, the loyal walker of geese, had heard the shots but decided it was just the boss shooting at a fox or something. No reason to check it out before finishing his dinner and watching that hot chick on television. But when he found his bloody-headed boss moaning and crawling on the floor, the boss's wife and kid dead in a heap, the safe open and the money missing, he almost peed in his pants. God help me, he thought, they'll think I took the cash. So he called the police.

This is how the cops, with all their trained experts and modern police methods, interpreted the crime, the crime scene, and the events that led up to it (and remember, if you object to the interpretation or to the language, this is your tax revenue at work, these are your public servants speaking):

Fat fuckin' Leon, like half the gossipy shitheads in this shithole town, musta seen his slinky-assed blowjob-lipped wife's fancy fuckin' car parked near the fuckin' church cottage and he musta known that the bitch was spreadin' her no-good waxed legs for the young stud shutterbug. And the dumb fat bastard also musta known that the fuckin' orphan with his bullshit pictures of churches and church steeples was playin' hide-the-salami with his hot-pants no-tits blondie daughter. Christ, all the zombie kids in town had seen 'em riding that bike together, goin' off to fuck in the bushes like a couple of fuckin' bunnies. So fat fuckin' Leon shot both the bitches, then waited for David. And when fuckin' David arrived for a friendly fuckin' dinner he struggled for the gun with fat fuckin' Leon, knocked him onto Qeer street with a piece of fuckin' fire-wood (bits of fuckin' bark were dug out of fat fuckin' Leon's fat fuckin' skull), then calm as a fuckin' hippo in a swimmin' pool, the stud sat there and ate his fuckin' fill of fuckin' goose (don't they eat nothin' else in this fuckin' town?) before he picked the lock on fat fuckin' Leon's safe (wearin' gloves, the smart bastard) and took off with the cash. That David was one cool fuckin' customer, the way he ate his fuckin' dinner with his two bitches dead on the floor and fat fuckin' Leon in front of him, his skull crushed like a fuckin' goose egg bashed by a sledgehammer. And then the fuckin' stud hooked up with his real girlfriend, the fuckin' rogue nun with the big fuckin' tits, and they hit the road, like Bonnie and fuckin' Clyde, sliding off the face of the fuckin' earth like shit off a hot shovel. . . .

So much for the official interpretation of events.

And who was there to tell it differently? Certainly not David and Sister Genevieve, they were long gone. And certainly not Leon. Yes, he lived, but the blow to his head caused his memory of the events of that evening to be completely erased. At the hospital for the criminally insane where he now resides in complete bliss, they say he has the mental capacity of a precocious three-year-old, though when he plays with himself and sings, "Maritza, Maritza, I am the Charlemagne Of The Geese," they do bring out the straitjacket.

A tragedy, everyone in the little town of —— agreed. An old-fashioned classical tragedy.

✣　　✣　　✣

The well-dressed man offered me the last stick of gum in his pack.

"That is all?" I asked.

"Take it, I insist."

I took the gum but didn't open it.

"I meant the story, Father Bernard. I think you will feel better if you tell me all."

"Well, you know the rest. Everyone knows the rest. The story is well known."

"We are not so far from Milan, Father."

"Don't call me Father. I am no longer a priest."

"Yes," I said. "But you have not been honest with me." I fixed him with my sad, almost-ugly face. "And you have not been honest with the police."

"For instance?"

"You did not tell them about David's photography."

"I gave them the pictures of churches and church steeples."

"And they gave them back to you. But you kept the pictures of women. . . ."

"David has no need of them where he is."

I let that one go.

"Allow me a few questions, Father. You received a letter from Sister Genevieve, yes?"

"How could you know that?"

"How I know does not matter, at least not yet. You disappoint me with your reticence. Actually, I'm disappointed in myself. I must be slipping. Usually they tell me all. But listen, and I will finish the story for you. . . .

"David and Sister Genevieve rode that motorcycle through the night. All the while they rode, David debated with himself whether or not to kill the sister. But he couldn't do it. Yes, he was bitter and cruel and maladjusted, but he wasn't a life-taker. So when the bike ran out of gas, David ditched it in a river. Sister Genevieve wrapped her nun's habit and cowl around some heavy rocks and threw them in the water, then draped herself in the checkered tablecloth that resembled Yassir Arafat's headdress (that, the briefcase full of money, some fond memories of little Michel, and the crazy nun with the big lungs were all that David had salvaged from his stay in the quiet little town of ———), and she hid in the woods while he walked to the nearest town and bought her some jeans and a T-shirt and sneakers. She really was a lovely young woman, you know. . . . So they settled in Marseille and lived very simply on Leon's hundred thousand francs. The immense horror of witnessing the murders, it seems, cured David of all his bizarre theories about churches and church steeples and women and his need to play doggie with young boys. He turned out to be a wonderful young man, gentle and sweet and very kind to Genevieve in that time. The transformation was miraculous. And when she found out she was pregnant, they exchanged their own wedding vows, under the eyes of God. He grew a mustache and cut his hair, and no one recognized them.

"Yes, they lived happily. He was quite changed, repentant over his old ways and quite in love with Genevieve. The change in him was remarkable, really. But Genevieve was ravaged with guilt. She knew she'd done a terrible thing and wanted to turn herself in, but knew also that if she did, then David would surely end up behind bars. So she stayed, figuring that any child born of their union would be blessed. She, herself, was damned, but the child would be blessed.

"They spent most of Leon's money on rent and food and on doctors and supplies for the baby (their only extravagance was a pair of crotchless panties for Genevieve); and when the baby arrived, a healthy, happy little girl they named Marie-Paule, because Genevieve had fallen in love with David over Sister Marie-Paule's soup, they were very happy indeed. And then one day, while David was out looking for a job, she went to a travel agent and spent the last of Leon's money on a plane ticket. One ticket. One one-way ticket. Then she sat down and wrote three letters. One to you, explaining all. One to David, professing her eternal love. And one to . . . well, let me hold that information for a moment. So she wrote the letters and posted two of them.

"That night they celebrated. David had landed a job in a pizzeria. So they drank beer and they made love, made love in every nook and cranny of the apartment, in every position imaginable—in the manner made famous by missionaries, in the manner made famous by dogs, in the manner made famous by Indian mystics and circus contortionists. . . . And after they'd gone to bed, she placed the letter for David in the baby's crib, along with the airplane ticket. And when the baby woke in the night and David discovered that Genevieve had gone, he wept. Genevieve had not wanted to do what she felt she had to do in front of David and the baby. I imagine she kissed them both in their sleep and cried a little, and then she went to the basement and did what she felt was necessary. She tore the checkered tablecloth into strips, tied them together, made a noose, tied the makeshift rope to a water pipe and hung herself."

Father Bernard—I should say, the man who once was Father Bernard and was now just a well-dressed man on the night flight from Toulouse to Milan—the well-dressed man wiped a tear.

"Yes," he whispered.

"Her dying wish was that David and their baby girl go live with her parents in Lille. So all three headed to Lille. The baby and the coffin rode for free. David was too grief-stricken to be nervous, too involved with the baby's needs to notice the commotion he caused. David, who had always been so aware of people staring at him, noticed nothing. And he was a fine father. You remember how the newspapers played up the desperado-with-a-baby-and-suicided-ex-nun-wife-in-a-coffin angle? You remember the airline's promotion? How sometime that week they would count their millionth passenger? Yes, as you well know, David was the millionth passenger. There was a brass band waiting in Lille, champagne and foie gras on the plane. Newspapers and television cameras waiting at the airport in Lille. Poor David. He was arrested the next day, after the good people in the little town of —— identified him from the television. Arrested and eventually convicted of stealing poor Leon's cash. But at least they let him bury Genevieve. Genevieve, whose memory he so treasured that he never told the cops she pulled the trigger. Poor Genevieve."

"Poor everyone," whispered the former priest.

"Yes, Bernard. Poor everyone. . . . Except for Bernard."

My eyes spoke the truth, but I did not condemn him. I was only telling it the way it was.

"Who are you?" he whispered. "Who are you to know all this? And who did she send the third letter to?"

"I am just a man you sat next to on an airplane. The man you felt compelled to sit next to and tell everything. I have seen David in prison and he has told me all. I have seen Leon in the mental hospital and he has told me what he can. I have been in the quiet little town of —— and I have learned many things. Perhaps you saw me there? Sitting or walking or leaning against a lamppost, getting my ear bent by nuns and cops and goose-walkers. Perhaps you don't remember seeing me. I don't blame

you, I have a very forgettable face. And now, here you are. . . .
But you have yet to tell me everything, have you?"

"No," he whispered.

"Louder, please."

"No," he said.

"You are going to Milan, yes?"

He nodded.

"With David's briefcase, yes? With David's pictures of
churches and church steeples and. . . . Tell me, it will make you
feel better."

"And the pictures of women," he whispered.

"Yes," I said. "There is that. The pictures of women."

"I found them," he said. "I wanted to turn them in to the
police," he said. "But they were so beautiful. David had seen
only ugliness. I saw beauty. I visited him in jail, heard his confession, and he said he didn't care what happened with the pictures. All he wanted was to be left alone."

The cabin lights were dim. He looked guiltily at the stewardess, loving her with his eyes, then looked back at me, strong
now, proud now, a bit angry now.

"I gave up my collar. I am no longer a priest. I can do anything
I want. Like any free man. I can even visit Leon's Maritza. . . .
Don't you see, the love that was missing from David's photos of
churches and church steeples, it's in his pictures of women.
Only he couldn't see it. And when you put one picture next to
the other, the women, with their softness and imperfect perfect
beauty and loving eyes, the women give the steeples their love,
their softness, their humanity. The spirituality of their flesh. It
works. I'm on my way to meet the publisher David contacted. I

don't feel bad or guilty. I've found out who I am. So something good has come of all this, no?"

"No," I said, taking the briefcase from him. His fingers let go reluctantly. "Nothing good has come of this. And you will not publish the pictures. They are David's. To do with as he pleases. He can sell them to the other prisoners to use as erotic inspiration, for all I care. They are his."

"Who are you?" he asked.

"I am just a stranger on a plane," I said. "Someone you have sung your blues to. A man with many passports."

I dipped into my pocket and showed him three different passports, all bearing my picture and all with different names.

"I solve problems. I invent solutions. I take muddy situations and make them clear. I am a human enema, a plumber of souls. And despite what comes next, you must know that I bear you no ill will."

"What comes next?"

"The toothpick," I said.

"The toothpick?"

He was puzzled.

"Where is the toothpick you stole from the bedside of the late Cardinal —— in the cottage by the apple orchard?"

He reached into his pocket and extracted a small velvet case. He opened the case.

"This toothpick?"

I nodded. There it was. The toothpick.

"That is what this is about? A toothpick?"

"Yes," I said. "I will return the photos to David, that is only fair, and the toothpick I will return to . . . to its rightful owner."

"But the Cardinal is dead."

"And his possessions belong to the Church. I will return the toothpick to . . ."

"You mean, to the . . . ?"

The gravity of the situation was creeping into his brain, slow and steady as an army of ants goose-stepping toward Bethlehem.

"Hush," I said, putting my finger to his lips. "No names. We call him the Big Kielbasa. The Big Polish Sausage."

I took the toothpick from its case and studied it. It gleamed, a dull beige gleam, quite old, very mysterious. I'd heard about this toothpick. It was a very famous toothpick, carved long ago by one of the famous African martyrs. Very strong, extra-long, quite sharp: good for getting food stuck back in the molars.

"The third letter," asked the former Father Bernard, "it was sent to . . . ?"

"Hush," I said. "We mustn't say; but yes, it won't hurt you to know, Genevieve sent it to Rome. To the Big Kielbasa. It told everything."

"This isn't about the pictures?"

"Heavens, no. He doesn't give a former-Yugoslavian rat's ass about the pictures. That's just my sense of what's right. Now, if you were still a priest, it might pose a problem. No, as I keep telling you, this is about the toothpick. The Big Kielbasa wants it back. And what the Big Kielbasa wants, the Big Kielbasa gets. He's a bit of a sentimentalist."

"And what happens next?" the former priest asked.

"What happens next? Why, you go where you're going and I go where I'm going. That's what strangers on a plane do, generally. . . . And now, Bernard, really, you must relax, really and truly relax. The time has come for you to relax. We are approaching Milan and you must relax."

The lights in the cabin were dim. The other passengers were snoozing. The pretty stewardess had ceased her bending and smiling and had taken her seat. It had been a lovely flight. Pleasant, on time, an excellent flight. Like a mother eagle, that plane was, proud and protective. The well-dressed man next to me took a sip of his drink and sighed, sipped and sighed and sipped and sighed and smiled and shrugged and looked out the window, at peace with himself, finally at peace, and that was the moment I chose to swiftly jam the toothpick deep into the tender hollow behind his head, where neck meets skull below the occipital bulge, right into his spinal cord, the magic place we in the business call "the brain's door." I slid the toothpick in and out and in and out, wiggling it gently to make sure.

There was very little blood and fluid to wipe off.

"You must understand," I told the dying man, placing his head against the headrest, smoothing his hair and closing his eyes, as the lights of Milan twinkled below, "I wasn't hired to do this. Only to get the toothpick back."

I placed the toothpick in its velvet-lined case and put it in my pocket.

"You see, Bernard, God has a soft spot for thieves, and so does the Big Kielbasa, but me, I happen to be a sucker for orphans. After Mother died, I was sent to an orphanage, and the priests who raised me whipped me endlessly, endlessly. Whipped me because they felt compelled to tell me things they couldn't even admit to God. So when I heard how fond you were of whipping the inno-cent orphans back in the little town of ——, whipped them for what?—for just being kids and following poor David's lead, poor David who had been whipped and violated by priests himself, I figured it was payback time. Nothing personal, this just seems right. Balancing the karma . . . It's ironic, of course, feeling as I do about priests, that I work for the Big Kielbasa, but it's the little ironies in life that make the journey interesting, don't you think?"

I unwrapped the stick of gum and started to chew. He wasn't a bad fellow, the former priest, not a bad fellow at all. He'd given me his last stick of gum.

"By the time that pretty stewardess you've been thinking of in such a healthy, un-priestlike manner discovers that you're not just drunk and catching a nap, I'll be hailing a taxi. And no one will remember what I looked like. Mine is a very forgettable face. They will scratch their heads and say: 'He was not a handsome man and he was not an ugly man,' and that is true, no? For better or worse, I'm somewhere in the middle, as Mother used to say, somewhere between Alain Delon and Jo-Jo the Dog-Faced Boy. . . . But that, my friend, is really another story and I don't want to bore you."

But the well-dressed man was beyond being bored. And as the plane descended toward Milan, my thoughts turned to Maritza, the stupendous Maritza. Yes, I would look her up, of course I would, any man in or out of his right mind would look her up, and as certain as wild geese fly north in springtime, I would bring her some foie gras, surely I would, bring her some foie gras and listen to her sing her blues. And maybe, just maybe, I'd let her whip me, for old times' sake.

THE BILLIONTH
BURGER

I MUST BE THOROUGHLY MAD TO be telling you this," said
the pale, pretty, British heiress with the sad eyes, sucking
vigorously on a cigarette in the bar car (specially ordered
for a group of wealthy Texans) on the train from Paris to Trouville. With each massive puff the red ember of her cigarette
glowed brightly and grew like a dog's erection, chewing off
almost half an inch of tobacco and leaving a wilted gray tube of
dead ash in its wake. "Thoroughly and utterly mad."

She was a thin woman, thin yet shapely, with the paranoid
darting eyes of Bambi in a butcher shop. In her early twen-
ties, she was, with hair the color of toasted wheat streaked with
gold, worn in the ringletted style favored by Renaissance portraits and horror-movie scream queens; and though her chest
was not supersized by any stretch of the imagination or
brassiere—only very, very nicely formed (uplifting to look at,
I have to admit) I was astounded by the amount of smoke she
was capable of drawing with each breath. Holy cow, I thought,
as rivers of smoke rushed out her nose and mouth, clouding

the car despite the excellent ventilation system, she must have quite the set of lungs.

A shaft of late-afternoon sunlight poked through the thick train window, sliced through the swirl of smoke and caressed the soft fine down on her neck, lingered lovingly upon the infinitesimal blonde hairs on her alcohol-rosy cheeks. Her fine nostrils, red-rimmed from recent crying, flared dramatically, snorted smoke like a teakettle on full boil. A blue vein of worry beat steadily in her temple. The skin sheathing her aristocratic skull was thin as onionskin paper, translucent. I could almost see her brain percolating.

She was delightfully appetizing, as charming as a Swiss diplomat without his wallet in a Cairo whorehouse, and as highly strung and ready to run as a racehorse on Derby day. It was time to set her mind at ease.

"You are telling me this," I said, reaching and lightly touching her bird-boned hand with its gnawed nails in a friendly, avuncular way, "because to keep it inside would be tantamount to suicide. That is the nature of a secret. If you let it sit and fester it will eat you alive, piece by precious piece, like a hungry cannibal eats a chubby missionary in a dark, smelly hut."

I fixed her with my melancholy eyes, my understanding, unsurprisable eyes, inviting her confidence, letting her know that my motives were selfless and pure, that I wasn't chasing after her swollen bank account or her sweet little derriere or even her extraordinary lungs which in the event of an auto crash could most probably double as air bags—no no no, I was offering her this sad, almost-ugly face of mine free of charge, as a sop to her sorrow, as a giant sponge for her pain, as if to say: "Let your sadness soak into my eyes, sweetheart, let it wash away like a spot of blood in an ocean of bleach, like a spot of bleach in an ocean of blood, let it go, let it go, let it go. . . ."

Yes, mine is a face so forgettable, so unremarkable, so ordinary, that she could dump her guilty knowledge with me and go on with her life untroubled, as if the secret had never existed and was at worst a dimly recollected fragment of nightmare seen through a hazy white film of gauze bandages.

"The only way to kill the cannibal," I went on, smoothly soothing her bubbling nerves with my voice, "the only way to keep the secret from chewing you alive, is to sanitize it, expose it to the scouring effects of bright sunlight and fresh air. Let the secret wither and die and you will be reborn. Think of it as a spring-cleaning for your soul. Banish your blues to the scrap heap of memory."

Snakes of smoke leaped and squiggled and coiled off the end of the cigarette as she took another enormous haul and considered my words, squinting through the smoke. Beads of moisture formed on the tall iced glass of Campari and soda in front of her on the table. It was the color of a medium-rare hamburger. Pink. Pink and juicy and wet, fizzing with life. The buzz and babble of American voices came in waves. And outside, the rich, cow-dotted French countryside rolled off into the distance, green with life, fat with farms, humped with hills.

"Yes, I see that," she said. "But shouldn't I be telling this to a psychiatrist or a priest or perhaps my best friend?"

The thin-lipped lovely lit another cigarette off the one she was smoking. Her fine brow wrinkled like an overbaked potato as she sucked. I have seen that look before, seen it many times.

She was almost ready to spill. The desire to tell all was growing heavier every second. Soon it would outweigh caution. All she needed was a little emotional push and she'd be over the edge, tumbling head over heels into the abyss of confession.

"You, Monsieur, are a stranger, a complete and absolute stranger."

"Let us say instead, just for the sake of argument, my dear, that I am a sympathetic ear," I said, waggling my ears for comic effect, an old and very silly trick, stolen, I must admit, from Orson Welles in *Citizen Kane*.

She reacted as I'd hoped she would, with a calm and relaxed laugh, a giggle really. A childish little bell-like tinkle that spoke of running and jumping and skinned knees, of chocolate bars and chewing gum and afternoons chasing butterflies in sun-dappled meadows. Of fresh pajamas and brushed teeth and soap behind the ears. Of kind kisses before beddie-bye. Of heartfelt prayers and cool, clean sheets and the sweet, clean dreams of childhood.

"So you're saying it doesn't matter who I tell it to as long as I dump it, get rid of the hungry cannibal?"

"Exactly," I said. "Send that nasty fellow back to the bush to find another victim."

And then, realizing that we didn't have all day, I decided to give her the push. I hated to shove that innocent child off the cliff, but it was necessary. . . . As if the spirit of Mussolini were watching over the French rail system, the train was running right on schedule.

"You could," I said, speaking very slowly and distinctly, as she took another savage yet contemplative pull on her cigarette, "you could tell it to a cow, if a cow was capable of understanding human speech."

Instantly her face crumbled. Her eyes became old and sad and cynical, glazed with hurt, and her body slumped, as dejected as a cuckolded spouse discovering the love-stained sheets and coiled-hair evidence of betrayal.

She laughed, a hoarse, rasping, bitter laugh, laughed and laughed. That bitter, grown-up laugh seeped from her soft cherry-blossom lips like raw sewage, at first a light, ugly trickle, then growing stronger and louder until it was a foul, disgusting torrent, a horrible, bloodcurdling roar splashing forth like the number one hit in the seventh circle of Dante's *Inferno*. And she kept right on laughing, laughing and laughing until twin tears streamed from the corners of her lovely eyes, framing the high cheekbones dotted with pointillist freckles.

"A cow?" she cried, her voice rising and breaking on a wave of desperate laughter. "You, Monsieur, must be bloody ruddy psychic."

And then it came out. The story. The strange, ugly story. Finally came out. No dillydallying. No more laughing. In a huge vomitous rush it came. Like the chubby missionary chased by the hungry cannibal, sprinting desperately for safety with shoelaces flapping and hair standing on end, the story rushed forth, fat with detail, twisted with emotion, stinking of fear, and greasy with nervous sweat. And as she told it, she smoked cigarette after cigarette, guzzled down Campari and soda after Campari and soda, making the poor bar-car waiter scurry back and forth as never before, loosen his bow-tie for the first time in fifteen years. Her eyes, locked onto mine, expected shock, surprise, disbelief—but I had no shock, no surprise, no disbelief . . . only compassion and comprehension. You see, I already knew the story. I was three jumps ahead of her. The truth was that I was there only to provide an ending. . . . That's what I do. I provide endings. Guilt-free, happy endings. That's where the artistry comes in. In the fixer profession that's what separates the men from the boys, the butcher from the Picasso . . . how one orchestrates the final moment.

✢   ✢   ✢

Our story begins with money. Lots of money. Birgitta Smedley-Ross came from money. Buckets and buckets of dirty, stinking, delicious cash.

Now, to understand Birgitta, our lovely, troubled, hard-drinking, chain-smoking heiress with the unfortunate coif on the afternoon train bound from Paris to Trouville, a heavy secret suffocating her spirit like an overweight Sumo wrestler lying atop an anorexic Geisha girl, it is necessary to understand the money. Where it came from, how it was earned. In other words: who got screwed and who did the screwing.

Now, the money wasn't always dirty. No indeed, for a very long time the money was clean as a sweet little bird's well-licked armpit, as sanitary as the Pope's toilet, if you will, and that earthly throne is, I can assure you from personal experience, as spotless and germ-free as the china Queen Elizabeth sets the table with when company comes a-calling. (Why, I remember the night a bunch of us were up at the Big Kielbasa's place in Rome watching the fights from Mexico on cable TV—there was

me, the Big K, Nelson (Mandela), Dez (Desmond Tutu) and
Jerry Lewis—don't ask me how he picks his guest list—and every
time one of us came back from the toilet (and here let me mention that a goodly amount of beer was being consumed and
Jerry especially has a notoriously weak bladder, perhaps as a
result of the early years on the road with Dean), the Big K
would rush into the inner sanctum and wipe up the errant
dribbles, regardless of whether or not it was during or between
rounds of the fight.) Yes, the money was earned in an honorable fashion. It was sweated for, and the sweat was as honest as
any sweat that was ever sweat, and it was cherished, cherished
and respected as only hard-earned money can be cherished and
respected; but by the time the money arrived in the hands of
Birgitta, it was covered with some extremely unpleasant crud
indeed, stuff you'd never in a billion months of Sundays find
hanging around the Big Kielbasa's throne room.

✛   ✛   ✛

Let us reverse the march of time and travel back to Italy in the
year 1894. The city is Venice. The place is the train station. The
time is morning. There at the Venice station in the early
morning, in the misty early morning, with the sun stuck way
back in the low, silver sky like a fist in a fat belly, with early-
morning pigeons scavenging on the platform for early-morning
scraps, there we meet Antonio Russo.

Ciao, Antonio!

Antonio is a handsome fellow of nineteen, blond and
healthy, with a broad chest, the youngest son of one of the oldest

and most distinguished glassblowing families of Venice. Next to Antonio, we find his brothers, Giorgio, Mario, and Claudio. The Brothers Russo. We will not greet the three older ones by name as they have little to do with our story; in fact, they are there at the station and here in our story only to say goodbye to Antonio. But let us state (parenthetically) that each of the brothers possesses the famed Russo lungs, by now a genetic mutation, and that during childhood, whenever one of them celebrated a birthday, the candles on the cake stood a snowball's chance in Guam of staying lit; and let us also state, for the record, that on the occasions when one of the large-lunged lads held his breath to demand an after-dinner sweet, Mama Russo (Susanna) would go right on with her knitting, add a few dozen stitches, maybe even finish the sweater, and if it was Papa Russo (Maurizio) being pestered, why he might consume half the newspaper and three-quarters of a bottle of wine before looking up to see if the brat had turned blue yet. It's a true pity the Russo boys weren't born in the era of jazz. They had the lips and lungs of Louis Armstrong, the chipmunk cheeks and chops of Dizzy Gillespie, the steady, long-blowing cool of John Coltrane, and the rare birdlike ability to modulate breath at subsonic speed of Charlie Parker, bending glass like the aforementioned virtuosos bent notes. Man, those boys could blow!

Yes, like his brothers, Antonio possesses the fabulous Russo lungs, the great magnificent Russo lungs, capable of blowing glass, of crafting intricate and delicate and delightful baubles, pricey bits of whimsy, sturdy useful vessels; and yes, Antonio has the Russo love of cash and commerce; but here Antonio differs from his siblings: he hates Venice. He considers it a two-gondola town. He wants more, much much more. Huffing and puffing glass for the next fifty years is not his idea of a meaningful life; so that is why he is at the station, and that is why Mario and Claudio and Giorgio are honking into their handkerchiefs like great elephants in mourning, rending the delicate silk to wet wispy shreds with huge screeching garlicky blasts of sad snot . . . for dear baby brother Antonio is taking the morning train for France, and from there a boat to jolly old England. . . .

. . . Liverpool, to be exact, where he changes his name to Tony Ross and opens an Italian restaurant.

Ah, but the good people of Liverpool are not yet psychologically and emotionally prepared for the wonders of spaghetti. They have no palate for pizza, no stomach for garlic, no curiosity for risotto . . . they are completely without interest in the many and varied gastronomic wonders of la bella Italia. And furthermore, to our young Venetian immigrant's abject horror, they prefer ale to wine. Tony Ross's restaurant sits empty as a Neapolitan wino's bottle.

The visionary dream of creating a Little Italy in Liverpool is dashed, but Antonio is determined not to end up back in Venice blowing glass, so he sets about investigating these strange English, tramping the streets and backalleys of Liverpool, eating in the most crowded restaurants, chatting with strangers, buying them pints of warm, pissy ale, observing the local customs, and he realizes, smacking his head for missing the obvious, that success lies in the familiar, and that more than rice pudding, more than tea and crumpets, more even than queen and country and flag and empire, more perhaps even than life itself, the British love their beef. Roast beef, boiled beef, bully beef, beef steak. Beef Wellington, London broil. Beef broth, beef liver, calf's liver, calf's brains, crusty golden pies bursting with steaming steak and kidney. Veal, marrow, tripe, blood pudding, blood sausage, ribs and tongue. Testicles, even. Yes, the British are Beefeaters from the word go.

So Antonio turns his failed spaghetti joint into a beef-and-ale house, and he prospers (the place is packed from breakfast until late at night), parlaying the one restaurant into two into three, buying a farm where he raises and slaughters and butchers his own cows, then more farms, more restaurants, a string of butcher shops, and in only a few short years of hard work he is far far richer than all his glassblowing forebears put together.

And so it comes to pass that after a brief courtship, facilitated by British beef and Italian poetry, Antonio marries Agatha Smedley, daughter of locomotive train magnate Arthur Smedley, and to seal this dynastic deal and permanently insert his not unsizable Venetian nose deep into the clenched rectum and cold, stony heart of his beloved's father, and to guarantee his cows permanent cheap passage to market and port (in a move that anticipates the spirit of late-twentieth-century American feminism) he tacks the Smedley onto the Ross and becomes Anthony Smedley-Ross, Esquire. Three out of every four tins of beef consumed by the British in the trenches of the First World War come from the Smedley-Ross factories and are branded S + M Beef, in honor of Antonio's parents, Susanna and Maurizio Russo.

How many men, how many millions of men were consumed

by war to make Antonio rich? How many men, how many millions of men died bloody, brave deaths in boots made from S + M leather, their bellies still gurgling with S + M beef, their bones strong from a childhood of S + M milk and cheese, to make Antonio rich? How many cows, how many millions of cows were consumed by men consumed by war to make Antonio rich? (And down the line, how many beef-related cases of colon cancer metastasized to make Antonio rich? Ai yai yai, my bowels ache just thinking of it.)

Agatha and Anthony have one only one child, a son, Osbert Wellington Smedley-Ross, known at home as Oz and at school as Beef Wellington, and between the wars Oz helps his father build onto the already substantial family fortune, branching into the gelatin market, selling the Americans beef lips and beef snouts and beef eyeballs by the thousand-barrel lot to make their hot dogs with. By the time Hitler and the gang serve the fresh war on the world table, the Smedley-Rosses are the biggest beef barons in the British Isles, possibly the biggest on the planet, with holdings worldwide.

✢　　✢　　✢

Let us skip the backstabbing backroom deals (the fact that S + M Beef supplied beef to both the Allies and the Axis powers), let us gloss over the Machiavellian manipulation of markets, the shrewd reinvestments, all the sweat and suffering (of others) and dirty dealing (by Smedley-Ross père et fils) that went into the creation of one of the worlds most fabulous fortunes . . . let us fast-forward to India, 1946.

✛   ✛   ✛

India in turmoil. India on the brink of independence. India gripped by the fever of change. Ghandi preaching passive resistance. And the British, wearied to the bone by war and the slow decline of empire, are about ready to pack up their tea bags and Union Jacks and set sail for home, their traditionally stiff upper lips drooping loose and soft as their guts after a heaping helping of Vindaloo curried beef (made four out of five times with beef from an S + M can).

Let us say hello to Egbert Smedley-Ross, son of Osbert and his wife Tallulah (a brewery heiress married to insure the Smedley-Ross restaurants a cheap source of ale), grandson of Antonio Russo: Major Egbert Smedley-Ross, adjutant to Lord Mountbatten and heir to the S + M Beef fortune, the future father of Birgitta. Major Egbert Smedley-Ross reporting for duty (in this strange but guaranteed true story).

Hello, Egbert!

What's that you're doing, Egbert? There in that dark bedchamber with the spinning ceiling fan, the sounds of all those hungry grumbling stomachs on that teeming Calcutta street outside the room muffled by the intimate rustling of bed sheets? Your crisp khaki uniform scattered all over the floor like banana peels in a monkey's cage? What are you doing, Egbert, with your white face clamped viselike on that young, handsome, Indian fellow's lap? Your red, bristly British mustache tickling his curlies . . . ?

"Oh, Major Egbert!" cried the young, passively unresisting, half Hindu–half Muslim in a melodic Indian accent, as the pressure reached its zenith and all his pent-up joy gushed forth, independent of his will (but sadly still dependent on an Englishman). "How do you do it?"

"Well you see, Ali," said Egbert Smedley-Ross with a satisfied smile, like the cat who's literally just eaten the canary, "just as you are the descendant of Indian dervishes and Kama Sutra—trained sexual athletes and hence are very comfortable on your knees or twisted up like spaghetti on a plate or whirling about the bed like a top, I am the descendant of Venetian glass-blowers and have inherited an incredible set of lungs. I can blow and suck like a bloody typhoon. It is my one great talent."

✤ ✤ ✤

Later that day, after the love, after the lunch, after the lingering languorous lunch- and love-flavored goodbye kiss, as Ali was gaily sauntering home to his humble hovel, whistling *Rule Britannia* off key, a few cans of S + M beef bulging deep in his pockets, a secret gift to his Muslim uncle, he was surrounded by an irate group of his countrymen who had decided to employ their own militant version of passive resistance on the traitorous homo-sexual. After dousing poor Ali with kerosene, the match was lit and tossed, and the gang just sat back and watched, passive as all hell, as the thin young man with the long fluttery eyelashes was burnt to a crisp, going from his own soft brown to Tandoori-chicken red to black in a matter of hellish screaming moments. And Major Egbert Smedley-Ross could do nothing but watch, his great breath powerless (these were no mere nineteenth-century Venetian birthday candles flickering atop a cake), watch and quietly weep from his window as his love went down in flames, watch and weep as a half-starving street urchin gleefully plucked two charred cans of S + M beef from the smoldering corpse and ran home for an instant beef dinner.

✧   ✧   ✧

That evening, Egbert visited Ali's family and tried to console them with a huge amount of cash and an ill-conceived gift of a case of S + M beef. (Those Smedley-Rosses! Always thinking a case or two of canned beef could solve any beef they got into!)

The family was inconsolable. Insulted by the money, even more insulted by the beef, they politely but firmly requested him to vacate the premises so that they could grieve in peace and arrange for the completion of Ali's cremation. But with the determination of a British bulldog, like a true Smedley-Ross, Egbert persisted. He wanted to do something nice for the family as a means of assuaging his guilt, and after a few weeks of entreaty, perhaps for no other reason than to be rid of the damned Englishman, they decided to allow him to take Ali's baby brother Ahmed with him to England as his ward.

✧   ✧   ✧

So Ahmed, now called Jack Smedley-Ross, the godson of Lord Mountbatten, grew up in Swallowville, the Smedley-Ross family seat, a huge estate in Hertfordshire, with many farmlands adjoining. At first an attempt was made to abide by Jack's Calcutta family's wishes that he be raised within the Hindu faith, feeding him vegetables and grains instead of cow products, but in 1948 (not long after old Antonio died, of natural causes, followed closely by the former Agatha Smedley, of heartbreak, followed closely by Osbert and Tallulah, in a plane crash), when Egbert married Prudence Pringle-Pratt (of the famous potato-fortune Pringle-Pratts) and Egbert and Prudence legally adopted him, she, as family matriarch, insisted that Jack be afforded no special treatment, that the sweet, handsome little fellow conform to the Anglican faith and beef-eating lifestyle of the rest of the family.

Said Prudence: "A true Smedley-Ross eats beef three times a day. And as for vegetables, his mother is a Pringle-Pratt, and that means potatoes, by Jove. Lots of potatoes."

Let us skip the details of Jack's beef-eating childhood, pausing only to mention that he grew sturdy and strong on a steady diet of meat and potatoes and Protestant hymns, and that Egbert and Prudence had five children of their own, Samuel, Simon, Cyrus (who do not figure greatly in this family history, as after university they emigrated to Argentina, Japan, and America, respectively, to help run S + M Beef International), and then finally, many years later, in 1973, as an unconscious and very surprising afterthought—an accident, if truth be known—the twins Bertram and Birgitta. Prudence was forty-eight years old by then (old enough that the servants checked the Guinness book of records to see if she might qualify as the oldest woman ever to experience the rigors and splendors of childbirth), Jack/Ahmed was pushing thirty, and Egbert, his once proud and very red mustache now a distinguished gray, was on the far side of fifty.

✠   ✠   ✠

I must take a break a moment, dear friends, for a deep breath. Yes, telling this story is exhausting. Traveling from Italy to Britain to India, and of course my home country France (where I met Birgitta on the train from Paris to Trouville), hopping to the nineteenth century and hurdling the years to the present . . . it makes me very tired. And all this talk of beef makes me hungry, very hungry. I believe I am in need of sustenance. Yes, I must step outside and visit my local neighborhood Fast Burger store, the most rapidly growing chain of burger emporiums on the planet. What? Are those snorts of culinary derision I hear? Are you judging me by my need for a burger? I ask you, all of you: who among you has not at one time or another zipped into your friendly, brightly lit neighborhood Fast Burger to satisfy that atavistic craving for beef within us all? The desire for the taste of blood and ketchup on the tongue, the warmth of fried meat in the belly. Who among you has not guzzled a cola, the ice-cold carbonated nectar of the living gods? Who among you has not stuffed strand after strand of crispy golden-brown fries down your throats? Who among you has not reveled in the grease, wallowed in the delicious slop? Why, if Louis XVI had tasted a Fast Burger, he would have ordered an outlet built right on the spot, within spitting distance of the throne, and he would have inhaled burger after burger, without chewing, until they ran out his royal ears. And had Marie Antoinette known the glory of Fast Burger's fries, why, her famous fate-sealing words might well have been: "Let them eat fries!" And it would have been so: the hoi polloi would have eaten fries, the Revolution would have been averted, and Marie could have kept her head.

So be not too proud, dear friends. Let those among you without the sin of chopped beef cast the first burger . . . I will only be gone for a few moments. Forgive this poor tired narrator, he needs a huge, delicious grease-dripping, artery-clogging Fast Burger right this minute. . . .

✛   ✛   ✛

I am back, my energy restored and my blood sugar count at an acceptable level. I will not belch on the page, I will not pick bits of burger from my teeth. No indeed, I am a gentleman—perhaps not a British gentleman like Jack Smedley-Ross, but a gentleman nonetheless—and I'm back, ready to jump right in, ready to dig into the meat and potatoes of the story, which, coincidentally, or not (you make the choice), concerns Fast Burgers.

✛   ✛   ✛

The Fast Burger chain was created by Jack Smedley-Ross, who despite being born in India, is as English as steak and kidney pie. A sharp dresser, a carrier of umbrellas, a ladies' man not unfamiliar with the British public-school practices that impelled his adoptive father Egbert to adopt parts of his elder brother Ali's anatomy back in Calcutta, mildly prejudiced against East and West Indians, given to incest (he seduced both Bertram and Birgitta at a very tender age) and fond of wearing ladies' underwear under his Saville Row suits, Jack is a very astute businessman who, as eldest son, has taken over the running of the family business from his daddy Egbert who, in his mid-seventies, now spends most of his days at Swallowville painting idealized portraits of cows and taking tourists on tours of his Museum of Beef, housed in a specially built airplane hangar.

While Egbert has been creating his museum the past ten years (collecting all manner of bovine memorabilia, from Antonio's first restaurant in Liverpool, imported brick by brick, to Antonio's first butcher shop, to Louis Pasteur's laboratory and the underwear Louis was purported to be wearing when he made his earth- and milk-shaking breakthrough, to an ancient Roman fresco of a spotted cow being milked by a naked Nubian maiden, costing five million US dollars, to the grease-spattered apron worn by the founder of McDonald's in his first restaurant, to an Andorran cave painting of a bull from the Neanderthal period—looking so very much like a bad Chagall that its authenticity was challenged until the carbon-dating tests were completed—to the yogurt spoon and chipped bowl used by the recently deceased hundred-and-forty-nine-year-old man in Georgia, Russia, plus various artifacts and beef-related tools and machinery, art and documents too numerous to mention) Jack has seen the Smedley-Ross market share shrink alarmingly. He has witnessed the rise of the fast-food joint and the death of the neighborhood steakhouse, the demise of the traditional Sunday family beef dinner and a horrifying trend toward the consumption of white meat, chicken and fish and pork; and though S + M Beef still supplies a healthy percentage of the beef for burger chains across the new Europe, Jack is worried. He is convinced that the fast-food craze is not just a passing fancy but the wave of the future, the shape of things to come, and so he decides, taking the bull by the horns, that S + M Beef must, absolutely must, capitalize its own burger division.

"We must control the whole process of nutritional delivery," Jack declaimed at the company board meeting, stroking his blood-red power tie with the Black Angus bulls. "From powerful papa bull shagging docile mama cow in the green field, to bovine embryo, to little cud-chewing cutie, to fat moocow, to slaughter, to butcher, to burgers in the bellies of consumers worldwide!"

"Huzzah!" cried the board of directors.

And Jack said:

"Let there be burgers!"

It was a natural. The Pringle-Pratt connection was tapped to insure a cheap and infinite supply of potatoes; the finest chefs on the continent and Nick Eliopoulos, owner of a famous Greek hamburger joint in New York City called Fat Nick's, were consulted to fine-tune the menu; and the African-American managers of two hundred and fifty McDonald's in the United States were lured to the fledgling organization at huge salary increases to get the first stores up and running (four stores to each manager), to teach the Europeans the intricate art of burger making.

As one of the Black Americans said to a group of Swedish trainees:

"Yo, my European brothers and sisters, you gots to slap the cheese like this, squirt the ketchup just so, lay in the tomato like this, and voila, baby, you got you a burger. From oven to mouth in less than fifteen seconds, wrapping and setting on the hot-tray included. You dig? And yo, Ingrid, don't go picking your nose on duty or it's your ass out on the street."

It took the Europeans a while to get the speed, to mimic the proper cheese-slapping technique, but soon they had it. And as far as picking their noses . . . well, only one employee, a Belgian of Taiwanese decent, found his ass on the street, his finger still stuck in his nose.

Indeed, let there be burgers! Clean delicious Fast Burgers!

And in a brilliant move that smacked of his great-grandfather Antonio/Tony Ross marrying his great-grandmother Agatha Smedley, Jack Smedley-Ross, longtime bachelor, fabled London swinger, took as wife one Lucy-Joy Klein, the American heiress to the most prestigious toilet-paper company on the planet, Kleinex.

Yes indeed, the S + M company was literally and figuratively covering their and their customers' asses. They had the cheese factories in Holland, the wheat fields for rolls in the US, the tomato farms in Italy, ketchup factories in Poland, lettuce patches in France, and onion fields and cows all over. They started with a thousand nearly identical stores dotted strategically about the new Europe, each costing upwards of two hundred thousand US dollars to construct, not including the cost of the real estate, sinking a few billion dollars total into the project, including the advertising. I'm sure you have seen the commercial where the still-fabulous Catherine Deneuve, sitting in a bubble bath, bites into a Deluxe Fast Burger, special sauce and ketchup and grease dripping pink off her classic lips as she whispers: "I like my men slow, but I love my burgers Fast!" It cost two million dollars to get her to say the magic words and another million to chew the burger for five seconds before the director screamed "Cut!" and she spat it out, but Cat was a real pro, they all agreed: the finished piece makes her looks like she's about to have an orgasm eating that burger. (Of course she hadn't been the first choice; they had offered St. Brigitte of the Homeless Donkeys ten million (what a coup that would have been!), but even at that price (that's a lot of donkey food she could have bought!), admirably true to her convictions, the Belle of the Beasts was unwilling to become the Belle of the Beef.)

And the people, the great teeming masses of Europe, on the go, on the run, too busy to cook for themselves, the people recognized a good thing when it was crammed down their throats, a superior product, guaranteed hot and fast and convenient, nutritious and delicious, delightfully scrumptious and sizzling and. . . . Stop me, or I'll have to run out again!

✦   ✦   ✦

Let us slow the story down, let us switch gears, let us get away from burgers for a moment and venture to a dingy little flat in the Brixton section of London where we meet Rhajiv, a British-born Indian of the Hindu faith, a telephone company employee with revolutionary leanings and a decidedly scientific mind, a card-carrying member of both Greenpeace and HOPCC (the Hindu Organization for the Preservation of Cow Culture). We will not greet him out loud, as he is hard at work in his kitchen laboratory, wearing latex gloves and a mask. He is busy fiddling with his vials and burners, test tubes and beakers and microscope, listening to the Sex Pistols . . . but let us sneak a peek at what Rhajiv, also known as Roger, is looking at under the microscope.

Cells. Cells behaving strangely. Cells breaking off and bouncing. Cells dancing madly, spinning like dervishes after drinking too much Italian coffee, an anarchic little dance of cellular disorder and death which amuses Roger no end.

"Tee hee hee," he giggles, like a mad scientist in a Grade-Z horror movie from the 1950s.

Tee hee hee, indeed.

What we are privileged to witness here, sadly privileged to be rudely spying on, I might add, is a moment of planetary signif-icance (akin to Oppenheimer and the boys splitting the atom): the isolation and creation of—a drum roll, please: Mad Cow Disease!

Yes, this is how Mad Cow Disease was born. Contrary to the theories being floated about by the natural-foods community and the liberal media and the left wing of the scientific-medical world that Mad Cow Disease is a result of years upon years of cows being fed hormone-enriched grain or munching pesticide-laden grasses or drinking chlorinated water or eating horribly diseased sheep parts, that Mad Cow Disease has been around for years, known about, the knowledge being sat on by the medical and scientific communities (mad, mad, conspiracy theories one and all!), Mad Cow Disease was created not so very long ago in Roger's kitchen.

Touched with the genius of madness and fueled by religious fervor and political purpose, Roger (having grown up in the London East Indian community listening to the diatribes of

Muslim fanatics and Hindu philosophers and of course the Sex Pistols), hates Christians and loves cows. Like Harry Truman before him, he has a vision. If a billion cows have to die to insure the future of the species, the cow species, that is, then so be it!

"I am striking a blow for cows everywhere and for the planet," he says to a white mouse named Major in a cage, smiling grimly as he feeds the little rodent some Basmati rice soaked in his special formula. "Otherwise, my little martyr, all the precious cow farts will eat away the ozone layer. The evil Beef-eaters will destroy the planet. But if I can stop people from eating beef by creating mass fear and driving the prices up, then cattle can go back to living normal lives, they will not be overbred, more rain forests will not be chopped down for grazing lands, the ozone will be saved, and Hindus, and Muslims and even those misguided revolting Christians can learn to live together and leave the cows alone. It will require great sacrifice on the part of the cow community, but great change demands extreme measures."

And by way of response, Major the mouse stares at him with thoroughly deranged eyes and runs full-steam into the bars of the cage, his limbs shaking spastically as he chews his own tail and froths at the mouth, head bleeding.

✠   ✠   ✠

London by night. Bertram and Birgitta Smedley-Ross are out clubbing, drinking champagne, dancing. They are also hunting, hunting for a lover. They both have the same requirements. He or she, it doesn't matter which, must be dark- and smooth-skinned, no hairy apes need apply. For whatever reasons, perhaps because each was seduced by elder brother Jack at an early age, they are both fixated on nonwhite nonhairy lovers.

✢   ✢   ✢

The jungle beat weaves a steamy sultry rhythm in Birgitta's blood as she takes the African girl's face in her hands. They kiss, a locking of lips, a mingling of salt and pepper, of cultures and continents. The international democracy of passion. Their hips grind, their pulses throb in syncopation to the mad, jagged bass line, while over in the strobe-lit corner, on a comfortable couch, Bertie, pale, pretty Bertie, the mirror image of his pale, pretty sister, down to the Victoria Falls of ringletted hair cascading onto his thin anemic shoulders and the Victoria's Secret brassiere under his pullover, chats up a handsome youth, a dark, cow-eyed fellow with lustrous long lashes who reminds him of big brother Jack.

It is, of course, Roger, and it is no accident that Roger is here. He has quit his job at the phone company and has been trailing the twins for weeks now, having gotten their names from the secret HOPCC files, the supersecret list of enemies, following them first one and then the other and now together, getting to know their habits and their haunts, their likes and dislikes, and he is appalled by what he has found: they are both bisexual, eat nothing but beef and potatoes, never give a beggar so much as a coin, and are, he strongly (and rightly) suspects, one another's lovers.

And that night, after the African girl goes off with another woman, his suspicions are verified. In the Hyde Park–Kensington flat they share, the twins treat Roger to a demonstration of the famous Russo glassblowing techniques, inflating him then deflating him then inflating him and deflating him and each other until it blows his mind, in addition to his beef and potatoes, to coin a euphemism . . .

⊹   ⊹   ⊹

Then begins an idyllic time. The twins take Roger on a Rolls-Royce tour England, visiting many of the Smedley-Ross holdings across the length and breadth of the country as well as the farms owned by their friends, and despite being exhausted by the twins' vast physical needs, Roger is happy, for his pockets are filled with sugar cubes soaked with his special formula. At each farm they visit, be it a Smedley-Ross farm or one owned by the competition, Roger throws sugar cubes into the fields and pens, and the cows lick and munch the poisoned sugar. Yumm.

⊹   ⊹   ⊹

"Dear Rog," said Birgitta one sunny afternoon, shortly after arriving at the family seat in Swallowville, far, far away from the prying eyes of the farmworkers, as they wandered alone in a field, having shed Bertie a way back to water the grass, as she took a colossally huge haul on her cigarette. "My darling love, why do you do that, throw sugar to the cattle?"

"It is the old Hindu influence," he answered with a sly smile. "Sweetness for the sweet cows."

"Oh, what a lot of mumbo jumbo and poppycock!" Birgitta snapped. "Don't you know that Hinduism is based on historical necessity? That the reverence for cattle derives from a decision made by community leaders in India long ago when it was calculated that there was more nutritional value in keeping the cattle alive to give milk than it would be to slaughter and eat them?"

Roger was shocked. Blasphemy! His eyes turned stormy, and he took his jacket off and hung it on a fence post like a British gentleman preparing for a bout of fisticuffs, then strode purposefully over to Birgitta and threw her to the soft thick grass, hiked her skirt high on her pale shapely thighs (with her knee-high socks and prickling golden thigh hairs, she looked enchantingly like a schoolgirl in a glossy British flesh magazine), tore her panties, and entered her savagely, like a rutting bull. And Birgitta lay back with a smile, her mass of ringlets resting on a cushion of cow patties, happy as a dreamy calf—finally she had provoked Roger beyond his Ghandiesque passivity—and as she lay there enjoying the wonders of the Orient, her brother Bertie sat on a fence nearby and watched, playing pocket billiards and sucking on a sugar cube found in Roger's jacket.

✛   ✛   ✛

Jack Smedley-Ross was squirting ketchup on Lucy-Joy Klein Smedley-Ross's impressive breasts and between her quivering thighs, preparing to treat her like a hundred-and-thirty-pound Fast Burger when he heard a strange howling and a series of loud crashes from downstairs.

"Don't sweat the load, Jack," said Lucy, playing the dual roles of Fast Burger and Fast Burger restaurant manager at the same time, grabbing him by the ears and pulling his head to her sizzling deliciousness. "You must eat me within fifteen seconds while I'm piping hot, or it's your ass out on the couch."

But Jack welcomed the excuse to exit stage left. He was tired of the toilet-paper princess's sex games, and he was worried: reports were coming in from his farms across Britain that the cows were behaving strangely. They seemed to be afflicted with some bizarre malady, some neural disorder. At first he had just ordered the cows sold to other herds, but now after traveling from farm to farm, observing the lunatic cows in action, the shaking heads, the frothing mouths, the jellied legs, he was having them isolated, studied, and then sold to the Cambodians and shipped to Southeast Asia to be used as detonators of live land mines.

If the public finds out about this bovine AIDS, thought Jack, we'll be up Shit's Creek without a paddle, as the Yanks are fond of saying.

Yes, Jack was tired. Tired and worried about the cows. And now this stupid cow of an American he had taken to wife for her toilet-paper connection was demanding service far beyond the call of marital duty. He yearned for the good old days of ladies' underwear and lemonade enemas. . . .

By the time Jack made it down the long and winding staircase to investigate, some ketchup caked upon his chin and Lucy-Joy sawing wood contentedly in bed upstairs, the living room was a wreck, and the whole family (save for Egbert and Prudence), wearing monogrammed pajamas and nighties, and all the servants, clad in cheap pajamas and nighties, were watching with shocked horror as Bertie, frothing at the mouth, clad only in push-up bra and see-through panties, ran into the walls and shook spasmodically, snorting and pawing the earth before each fresh run.

"Drugs," thought the butler.

"Inbreeding," thought the upstairs maid.

"Divine retribution," thought Roger with an inner smile.

"Like the crazy cows," thought Jack with a shiver as the cook, a large Jamaican woman with eyes as black and fiery and determined as Sitting Bull the Indian, hit poor Bertie over his curly head with a heavy skillet, temporarily putting an end to the insanity.

✛   ✛   ✛

Old Egbert had slept through the previous night's brouhaha. He awoke refreshed, and after sucking a good few roomfuls of fresh air he went to the Museum of Beef to hang a recently painted portrait of the Laughing Cow lying on a chaise longue, womanly udders flopping this and thataway, in the classic style of Reubens.

✛   ✛   ✛

All the Smedley-Rosses had slept late save for workaholic Jack, who had taken an early-morning helicopter to the S + M company headquarters to coordinate the Fast Burger chain's billionth burger promotion. Yes, in less than a year, Fast Burger had sold close to a billion burgers. It was the fastest-growing hamburger chain on the planet. Now, given a choice, many

Europeans were choosing Fast Burger over McDonald's. So it seemed appropriate that the company do something extra-special to celebrate. The former prime minister and one of the boy princes and a top transvestite pop star were being considered as candidates for the billionth burger. The board was in favor of the prince, Bertram and Birgitta favored the transvestite, but Jack, ever the patriot, was leaning toward the gallant old prime minister.

✢   ✢   ✢

Bertram was sleeping soundly, a large lump on his head, but really none the worse for his midnight episode.

✢   ✢   ✢

Roger was lying back in bed like a pasha, enjoying Birgitta's morning breathing exercises. Unbeknownst to him, though, the upstairs maid had taken his jacket to be cleaned and pressed. And when she found the sugar cubes in his pocket she said to the downstairs maid, "Bloody little thieving Paki. Doesn't know a patch of clover when he stumbles into it. Sweet little Birgitta's up there sharing the family glassblowing secrets and the ungrateful brown bugger's gone and nicked the sugar." And so, ever loyal to the Smedley-Rosses, she put the sugar back in the pantry.

✢   ✢   ✢

Brunch was jolly. The day was warm. Roger was in shirtsleeves.

Too warm for his jacket, so he hadn't yet noticed the missing sugar cubes.

All the Smedley-Rosses drank mimosas, champagne and orange juice, all except Old Egbert, who drank tea with milk and sugar. (Need I say which sugar?) And they ate steak and eggs with potatoes. Old Prudence nodded her head with approval at the way young Roger ate three helpings of potatoes, though his refusal to eat beef or imbibe alcohol at breakfast (or anytime) seemed downright unpatriotic.

"Perhaps," she said, "Roger, some Pringle-Pratt was in Pakistan and you have our blood running through your veins, you do so love your spuds."

Roger didn't bother telling these disgusting creatures that he was a British citizen, a Brit of Indian heritage born in London, a terrorist sworn to destroy the British beefmaster class and restore cows to their rightful place of honor and dignity in the world. . . . No, he politely excused himself to take a walk.

✢   ✢   ✢

Old Egbert caught up with young Roger as he approached the Museum of Beef.

"Sunny day," said Lord Mountbatten's former adjutant, still spry despite the heavy load of years he was carrying. "Keeps the bloody tourists away. How'd you like a private tour of the museum, young man?"

"It would interest me greatly, sir."

"You know," said Old Egbert as they stood before Tony Ross's first restaurant, recreated brick by brick in the Great

Hall of Beef, "you remind me of someone I knew years ago in Calcutta."

"You know what they say," said Roger with a malicious grin. "We all look alike."

"No, no, not that," said Old Egbert, looking at the very first menu from Tony Ross's aborted Italian restaurant in Liverpool, preserved under glass like the Magna Carta, glancing at such then-unappreciated items as Risotto Milanese, Eggplant Parmigiana, and Veal Marsala. "You really do remind me of him."

Old Egbert continued with the tour, all the while thinking back to his great love Ali, lo those many years ago in Calcutta. They were now in Tony Ross's first slaughterhouse. The cloying stink of ancient dried blood made Roger nauseous.

"Smell that, boy?"

Roger nodded yes.

"That, boy," pronounced Egbert, breathing deeply and sighing contentedly, "that is the smell of money. You've heard people say that time is money? Wrong wrong wrong, my boy. Time is peanuts!" he cried. "Time is the soap that washes history's ass!" His old eyes blazed with conviction. "The truth is that blood is money!"

Roger felt the Pringle-Pratt potatoes rise in his gorge. . . . The bloodstained draining troughs, blood turned faint and black with the passing years, the heads of the sledgehammers worn smooth from countless unions with the skulls of cows, the sharp bloodstained knives, razor-sharp, the bloodstained butcher tables: a money factory, a factory of death, he was in the belly of the beast. . . . He could hear a billion cows plodding

toward their doom like Jews to the gas chambers, their resigned
hoof beats echoing in his brain like tom-tom drums in the
jungle: "Run now, run, the white man's coming, grab your
babies and run, run!" But there was nowhere to run to . . . not
for Jews, not for the tribesmen, not for the cows. They were
caught up in the bloody warp and woof of history. The poor
sweet docile cows had been trapped. Victims of the planetary
beef mania, the red-meat hysteria. Roger groaned. He could
feel what the cows had felt: the fear, the sorrow, the sure,
marrow-deep knowledge of impending death . . . and now,
slicing sharply through his consciousness, a billion bovine
screams of terror echoing across the years, mooing the ultimate
moo-cow blues as the heavy sledge arcs gracefully through space,
smacking them between the brown, liquid eyes, the dull thud of
iron hammering onto skull, dizzy, groggy, skullbones dented,
sometimes cracked, neurotransmitters firing wildly, legs rubbery,
but still alive, yes! as the sharp knife in the blood-dripping hand
expertly slits their throats, blood pumping in great gushing gey-
sers, pain inconsequential, blocked out by the hovering shadow
of impatient dark death, a sad, pointless death after a sad, pointless life of slop-eating slavery. . . . And for what? So that some
bloodthirsty Brit could eat a steak, a bloody juicy steak? So that
some pasty-faced voyeuristic Brit with bad teeth and ice-cold eyes
could stand in an air-conditioned supermarket and get a goddamn hard-on while looking at the obscenity of raw red beef
marbled with fat, packed in clear plastic?

The misery of a million dead cows crowded Roger's vegetarian heart, tears ran down his face, and he fainted.

When he awoke, he found himself with his pants around his

ankles, lying in a draining trough, the old man's face performing the by-now-familiar Russo glassblowing routine on his crotch.

"No!" he groaned, begging, pleading to the insane old man. "Have mercy. . . . Please, no."

"Nnysss!" came the muffled cry. And Old Egbert's eyes glittered madly. He was flying high on a combination of passion, memory, and Mad Cow Disease.

"Stop it, please!" Roger grabbed a handful of the cottony hair and yanked, but Old Egbert would not budge; and with a sickening feeling in his gut, much like the first time he ate a cheeseburger as a child, Roger felt the silver bristles of the old beef baron's mustache tickle his belly, and against his will he felt himself pumped and pumped until he was about ready to explode. . . .

"No!" he screamed, and his scream echoed in the cavernous room like that of a solitary brown cow being led to slaughter . . . and then he reached, stretched his hand, groping, groping . . . his fingers wrapping around the smooth, wooden grip of the heavy sledgehammer . . . lifting it with difficulty now, holding it high now . . . and now letting gravity and strength born of terror do their work, bringing it crashing down onto the old man's snow-thatched noggin.

Kkklack!

Egbert's eggshell skull was split wide open, his brain was exposed, a vague yellow-gray color like the polluted evening skies over Manchester, yet the unbearable suction continued, continued, and Roger felt the life being sucked out of him by Egbert's massive dying breath. He did not want it to end like this. . . . Yes, he'd done his part for the preservation of cow culture, but he was too young to die, and he realized in a flash of insight that he loved Birgitta, really and truly loved her. . . . And it was with tremendous effort, an effort born of abject fear of emasculation and love for Birgitta, that he was able to pry open the clamped powerful jaws and raise the now-dead head from his now-deflated spout; and there he sat for a good minute and a half, feeling the stale beef-scented wind of the old man's final enormous dying breaths blowing him dry.

Praise Shiva, the evil beef baron was nearly dead, and Roger was intact, having just escaped circumcision or worse. He bowed his head and said a prayer, then stripped the old man and hung him by the feet from a chain, winched him above the trough, the rusted metal creaking as he swung. . . . And then Roger did to Old Egbert what Old Antonio had personally done to so many poor cows: he sliced his throat and bled him dry.

We will skip the details of the amateur butcher job. We will not mention the shockingly huge size of the old man's lungs. We will jump right past the burning of Old Egbert's Banana Republic safari suit, Topsiders, and silk undershorts with the monogrammed cow in Tony Ross's pizza oven, the fire fueled by the portrait of the Laughing Cow and other flammable memorabilia. We will edit the telling of Roger's somber burial of teeth and bones and buttons and zipper and jewelry, the scrubbing of the utensils and troughs; and by all means let us not watch the close-up of Roger running the hunks and filets of the old man's remains through the antique meat grinder. Suffice it to say that three hours later, when Roger left the Museum of Beef by a back window and made his way to the manor kitchen, he did so holding a large package of chopped Egbert which he placed in the refrigerator.

"Don't mind me, Cook," he said. "Just leaving some chopped turkey in the fridge. Hindu dietary restrictions and whatnot."

Cook just watched as the cheeky Paki strolled off, whistling a Sex Pistols tune.

"Rass clott!" she swore, Jamaican style, opening the package. "De coolie bwoy gon gyet m'black rass fired, bringin' white meat into de Smedley-Ross household!"

✛   ✛   ✛

In Jack's absence Lucy-Joy Klein Smedley-Ross was amusing herself by playing naughty nurse to Bertram. Instead of the traditional sponge bath, however, she was administering a good hard tongue bath, not up to Smedley-Ross standards, thought Bertie, after all she's only a Smedley-Ross by marriage, but rather pleasant nonetheless.

Ah, thought Lucy-Joy, getting atop to play horsey, he might have a lump on his head, but he's also got a lump where it counts: he's really getting into it! He's frothing at the mouth and twitching like an epileptic in a Dostoevsky novel!

✛   ✛   ✛

And as the cold rain fell steadily upon the red-slate roof of Swallowville, the Smedley-Rosses hunkered down for a long weekend of thick quilts, roaring fires, board games, glassblowing exercises, and tea with sugar.

✛   ✛   ✛

And no one missed Old Egbert for days and days.

✛   ✛   ✛

Birgitta sucked down the last of her latest Campari and soda.

"That was two months ago," she said.

"And Roger admitted the murder?" I asked, already knowing the answer but just checking on her honesty quotient.

"Yes," she said, opening a fresh pack of cigarettes, snaking one out and igniting it with her monogrammed gold lighter. "He admitted everything. No regrets either. When he realized his sugar cubes were missing and that he loved me, he warned me not to drink any sugar in my tea and told me the whole bizarre story."

"Do you feel better?" I asked. "For having gotten it off your chest?"

"Yes, Monsieur, I do," she said with long long Russo-breathed sigh. "I really and truly do. As if the hungry cannibal is far far away. . . ."

"That is good, very very good. . . ." I said, encouraging her as she smoked, still marveling at the way she able to conquer a cigarette with only a few killer puffs. "So what happened next?"

"No idea," she said. "I took off. I felt betrayed: by Roger, by love, by passion, by my past, by life itself. I needed some time for self-reflection, to find myself. I've spent the past eight weeks scuba diving in the Galapagos Islands. Just got back to London yesterday. For the billionth-burger celebration."

"Ah, Birgitta," I said, shaking my head sadly. "Lying does not suit you."

"I don't have the foggiest notion what you mean, Monsieur."

"I mean, deal girl, dear, sweet, large-lunged lass, I mean that you are holding out on me. Keeping things to yourself. Naughty naughty. Fabricating stories to cover your ripe delectable rear end, if you will. I can smell out a lie like a blind perfume maker can smell a cow turd in a bowl of vichyssoise. You cannot hide the truth from me. I know what happened. I know where you've been, what you've been up to, you and Roger, and it wasn't scuba diving. . . . Not that with your amazing lungs you would even need an oxygen tank. . . . No, dear girl, you've been exploring the depths—but not the depths of the ocean, nor the depths of despair—no, you've been frolicking like a slippery sexy little eel in the depths of betrayal. . . . Dear dear Birgitta, if you do not tell me all, then the cannibal will continue to nibble away at your delicate body, bit by lovely bit until. . . ."

She touched her breast, then her nose, looked at me, the darting Bambi eyes growing foxlike with jungle cunning. I could see the fresh lies formulating behind her pale, almost translucent forehead. I shook my head.

"The truth," I said. "Tell me the truth. The truth shall set ye free. . . ."

"Fuck a duck!" she cried. "You're from the bloody press!"

"No, but I am not here on this train by accident."

"Apparently not," she said, snorting frostily, her voice icy as February in Finland with suspicion. "I think you should leave me now, and if you publish one word of this, my family, what's left of it, we'll sue your measly reporter's ass back to the Stone Age. . . ."

"Calm yourself, my dear. I am not from the media. *Au contraire*, publicity is my enemy. In point of fact, I happen to be employed by a large ecclesiastical organization," I confided, deciding that now was the time to show her a few of my cards, ease the story out of her like a skilled obstetrician pulls an unwilling baby from the warmth and safety of its mother's womb. "In the security-intelligence division."

"Ha!" she snorted with bitter mirthlessness. "That's a good one. But I suppose it's not far from reality. We English have come to worship at the altar of tabloid scandal. Which 'church,' Monsieur? The *Sun*? The *Daily Mirror*?"

"No, my dear, a real church, one based in Rome. . . ."

"You work for the bloody Po—?"

"Careful now. No names. We call him the Big Kielbasa, the big Polish sausage."

"Ludicrous."

"Perhaps," I said, lighting her fresh cigarette and watching her suck and suck and suck, three huge sucks and the cigarette was done, and the smoke was coming out of her hair and nose and mouth in great cloudy drifts.

"But let me explain. Six weeks ago the Big Kielbasa got a call from a good buddy of his in Canterbury, England, one of his best friends in fact. Let us call this friend Archie, Archie of Canterbury."

Birgitta's lips rose at their lovely corners into a wicked grin and she sneered in disbelief.

"What is so incredible about that?" I asked. "At that level they're all friends. They put aside ideological differences and just enjoy each other's company. I mean, who else can really and truly empathize with the burdens and dilemmas of vast responsibility and leadership save someone else in a similar lofty position? Why, I've seen the Big Kielbasa and the Dalai Lama play ping-pong until three in the morning. And the closest they ever came to an argument was whether or not a backhand winner by the Lama had nicked the table. . . .

"Anyhow, ping-pong aside, it seems that an Anglican priest had reported a curious incident to his superior, who in turn reported it to his superior, and so on and so forth up the pecking order until Archie got ahold of it. Now, Archie was stumped what to do. The situation was potentially very embarrassing, so extremely sensitive that he called the Big K for advice—he really does look up to him—and the Big K, cognizant of how compromised Archie's security forces and even the British Secret Service are these days due to tabloid infiltration, the Big K suggested that Archie allow him to send his top man in to find a solution. . . ."

"And that would be you," she said, like a wise child not buying the bedtime story. "You would be the Vatican fixer."

"Yes, that's me," I said humbly. "So I jump a jet—I do so love travel, talking to people on planes, on trains—and I go to England. I make my way to Swallowville. Yes, don't look so shocked. While you and Roger were off scuba diving in an ocean of love and deception, I was cleaning up your family mess. An interesting bunch, your family."

"The hell you say," Birgitta said with a loud derisive snort. "My family, all except Jack, are dead. Killed in a fire. The Swallowville mansion burned down."

"No, my dear, that is only what the press was told. That was the cover story we concocted to hide the truth. I will, if you refrain from such time-consuming outbursts, I will now tell you what really happened.

"Shortly after you and Roger vanished, your brother Bertram, his brain addled by Roger's special formula, decided that he was not a human being at all, that in fact he was a bull. Now what does a bull do best . . . ?"

She motioned me to tell it.

"Yes," I went on, clucking my sorrow, "he raped the poor innocent maids and the West Indian cook and even Charlie the gardener, no great beauty queen, and afterward he killed them all, I'm sad to say, crushed their skulls with a fire poker and buried them out back. Now, Lucy-Joy, your American sister-in-law, had gone equally mad, infected as she was from having slept with Bertie. She was holed up in her room watching television behind a barricaded door and eating rolls of toilet paper. And all this time Jack was at company headquarters, coordinating the billionth burger celebration. He had no idea at all what had transpired back at Swallowville in his absence.

"How could he know that Bertram had wiped out the entire staff? How could he know that you and Roger had slipped off into the wind? How could he know that Bertram was now completely bananas, having decided that a proper bull needed a proper mate to keep company with? Yes, your brother had become what you Brits so aptly term 'a nutter.' A complete and utter nutter. He went down to the fields and lived there for three days in his bra and panties, eating grass and crawling about on all fours, mooing at the cows and trying to find one that might accommodate him. The farmworkers just ignored him. The rich, they knew, were a bit different, and if a

Smedley-Ross wanted to live with the cows instead of in a comfortable mansion, why, who were they to tell him he couldn't? It looked like Bertram was to be a very lonely little bull indeed, that is until he met Ludmilla."

"A Russian in Swallowville?"

"No, a Holstein, a lovely black-and-white spotted calf he called Ludmilla for some unfathomable reason. When I came onto the scene, they'd taken over your late father Egbert's suite. They were eating grain and vegetables and making love on the master bed under the great mirrors on the ceiling. Ludmilla was wearing the late cook's brassiere and a bonnet Bertram had borrowed from the wax figure of a sixteenth-century Welsh milkmaid in the Museum of Beef. They seemed very happy."

"I don't believe you for a second," said Birgitta with dismissive laugh. "That's the most preposterous bullshit I've ever listened to!"

"It's a hard one to swallow, I'll admit," I said, reaching into my pocket for the photos. "I figured, even Archie and the Big K, a pair of gents who have heard it all, I figured that they might demand some verification, so I immortalized it on film. Human beings might lie, but undoctored Ektachrome is a stickler for the truth. Regard: the Kodak moment."

Birgitta took a long look at the photos. They were good clear shots, and the features of her brother, distorted by lust and the effort to please his partner, were unmistakable. Ludmilla? Birgitta couldn't have known Ludmilla from any other black-and-white calf, but whoever the comely young bovine mademoiselle on the business end of Bertram's efforts was, she certainly seemed to be enjoying herself, twitching her tail and straining her buttocks to receive the thrust of a very determined Bertram Smedley-Ross's arguments.

Poor sophisticated Birgitta's face shattered like glass, piece by pretty piece, until it was a quivering collection of mismatched parts.

"I want my mummy!" she wailed plaintively, then whimpered so loudly that a few nearby Texans overcame their native politeness and looked over to see what the commotion was about.

"Your mum . . ." I whispered gently, sighing, holding her chilled hand with its gnawed nails and lighting a cigarette for her, sticking it in her lifeless lips. "I am sorry to inform you that dear Prudence, going slowly mad from tainted sugar, happened upon your brother in flagrante delicto with his spotted sweetie and started to scream like a banshee, not because he was making love to a cow, no, but because her mind had flipped into another dimension and she was convinced that Ludmilla was a Catholic girl from town. 'No Catholics in our family!' she yelled, drooling madly and turning red as steak tartare. 'No Catholics in our family! Keep the bloodlines pure!' So to shut her up Bertie clonked her over the head with his loyal fire poker and sewed her lips shut with fishing line. When your mother awoke she could not yell. And then the disease completely engulfed her brain and she felt impelled to run into walls, which she did until she died."

Birgitta wept, great slick streams of salty tears running down her freckled cheeks. I reached a hand, touched the soft skin, tried to stem the sad tide, but it was a useless gesture that left me feeling useless and melancholy. There was nothing to do but continue with the story. Get to the end so that I could do what I was sent for.

"Now the previous day," I continued, speaking quickly, for we were not so very far from Trouville, "Bertie had phoned the local clergyman and asked him to come to the house for a private discussion of the utmost importance. Knowing how much the Smedley-Rosses had contributed to the church over the years and what devout Anglicans they were, especially your late mother, the priest jumped into his Jaguar, bought with the overflow from the money Jack had given them to build a new AIDS hospice, and he drove on over to see what Bertie wanted.

"In a word: Bertram wanted marriage. He wanted to legitimize his union with Ludmilla and make her Mrs. Smedley-Ross. The priest noted the way he frothed, he noted the happy, satisfied look on Ludmilla's face, he noted the bloodstained poker in Bertram's hand, and he thought he'd landed in some LSD-fueled scenario written by D.H. Lawrence, so to get out of the house he said, OK, he'd arrange for the wedding. Well, of course, such a union, it goes without saying, would be impossible under current Anglican regulations, so upon returning to the parish he called his superior who called his, and so on, until the Big K sent me to check things out.

"When I got to the Swallowville lands, I stopped to speak with the farmworkers. They had not seen anyone for days and were worried. So I was very careful. When I walked into the mansion, I found Bertram and Ludmilla making love in front of a great roaring fire. Being a gentleman, I did not disturb them but made a tour of the premises. I found Lucy-Joy dead in her room, choked to death on an overly large mouthful of toilet paper, the television still blabbing away. She had literally bitten off more than she could chew. . . ."

"Lies," Birgitta said with a whimper. "All lies. Horrible, ridiculous, cruel, cruel lies. Everyone died in the fire."

"No," I said. "Truths. Truths stranger than fiction. And Jack and I covered these sad truths, buried them deep. As far as the world is concerned, there was a fire at Swallowville and your whole family was tragically immolated. . . ."

The rest I told her quickly, for we were now very very close to Trouville. She was no longer surprised by my words, she no longer fought the truth. We sat there, and I spoke and she listened, and she let the truth wash over her, and in a way, it did set her free. She became very relaxed.

I told her how I'd found the bodies in their shallow grave, already dug up by local dogs who themselves became infected with the bovine malady. I told her how Bertram opened his heart to me and told me all. How I'd locked Bertram and Ludmilla in the barn. How I'd found Egbert's bones and jewelry and zipper and buttons and teeth buried behind the Museum of Beef. How I'd called Jack. How he and I had smoothed the local police with contributions to their favorite charity: themselves. How we'd placed what remained of the bodies in the house and torched it. How Swallowville burned, a magnificent fire seen for miles around. How the local fire companies unfortunately discovered their hoses had somehow been cut by vandals . . . (Jack shelled out some serious grease for the cover-up . . .). How Swallowville had burned to the ground. How we'd found the dead bodies in the mansion, including Bertram's. . . .

"But you said that Bertie was in the barn, safe."

"Yes, Bertie was safe. Bertie and Ludmilla both. We just reported him dead."

"Where is he?"

"All in time, my dear," I said. "Well get to that."

So I went on. Telling her how we'd traced her and Roger to Roger's Brixton flat. How we'd observed her living the life of a British Patty Hearst, a revolutionary's lover wearing a black beret and secondhand clothes, living amongst the poor, totally incognito, eating vegetables and grains. . . .

"It must have been a good experience for you," I said.

"Yes, not bad. Roger is a wonderful lover. The food was bloody awful but the sex was splendid. I had to nip out now and then to sneak a Fast Burger, but other than that it was a marvelous adventure. . . ."

She paused, the tears all dry, confident now, thinking she was home free. She lit a cigarette, inhaled like a vacuum cleaner, and spoke:

"So if you know so much, Monsieur, what happened next?"

"No," I said. "It will be better for your conscience to tell it yourself."

"Why not," she said confidently. She was back to being Birgitta Smedley-Ross, heiress in charge.

"Well, Roger and I decided that just getting the disease out there in the world wasn't really enough, you know. We had to make a statement, a loud statement, a political statement, like the Sex Pistols farting in the Queen's ear, like spitting in society's jaundiced eye. So we got jobs in the Piccadilly Fast Burger. The flagship restaurant. I knew from Jack's speeches at the dinner table that the whole billionth burger celebration was being geared to take place there. That in fact the billionth burger was to be eaten by none other than the Iron Lady herself, that silly, stupid cow, Margar—"

"No names," I said. "I know who. Let us refer to her as Helmet Head."

"Fine, fine, Helmet Head. So we took the job, and a foul horrible job it was. Those greasy patties of meat, those greasy salty fries, I started to understand Roger's objections to beef. . . . But we worked and worked and I can tell you this: the life of a minimum-wage earner is exactly what its cracked up to be: bloody hell. . . . And so bloody sad. . . .

"So the day of the billionth burger arrived. Was it just this morning? God, it seems a million years ago. . . . Roger got up early and went out to buy me a few packs of ciggies, but he never came back. I suppose he lost his nerve; but I went ahead, put on the silly uniform, and went to work at Fast Burger. We had molded the billionth burger days before, from the meat Roger brought back from Swallowville. We made the burger and threw the rest in the garbage. My father's remains. White meat, yes, but cooked, lying inside a bun, covered with lettuce and tomatoes and cheese and onions and ketchup, dripping with special sauce, it would be indistinguishable from a real Fast Burger."

"How did it feel, holding your fathers . . . meat in your hands?" I asked her, for I must honestly say that in my many years as a plumber of souls I'd never met such a one as her, so ultimately cool and adaptable to the shifting morality of a situation. "I mean, how did it feel to squish it between your fingers?"

"Feel? Well, it felt like burger meat and it cooked up rather nicely. . . . Oh, you mean how did it feel, from a psychospiritual angle? Hmm, rather powerful if you must know. Powerful . . . and painful. . . . After all," she said, blinking back a fresh tear, looking at her fingernails, scratching some flakes of dried meat off, "that was my bloody dad. . . . But I barely gave it a thought, it was like I was programmed. . . . The cameras were there, the TV cameras and the radio hookups, and all the security forces and Helmet Head and even the young prince and his mum, the princess of—"

"Helmet Head ate the burger?" I asked.

"She must have!" said Birgitta gleefully. "I didn't actually see her eat it but I assume she did. . . . I hope she dies a painful and horrible death for what she's done to Britain. . . . But suddenly dear Jack was there, in the kitchen, and he hustled me out of there by the back door, God knows how he recognized me in that Fast Burger uniform, and he put me in a limousine and told me that the police were wise to me and Roger and that if I didn't want to be arrested I must take a plane to Paris and then this train. He had an outfit for me and makeup and a carton of cigarettes and my lighter, my passport, and some money, and he told me that a large steamer trunk with everything I love from Swallowville would be waiting for me at the station in Trouville. I am supposed to go to a certain cemetery in Trouville to receive further instructions. I wonder what happened to Roger. Was he arrested?"

Just at that moment the mechanized voice announced the station stop:

"Mesdames, Monsieurs . . ."

"We're here," I said, helping her to her feet as a proper gentleman should, perhaps not a British gentleman like Jack Smedley-Ross, but then again I have never worn ladies' underwear nor submitted to the tart tangy pleasures of a lemonade enema. . . .

We made our way to the exit. It had been a lovely ride, a terribly pleasant journey. She was a little tipsy now. I helped her down to the platform.

"Roger is out of harm's way," I said as we headed over to where the baggage was being unloaded. "And Helmet Head did not eat the burger, nor did the little prince. The burger was taken into custody, as was Roger, hours before. We picked him up when he left the apartment to buy your smokes, and I personally questioned him. Roger told everything."

"Did he, now?" she asked as we watched four strong men strain to load a large steamer trunk into the open back of a pickup truck that had been rented in advance.

"Yes, he squealed like a white mouse in a bath of acid. That's how we managed to grab the billionth burger; but your brother Jack, well, he's a proper British gentleman and he decided to give Roger a choice."

I tipped the men and took the keys, helped Birgitta into the front seat. There was no passenger-side airbag, but then again we weren't going far, and we weren't in a hurry, and I'm an excellent driver, and of course she had those huge inflatable lungs. . . .

We drove. Ah, how very green and fresh it was. You could smell the sea.

She lit another cigarette.

"Yes," I said. "Roger was left alone in his cell with . . . with the billionth burger. The one meant for Helmet Head. You see, given the option of life in prison or eating the diseased burger, Roger rather gallantly chose . . . suicide. He ate the poisoned burger."

"Ah well," she said, lighting a cigarette and taking a deep philosophical pull. "To each his own cup of hemlock. He was a nice fellow and very good in bed, for a vegetarian, though I do believe a meat-and-potatoes man has more staying power, but as they say: easy come, easy go. *C'est la vie.*"

"Yes," I said, matching her, two clichés for two clichés: "Those are the breaks. Here today, gone tomorrow. . . ."

"I wonder," she mused, as we cruised the superb country-side, so fresh, so wholesome, so lovely and sunny and innocent after the cold, dark, rainy strangeness of Britain, "why this cemetery, why this town, and who am I to meet?"

"Me," I said. "You are to meet me."

"Of course," she said. "How bloody stupid of me."

"Well, here we are," I said. It was a quiet little country ceme-tery, rather pretty, old gravestones, green grass, a gentle breeze. The French dead were very peaceful. We got out of the truck.

"Yes," I said. "It's been a busy day. I had to take the S + M company jet with this trunk to catch up with you in Paris."

Birgitta stood by smoking while I climbed into the back and unlocked the trunk, opened the lid.

"Bertie!" she cried.

There, crammed into the large trunk like S + M beef in a can, were her brother Bertram, clad in push-up bra and see-through panties, and his sweetheart, Ludmilla the little Hol-stein calf.

"They're dead!" Birgitta exclaimed.

"Hardly," I said.

Ludmilla wore a triple oxygen tank, a face mask, and the old Welsh milkmaid's bonnet from the Museum of Beef. Her lungs, under the late cook's brassiere, were rising and falling gently with the canned air. Bertram's face was pressed against the keyhole. His Smedley-Ross bellows had been gulping air through the lock since London.

They unfolded themselves and stood, stretching, both a bit wobbly, frothing some, blinking madly in the late-afternoon sun. I pulled the ramp down and helped them off the truck. Birgitta embraced her brother. . . . They kissed warmly.

"We're here?" Bertram asked me.

"Yes," I said, unstrapping the tanks from Ludmilla, taking the face mask off, allowing her to breathe the fresh air of Normandy. "Just as you wished. Jack wanted it this way. He loves you both very much. . . ."

I consulted my little map of the graves and led them, led them toward (my version of) the spot Bertram had spoke—about, spoke—about at such length and with such longing. We walked, the four of us, two men and a cow and a large-lunged lovely. We stood by the grave, the grave of Gaston Flaubert. I put on my collar, my white priest's collar. (Oh yes, I am ordained, long ago. That's how I came to the attention of the Big Kielbasa. It's not something I talk about much. . . .)

"We are here today," I said solemnly, "to join Bertram Smedley-Ross and Ludmilla Holstein-Friesian in the bonds of holy matrimony. . . ."

So I went through the ceremony. And when it came to the moment when I asked the assembled throng—Birgitta, a bunch of dead Trouvillians, and the ghost of Gaston Flaubert—whom amongst them had any objections, Birgitta was about to voice ten or twelve thousand fairly rational objections, but then she saw and finally understood the love in her brother's eyes, she saw and understood the sweetness and docility in his intended's eyes, and she saw the foam and flecks of blood on both their lips, the spastic legs, the rapid blinking, and she knew there was not much time. So with tears running down her face, tears of sorrow, tears of joy, she swallowed her objections. . . .

"You may now kiss the bride," I said, and Bertram smiled and closed his eyes, put his arms around Ludmilla and kissed her sweet wet snout, and that was the moment I chose to pull the two loaded and silenced Derringers from my pockets and place them against their heads and pull the triggers. . . .

"Yes," I told Birgitta as we looked at the two star-crossed lovers lying there entwined on Flaubert's grave, joined forever in love and death, "at the height of their joy I have put them out of their misery. That was what Bertram wanted, his final wish . . . he knew he was dying . . . he wanted to be married at the grave of the man who wrote *Madame Bovinary*."

"*Madame Bovinary*? But Flaubert's book was *Madame Bovary*."

"The Mad Cow Disease," I said, shaking my head sadly. "It gives one funny notions."

"Excuse me," she said. "But as I recall, the chap who wrote that tedious volume was Gustave Flaubert—not Gaston."

"You get an A-plus in French Literature, my dear. Yes, it was Gustave, but when I called the cemetery experts in Paris, and they informed me that Gustave was buried in Rouen, I said to myself, no, that's no good. I've never forgiven the town of Rouen for flame-broiling Joan of Arc. . . . So I asked, was there another famous Flaubert in their registry? And they said yes, Gaston Flaubert."

"And what, dare I inquire, is Gaston famous for?"

"He's the man who invented the crotchless panties."

"Quite," she said.

She watched and smoked, a very classy and serious and beautiful young woman, smoked and watched and watched and smoked as I carried the trunk and placed it in an open grave next to Gaston Flaubert, arranged for in advance by the organization back in Rome. I pulled the bodies over and managed to get them in. I shut the lid of the trunk. The shovel was waiting, as ordered by the folks back in Rome, as paid for by Jack Smedley-Ross. Birgitta threw a handful of dirt onto the trunk, and then I heaped the rich brown earth, filling the grave, working hard in the setting sun.

"And now," said Birgitta when I had finished, "where is my grave?"

I turned from my labor, and there she was, standing naked and magnificent, her very, very nicely formed breasts taut and proud in the warm gentle breeze, her insouciant rear end jutting.

"Your grave?"

"Yes, my grave, my burger, my bullet."

"Whatever are you talking about?"

"Aren't you going to kill me?"

"Don't be mad, my dear," I said, pulling a burger from my inner pocket. I'd been holding it since London, thinking about it with longing. Nothing like listening to a confession to make me hungry. I was ravenous. I opened the paper and said a little prayer, asking the burger's forgiveness. . . . And then I raised it to my lips. . . . Sure, it was cold, but my goodness, I thought, biting into the soft bun, feeling the deep beef flavor explode in my mouth, it was delicious, truly, truly delicious, indescribably delicious, delicious and delectable, delightful and. . . .

"It's a Deluxe Fast Burger," I said, chewing the pink juicy beef perfection. "Guaranteed safe, from the second billion. Have a bite."

"Don't mind if I do," said the pale, pretty heiress, taking the burger and chewing elegantly. "Don't mind if I do," she said, ketchup and grease and special sauce dripping pink from her sweet cherry-blossom lips.

"So you're not going to kill me?" she asked through a mouthful of beef, as the warm breeze tickled the grass around Gaston Flaubert's grave and rustled her ringlets. I put my collar away in the pocket with my left-hand Derringer.

"No," I said. "Not even if you begged. There's been enough death in this story as it is."

She came to me then, kissed my lips gently. I licked a spot of ketchup and special sauce off the corner of her mouth. She pointed to a distant field where a large bull stood, head bowed, munching grass, oblivious to the human comedy.

"And I won't have to . . . service him?"

"Not unless you want to, I said. . . ." And whip me with a cat-o'-nine-tails if I didn't detect a glimmer of disappointment flit across her eyes. "No, my dear, the karma is clean now."

And she sighed, soft and smooth in my arms, smelling only faintly and not at all unpleasantly like a Fast Burger and fries plus an after-dinner cigarette.

"But there is something . . ." I said, touching her wild smoky hair, "something I've been thinking about for days and days now, hoping and wishing and dreaming about like a child looks forward to unwrapping a precious gift on Christmas morning . . . I would count it an honor, Birgitta, a marvelous and delicious honor . . . if you would see fit to grace me with a hands-on demonstration of the fabled Russo glassblowing methods. . . ."

"And I, Monsieur, would be honored to demonstrate," she said graciously, kneeling on Flaubert's grave, unwrapping my package with deft, bird-boned fingers, "the various techniques. The family secrets, if you will, all the way from Venice to Liverpool to India and back. . . ."

And then I felt her breath, soft at first, delicate as a thought, soft and sweet as velvet dipped in honey, the first heavenly inhale, stirring something deep inside me. . . .

"And you know, Monsieur," she said looking up at me with a smile. "You were right. The truth has set me free. I feel like a new woman. Thank you."

"No," I said, leaning back against the gravestone with a sigh, closing my eyes. "Thank you."

"You know," she said seriously. "I think I'll quit smoking."

And that was the day Birgitta Smedley-Ross quit smoking cigarettes. And as I found out that evening, the stars twinkling above the grave of Gaston Flaubert, as she inflated and deflated and inflated me, again and again with an infinite variety of Venetian flutters and trills and arpeggios, it didn't at all hurt her magnificent glassblowing technique. . . . In fact, maybe it helped. Yes, I might even venture to say that it helped. . . .

✢   ✢   ✢

But she never did quit eating beef, despite the dangers of Mad Cow Disease. And neither did I. Because wherever you might happen to find yourself in this crazy, mixed-up world of ours, wherever there are men and women fighting the good fight, living a dignified decent existence on the go, you're never very far from a Fast Burger. . . .

Yes, as Sir Jack Smedley-Ross, knighted by the queen for his patriotism and contributions to the British beef industry, said to Mother Teresa when she cut the red ribbon at the first Fast Burger in his hometown of Calcutta, India . . . as Sir Jack also said when he signed the deal to put a Fast Burger franchise on the moon . . . and as Sir Jack, one of the richest men on the planet, famed London swinger who so loves his lemonade any which way he can get it, likes to say to anyone who happens to sit down at the Smedley-Ross table in the new mansion in Swallowville (be they Muslim, Christian, Buddhist, Mormon, or even Hindu) . . . as Sir Jack has ordered chiseled onto the headstone waiting for him at the private cemetery in Swallowville, out behind the Museum of Beef . . . as good old Jack (born Ahmed) is fond of saying:

"Damn the karma! Let there be burgers!"

The Trillionth
Shit

Shiiiiiiiiiiiiiiiiiiiiiiiiiiiiiiiiiiiiiiiiiiiiiiiiiiiiiiiiiiiiiiiiiiiiiiiii-
iiiiiiiiiiiiiiiiiiit!" screamed the drunken man in the
stained, stinking, but strangely stylish brown rags as he
weaved and wobbled his way down the Metro station platform,
his zipper wide open to the roaring breeze of a departing train.
"My life is shit!"

He stood above me, swaying on booze-rubber legs, dread-
locked hair sprouting wildly from his taut-skinned skull, his
ravaged, brown, cherry-veined eyes begging me to contradict
his self-assessment—which in all honesty I couldn't—he really
did smell like shit.

"Shit is natural," I said, adopting the low, slow, soothing tone
they taught us back in the seminary—that special verbal honey I
have in the past used successfully to ease the rage and pain of over-
worked postal workers, rabid dogs, and the two psychotic, suicidal
violin-playing, lesbian grandmothers from Lyon I talked off the
ledge at Notre Dame—capturing his tragic eyes in the soft magnetic
blanket of my glance. "Shit is the most natural thing in the world."

"But I'm sick of shit," he whined loudly, the words echoing syllable by sad, slurred syllable in the tiled station as he plunked his ragged rear end down next to me on a bright-red seat with a gargantuan whooshing sigh, his long legs splayed wide open, grit-blackened toes wiggling from the open ends of his overaged-Camembert-stinking Nike sneakers, the self-pity oozing from each and every grimy pore of his handsome, defeated, café-au-lait face.

"Sick to fucking death of shit," he muttered, sucking on a bottle of cheap, red Burgundy, one of three he'd imported into the Metro in an ancient, plastic, FNAC sack, his full, sensuous lips quivering, glistening purple with wine-thick spittle.

"I'm sick of the world shitting on my head!" he wailed, oblivious to the curious stares of the few waiting passengers. "Right smack on my fucking head! Splat!"

He indicated some crusted lightning bolts of crud—like slashes of Indian war paint—decorating a forehead camouflaged with frayed filthy ropes of matted hair.

"I've had it up past my eyeballs with shit," he said, calm again. "I've tried to escape the shit, Monsieur, really I've tried, but I can't. I'm trapped in shit, buried in shit . . . I wake up in the morning and it's like my eyes are stuffed with shit. I try to hear the little birds singing their happy little songs but my ears are clogged with shit, not even a twitter penetrates. No sunlight, no birdsong—"

"No shower," I put in, not out of cruelty, no, but to force him deeper into the bowels of his blues, down where the dark is so profound and frightening that not even a glimmer of dishonesty can survive.

"Laugh at me, Monsieur. Go ahead," he begged, "laugh. I'm an easy target. You can smell me a mile away. Here comes Mr. Shit, the walking talking piece of shit. Just a giant squishy turd with memories—And the memories . . . oh God, even the good ones, they're slowly turning to shit. . . ."

I looked at the man. In his beat-up yet somehow elegant rags (really like some sort of aristocratic visitor from a post-Apocalyptic future), his soul swimming in a brimming pool of self-pity, he would be an easy one to drain secrets from. Like a Russian communal toilet that's been stopped up since the salad days of Brezhnev, Mr. Shit was in dire need of a good flushing. And I was just the man to do it.

"Can I tell you a story?" he asked, his eyes darting from me to the approaching Metro, then back to me, then back to the Metro—back and forth like an Olympic ping-pong match.

"Go right ahead," I encouraged him, though I already knew much of what he was about to tell me. But if it's a really long story I might have to excuse myself to go take a . . ."

"Thank you," he said gratefully, releasing another massive sigh of relief from deep within, much like the sound made by the groom at the first wedding I refereed. . . . The brave young fellow had been holding a giant noxious flatulence all during the ceremony, painfully suppressing it because he didn't want to upset his (cosmetically) blushing bride, but then, the deal-sealing kiss out of the way, the old girl herself went right ahead and beat him to the punch by delivering a viciously long, loud, smelly, honking number in the key of C, followed by a two-fingered nose-pick just to let the poor dupe know what he'd bought into for the next fifty-odd years. . . . So now, liberated from the constraints of courtship modesty, the freshly married groom (literally) threw caution to the wind and let go with an enormous atomic blast of rancid gas of his own, a mournful, keening, rotten-egg trumpet, blare from the depths of his resigned being. . . . And that's how I left them: standing there, no more secrets, no more masks, man and wife, blasting and honking away, picking their crud-stuffed noses, blasting and honking and picking, cackling like schizophrenic chickens till death do them part. . . .

"Thank you," Mr. Shit said, sighing once again and scratching his scabbed scalp as the harried Paris citizens streamed off and on the train, headed wherever, to see whoever, to do whatever. "I'm feeling better already."

Ah, but it was too early for the healing. I didn't want him feeling good yet. I needed him raw and hurting, his nerves on edge, his senses sharp as Jack the Ripper's Swiss Army knife. I had to stretch his heartstrings back to the snapping point.

"Metros are like girl's asses," I told him rather coldly, as the butt end of the train disappeared into the black tunnel. "You miss one—no big deal—all you have to do is wait a few minutes. There's always another one coming along."

His eyes took on the glazed, dazed, hurt look of the man who's played at love and lost, lost so badly that he cannot see the world of future possibility; all he can see is the world of what was, what might have been. All he can do is look inward and stare helplessly as the ferocious hyenas of mocking memory rip and nibble and suck at the festering bloody wounds where Cupid's arrows are lodged painfully and seemingly eternally in his heart.

"Oh no, Monsieur, you're wrong," he said, shaking his head sadly, his eyes taking on a dreamy milky cast. You're completely wrong. Each ass is unique. Each ass is special. Each ass has its own personality. . . . Each ass is a universe unto itself, the most beguiling and powerful part of the female human anatomy, the seat of the soul, the entrance to heaven. . . . And my girl has. . . . She had. . . . Well, hers is. . . . It was. . . . Well, in a word, it was glorious, spectacular, incredible!"

"That's three words."

He ignored me, lost in the labyrinth of anal memory.

"The way it jutted, Monsieur, the way it curved—*ooh la la!* to an infinite power! The delicacy, the spectacular insouciance, the sense of humor, the perfect statue smoothness, the roundness, the fabulous way her little puckering bud of anus smiled when she—"

"You've convinced me," I broke in. "I will have to completely reformulate my philosophy of the rear end. But back to the story. . . . Pardon my confusion, but is it a story about an ass or is it a story about shit?"

"Why," he replied, surprised, "both, of course. How can you separate the two? Romeo and Juliet, sperm and ovum, crime and punishment, Laurel and Hardy . . . ass and shit. Without one, the other has no meaning. Like the man said, I shit, therefore I am."

"Which man said?"

"Some guy I met in a bar. Let me ask you this, Monsieur: What came first, ehh, the chicken or the egg? The ass or the shit?"

"You're a deep thinker," I said. "And what have you concluded?"

"Well . . ." he said, using a throwaway lighter to ignite half a grubby cigarette he had scrounged off the platform, puffing away contemplatively, brow furrowed like some pedantic bow-tied washed-up old fart of a writer on some unwatched cable TV talk show. "I have given many hours of mental sweat to the subject—after all, I am an égoutier, a sewer man. . . ."

His voice downshifted into a melancholy gear, and he sobbed quietly. A large tear plopped from his eye onto the burning coal of his cigarette, extinguishing it with a stinky hiss.

"Or at least I was a sewer man. . . ."

All we needed were the two psychotic, suicidal, lesbian grannies from Lyon playing their violins.

"You see, Monsieur," he said with his trademark sigh, his cheeks wet, "I was born for the sewers. It was my destiny. My father was an underground man, my grandfather before him, and his father before him, right on down the line back to the 1850s, the time of Napoleon III, when the engineer Belgrand built the Paris sewers. Yes, you might say that a healthy appreciation of shit runs in the family."

"And with all that genetic preparation, what have you decided?"

"I've decided that it's all shit."

"But which came first?" I prodded his wounded spirit. "The ass or the shit?"

"The ass, Monsieur," he answered sadly, without hesitation. "For sure, the ass. God created his own ass so that he could shit us humans. And that's what we are, that's what life is, what love is—nothing but shit."

"Charming," I said.

"The truth hurts, Monsieur, but think about it. What is this planet? Just one big piece of shit, getting shittier and shittier all the time. Am I right or am I right? And the sun—nothing more than hot bright shit. And the moon? Cold, dimpled, Swiss cheese shit. And all the solar systems and galaxies and meteors? Just shit, shit, shit in various stages of hot and cold and putrefaction."

"And the Big Bang?"

"The first big shit, where the whole damned shit-storm got started."

"You depress me," I said.

"Don't feel bad, pal," he said, putting an arm around my shoulders. "I depress myself."

But I had to get him back on track, steer him away from our blossoming friendship, take his mind off toilet cosmology, scatotheology, anal-fecal philology, and back to the story, so I added: "No wonder you lost your job."

"You think jobs are like Metros?" he roared. "Another good one will come along any minute? You, Monsieur, if you don't my saying, have some very sick ideas. Shame on you."

"How did it happen?" I asked gently. "How did you lose your job?"

He took a deep breath, sighed yet again, swigged some more wine. I opened a lollipop and started to suck slowly.

"It started like this, he said, tranquil as a turtle in the noonday sun, grateful to be telling it. "One day, after eleven years on the job—and by the way I didn't get the job through family connections, I had to pass a battery of difficult tests—one day I was down in the sewers, checking water and electric pipes, reading gas levels, cutting away tangles of plastic bags and six-pack links with

wire-cutters, making sure that the shit was flowing, I was sepa-
rated from my partner and I saw . . . well, I saw a ghost. Sweet
mother of God, I said to myself—making the sign of the cross,
though I hadn't been inside a church for a dog's age—a ghost. A
ghost with red eyes and the most extraordinarily exquisite white
ass on the planet. . . ."

✛   ✛   ✛

"I'd like this to be on the record," I said to the Dispatcher, two
weeks before I arranged to run into Felix, the tortured shit- and
ass-obsessed man in the Paris Metro, as we rode the golf cart away
from headquarters beneath the streets of Rome. "I am not particularly happy with the assignment. I think I'm due a vacation."

"Vacation from what?" growled the Dispatcher, her words
greased with a thick coat of sarcasm, as she puffed away on her
little Clint Eastwood Spaghetti-Western cigar. "Your life is
nothing but fun and games, tiptoeing through the tulips, trip-
ping the light fantastic, putting on the Ritz. Time to put your
nose to the grindstone, your shoulder to the wheel. A little
hard work never hurt anyone."

I gave her a look. Did she really say all that? All those tired
clichés strung together to tell me to fuck off. What a pain in the
ass she was. Her predecessor had been such a nice fellow, a true
human being who actually understood the pressures of the job
and gave a shit about his agents, but this Dispatcher was so cold
and clinical and cynical and uncaring—she gave me the creeps.
And it wasn't just me. Everyone in the organization felt it. Even
people in other services felt it. I remember when she first came

on the job. A colleague in America, a top-level operative at the company based in Langley, Virginia, asked me to write a confidential evaluation of her for their files. Though written well over a decade ago, my letter still sums her up as well as anything I might say now. I quote myself:

"The Dispatcher is a tiny person, as small as a ten-year-old child, with an ageless pixie face and small rotten teeth the color of American Indian corn: black and red. She speaks in a deep rumbling voice, like a pneumatic drill breaking up street, and eats like a dieting sparrow. She drinks nothing but Bacardi and Coke, from breakfast until late at night, and smokes small Brazilian cigars, one after the other, except when in the presence of the Big Kielbasa (our CEO, who can't abide smoke on account of his fragile health), and then she sucks on red, flat lollipops she buys by the gross from Germany. She wears military fatigues at all times. Her silver hair is cropped short as a commando on patrol in the jungles of Borneo. She never seems to sweat or stink, even when conducting long, grueling, Kung Fu training sessions; and because none of us in the security-intelligence division has ever seen her leave her desk to make a choice between the ladies' and the men's rooms, despite the mass quantities of Cuba Libres she pours into her tiny frame—and even though she answers to Signora—there remain some grave doubts as to her gender. She is one of great mysteries of the Vatican.

"The Big Kielbasa himself, to whom she seems completely and fanatically loyal (she came on board to head the division at his personal request after the assassination attempt), once told me after a few too many beers that as a child she (he?) escaped from a concentration camp to become one of the top assassins in the Polish underground, and that was when he first met her. Is she Jewish originally? Is she Catholic? No one cares and no one cares to ask. Just as no one really cares or cares to ask if she pees standing or sitting or hanging from her toes like a bat. It's totally beside the point. The point being that her knowledge of sudden death is so immense and frightening that she commands complete and utter respect. Poisons, needles, knives, guns, bare hands, creating a lethal weapon from whatever is available, she is a master. Or perhaps I should say a mistress.

"Rumor has it that she spent the postwar years in China, working for the Chairman, and later in Tibet, studying with the old ones, and after that in the USSR. It's said that she can slash your throat with an American Express card, cut off your air supply with three garbanzo beans (two stuffed up your nostrils and one down your windpipe), touch your chest with her pinkie finger and cause instant cardiac arrest. Legend has it, and please don't laugh, that she even once tickled a Bulgarian double agent to death. And I've heard it whispered—on the squash courts, in the sauna, in the gymnasium bar—that she is perfectly capable of killing a man in his sleep from a long distance. That she can enter your dreams and short-circuit your brain and change your status from breathing to decomposing in a microsecond. That she can turn herself into a bird and fly across the night earth, tear your eyes out with her talons and be back at her desk in Rome for a breakfast of Brazilian stogies and Bacardi and Coke: a shaman. . . . I don't actually believe a word of this—except for the credit-card method, which I can personally vouch for (I never leave home without it)—but whatever her gender, and even though I'm no slouch in the business of sudden death myself, she is not a person to make angry." End of quote.

I was thinking about this evaluation as we approached the pizzeria basement, the exit we agents take from the Big Kielbasa's place, and I shivered. Nothing in the intervening years had changed. The Dispatcher was exactly the same physically, and she still gave off precisely the same creepy vibes. Like playing pinochle with a corpse.

She put a hand on the Swiss Guard's shoulder and told him to exit the vehicle and leave us alone a few minutes. The guard walked away and stood at a polite distance of fifteen meters, on alert, trembling, shifting uncomfortably as if something rather unpleasant had come to pass in the rear section of his bikini briefs.

I looked at the Dispatcher, the little Brazilian cigar smoking in the corner of her wicked angel face. Oh shit, her features were relaxing. I've seen that look before, seen it all too often. There was no mistaking that easing of facial tension, that unwrinkling of stress lines, that huge soft release of breath: a confession was coming. I could no sooner stop it than an Egyptian swimming pool maintenance man could have stopped Moses from parting the Red Sea. Even people like the Dispatcher (why, even the Big Kielbasa himself . . . but that I must never speak about), even professionals whose job it is to hold onto things, guard secrets with their lives, they just cannot resist telling me things. They look into my sad, almost-ugly face and, no matter their age, sex, color, or creed, it's as if they're looking into a mirror, a deep, penetrating, X-ray mirror that goes beyond the surface to reveal that crowded repository of life's wounds deep within us all, that vulnerable place we call the soul, and all the shit, all the self-pity, all the regret and guilt and sorrow and hurt they've kept bottled up for years, it all just surfs forth, frothing like champagne bubbles, on a silver wave of words.

"I was fourteen," she said, in a slow, dreamy voice, wholly immersed in the past, the gravel in her voice muffled like the first rumble of an avalanche, and I could see the little shitty turds of memory pooling together like mercury from a busted thermometer, preparing to bubble into the light.

"I've never told this to anyone," she added.

(Ah, if I had half a franc for every time someone has dropped that phrase in my ear I'd be rich as . . . well, I'd be as rich as the Big Kielbasa.)

"It was back in the war," she went on. "The Nazi guards were using me for their pleasure, passing me around like a bottle of cheap schnapps. After violating me they would lounge about and drink beer and sing the praises of the Führer until they passed out or were ready for round two. This night they gave me candy, a red lollipop. One by one they passed out. I tried to suck the pop, but my mouth was so dry, the candy wouldn't melt. Then Jurgen, my chief tormentor, woke up and approached me, huge, red of face, his weapon of choice swollen with sick desire. . . . He was coming to degrade me again. . . . I bit the lolly, creating a sharp shard of red candy on the end of the cardboard stick, and with a decisive backhand motion I slashed him across the throat. Just so," she said, demonstrating with a swift, almost invisible stroke of her cigar far too close for comfort. I gulped.

"Got his jugular the first time," she said with pride. "My first kill. Nazi bastard bled like a stuck pig. Then I did the others with my trusty lolly, cutting throats, poking eyes with the fuzzy end. And after they were all lying there, dreaming the big Nazi dream of huge pink Aryan breasts and piles of rotting dead Jews, I went out the window, sucking that bloody lollipop on the road to freedom."

"Why have you told me this," I asked.

"Because," she said with a sigh, "I've been holding on to it for over fifty years and I needed to dump it. . . ."

There was more, I could tell, much much more. Her eyes were still chock-full of shit, her sigh still had a toilet stink. She was holding back. But I didn't need to hear it. I really didn't. I had my own shit to deal with.

"I feel better," she said, smoking. "I feel much better. What they say about you is true. Your eyes absorb all the pain. . . . And now, now I owe you . . . but also, you owe me. You are my creature, yes? My dog. When I say bark, you bark. Yes? When I say sit, you sit. Yes?"

"When you say shit do I shit?"

"Don't fuck with me. I know you've been taking liberties with your vows. I had you shadowed after the toothpick job. I know about Maritza, and I know all about Birgitta the burger heiress. If the Big K found out, he might insist you be defrocked or, perhaps worse, that you be sent to America for rehabilitation, for purification. Up at the retreat in New Mexico with all the pederast priests. America, think about it. Nothing but you and fifty pederast priests and some lonely coyotes, not a girl or a jar of good foie gras for a hundred kilometers. And knowing your history of growing up in orphanages, I don't think you'd be very happy. So no more whining. You will take the assignment and you will carry it out. And remember this, the Big Kielbasa loves you like a son, and that buys you a lot of slack around here, but son or no son, there's still plenty of rope to hang you with. No fuck-ups and no more complaining, or else you deal with me."

"Put that way, I don't see how I can refuse."

"Damn right. And I want reports by phone, in standard code, every two days."

"That is most irregular," I said. "Usually an agent in the field makes his own decisions and plays the game as he sees fit. May I ask why?"

"None of your business!" she hissed, snakelike, and I admit it, friends, I blanched. I, who in the service of Ultimate Good have sent more souls packing on to the next life than a Chicago ghetto fire, a Pakistani train wreck, a British serial killer, and a Middle-East terrorist bombing lumped together, I actually drew away from her.

"Here," she said, handing me a pocketful of lollipops. "Take a few. They might be useful. No guns and no cigarettes where you're going. I'm sorry I blew my top."

"No problem," I said. "But I quit smoking years ago."

"Yes," she said, "But you might be tempted. And oh," she added, handing me a small, brown, paper package tied with string, "you forgot these in your locker."

Inside were twelve collars, cleaned and pressed, easy on the starch like I like them, from the Chinese laundry at the Vatican.

Yes, I was on assignment once again.

✠   ✠   ✠

I hadn't been to Lourdes in years, but some of the happiest summers of my teenage years were spent there, in that Disneyland of
the spirit, pulling carts loaded with invalids from their hotels
down to the sacred grotto where we would immerse them in the
pools of holy water, getting down there ourselves, dunking
them, pouring pitchers over their heads, healthy young bodies
holding the sick and elderly and crippled.

And it was at Lourdes where the beauties of faith became
apparent to me. I saw the lame walk, I saw the consumptive
breathe clearly, I saw the old feel young and frisky as colts in
green pastures, as randy as young bulls in their first season of
rut. Yes, these things I witnessed with my very own eyes. . . .

And it was there, at Lourdes, where I actually participated in
a miracle. Two miracles, really. The first impelled me into the
priesthood and the second, well, the second dictated the kind
of priest I became.

Miracle number one: One day an orphan called Ludo, my
best friend at the time—now a very successful life-insurance
broker in Marseille specializing in policies for Corsican gangsters—
one day Ludo and I were carting our sick charges down to the
pools. His was a fat blind man and mine a thin stroke victim who
could neither walk nor speak. Already fascinated with percent-
ages and odds, an interest that in later life would contribute to
making him a top insurance agent, Ludo bet me that he, a tall
boy, could deliver his heavy charge to the grotto, the former pig-
watering hole where Bernadette had seen the virgin eighteen
blessed times, before I, an average-sized boy, could deliver my

119

lighter load. He would spot me ten meters and ten seconds. Whoever lost the race would buy the other a bottle of wine. So off we went, running madly through the crowded streets of Lourdes. By the time we passed all the gangs of shocked pilgrims and invalids and priests and nuns and were nearing the finish line, the stroke victim and I were leading Ludo and the blind man by five meters. That's where I made my mistake. Looking back to gloat, I tripped over a dropped candle and went flying. The cart kept going, passed the finish line and veered wildly, crashing into the grotto wall. The poor stroke victim was sprawled on the ground, crumpled like a used tissue, bleeding from the head, right on the spot where Bernadette had seen the Virgin.

Oh Lord, I thought, overwhelmed by the enormity of my sin, not even feeling the pain of my scraped hands and knees, the moment of victory is the moment of ultimate defeat: he's dead. I've killed him. Out of pride, out of the pride of the competitive ego, the lust for superiority, out of the pure hateful hubris of youth, I've killed a pilgrim, a poor, helpless invalid.

"Make him live, dear God," I said aloud, tears streaming down the beardless cheeks of my sad, almost-ugly young face. "Make him live, and I'll serve you forever."

And no sooner were those words out of my mouth than up popped the invalid, cursing me like a transvestite hooker who's been stiffed on payment for a job well done, cursing and coming at me with hands poised for strangulation. . . .

Formerly a wordless vegetable, the man was now as good as new, better perhaps. The moment of ultimate defeat had been trans-formed into the moment of ultimate victory: a miracle. . . .

And so my fate was sealed, and despite the prolonged whipping

Father M—— graced my rear end with that afternoon after they pried the stroke victim's iron fingers from my well-throttled neck, I followed a winding prickly path to the priesthood. And even though I never really liked or trusted priests, and even though I never bought into the rules of the game, I lived up to my part of the bargain and ended up wearing the collar with pride, and eventually, after a few years of normal clerical duties, I was called to serve in the most difficult, soul-challenging branch of the organization, the security-intelligence division. And I have served with distinction, if I do say so myself.

But the second miracle, the event which brought me even closer to God, ah, it occurred that very same night.

On the field across the river from the grotto, fueled by the bottle of wine that honorable Ludo bought me in payment of our bet—in view of the statue of Bernadette, in the warm cup of green valley with the cloud-crowned mountains standing guard—I, a humble orphan accustomed to the sharp whips and harsh words of priests, I, a man-child born to violence and sin, first experienced the blessed glories of the flesh. Ahhhhhh, I thought, as I held the sweet little cutie from a local convent school, presently a nun who shall go nameless here (we must always do our damnedest to protect the innocent) . . . Ahhhhhh, I thought, as I held the dear sweet warm lovely girl in my arms, now that's heaven. . . . I remember she wore (rather briefly I must admit) the cutest, cleanest, little blue pin-striped outfit, and she never did take off her old-fashioned nurse's cap, and from the things she did, the way she coaxed the pain from my poor scraped and whipped and throttled flesh, replacing it with thoroughly adult pleasures, I knew that somewhere down the line, in the not-too-distant past, the good priests must have singled her out for special instruction. . . . Ah, but that really is another story.

✢   ✢   ✢

As the taxi crawled its way down streets packed with shops selling tourist junk—medallions and plastic water bottles with the Virgin's logo, walking sticks and Lourdes baseball caps—as we picked our way through masses of shining-eyed pilgrims, hymn-singing, hardhatted, blue-shirted, red-kerchiefed, burly miners from Belgium drawing invalids in carts, bands of pious young pretties in long skirts pushing squadrons of poor, drooling, lolling-headed miracle-seekers in wheelchairs, past all the nuns and priests and camera-wielding tourists of every shade of the gorgeous melanin rainbow, I thought about the Dispatcher. Whatever the truth about what lay under her underwear (and at this point, after her little wartime fairy tale, I'd decided she likely fell on the female side of the fence), whatever the secret hurts she was clasping close to her flat bosom and might yet release to my care, she was as tough and potentially mean and unpredictable as Joe Stalin with a urinary tract infection. My ass was on the line if I crossed her. And the Big Kielbasa, whom I loved like the father I never knew, I didn't want to hurt him. He was so kind, so sensitive, so blessedly innocent, so simple—good Lord! the man wore bowling shoes and Mickey Mouse underwear under his robes! He knew nothing about my methods or my tastes. I could see his reaction if he found out what I'd been up to, lo these many years, in the name of peace. The profound disappointment. Yes, he'd forgive me, that was his nature, his philosophy—but the pain, could his good, tired heart, so battered by the sadness of the world, could his sweet heart bear the pain?

I was chewing this over in my mind as I paid and exited the taxi. I'd been thinking about it since Rome. And I was still thinking about it as I walked through the church compound gates, anonymous in my collar among all the pilgrims and clerics, and I came to the conclusion that my service in the organization was reaching a new phase, possibly coming to an end—maybe it was time I voluntarily moved on. It was one thing taking on the confessions of common citizens, the run-of-the-mill crap I hear all the time: incest, murder, sexual gluttony, and cannibalism (yes, it weighed on the soul, but I was dealing with it)—that was one thing, but now the Dispatcher, our very own living Angel of Death, was using me as a private dump, her personal toilet. It wouldn't be long before she began to resent me, and if that happened there was no telling what she'd do. I'd be, as our young American cousins so aptly put it, up Shit's Creek without a paddle.

Yes, I thought, to protect myself I'd better get a paddle, I'd better do as old Ludo would advise, get myself some life insurance, I'd better get busy and write my cases out. . . .

And besides covering my ass, I thought, it will be good therapy. The act of telling might just relieve some of the inner pressure that's been building up within me. All the bodies, all the doubts, all the shit. . . .

Physician heal thyself, plumber clear thy pipes. . . .

✢ ✢ ✢

"Good to see you again, Father," said the tall old priest with the white hair. "I remember you as a teenager. Even then God was using you."

No shit, I wanted to say. And I've still got the scars on my ass to prove it.

"Good to see you too, Father M———," I said, shaking the familiar old priest's familiar hand, less frightening now that it wasn't holding a whip. "Tell me, what's the buzz? What's up?"

"Attendance is down."

"So I've been told back in Rome."

"Yes, attendance is down, and we don't know exactly why, but we've been noticing this trend for a while now. The hotel registries indicate that we are getting fewer and fewer pilgrims from Paris and the suburbs around Paris. Why this is we're not exactly sure, but we'd like you to speak with a priest from Paris. . . . He's a bit off the deep end. . . . Well, you be the judge. He's been getting treatment, and though we can't make head nor tails of what he says, we think he might know something important. . . ."

The old priest led me to a private pool of holy water reserved for members of the clergy. I stood in the dim, humid room feeling the sweat roll down under my collar, remembering all God's special children: the lame, the twisted, the blind, the limbless, the infirm of body and spirit, all my fellow sinners in faith seeking sweet earthly release from the burdens of flesh. . . .

The pool sparkled, its surface slick with rainbow streaks—the nervous sweat and the mingled oil of the imperfect—the sad lovely grease of hope. . . . And in one corner, a pale man, youngish, his thrashing arms held by the strong grip of a brawny teenager, babbled away.

"Let there be shit. Shit is fine! Shit is the way! Shit oh shit oh shit oh shit! SHIT SHIT SHIT!!!"

"How long has he been this way?" I asked.

"We don't know. He came here with a young woman. He asked that she be allowed to take the waters, but after hearing him babble about the sh . . . we reported to Rome and they decided that he needed more help than the girl. So we've had him in the pool for three days now. He keeps babbling away about sh . . . Always about the sh. . . . "

"Don't worry," I said, clapping the embarrassed old priest's trembling old shoulder. "We'll soon get to the bottom of things."

I stripped to my Calvins and immersed myself in the pool.

"Leave us alone now," I called, my voice echoing in the dim room. "Please."

After the teenager and the old priest had gone, I paddled over to where the young, waterlogged, Parisian priest stood holding on to the edge. His skin was as wrinkled as an albino prune—he'd been in the bath that long. The water was neither cold nor warm, it was very calming, peaceful really, if truth be known, like the amniotic syrup of our mothers' wombs. The priest had calmed down, his eyes had grown peaceful. Already my special magic was at work, radiating through the water in waves of serenity.

"And so, Father," I began, firm and authoritative, "what's all this shit you've been talking about shit?"

"It's true! Shit is the answer! Shit is the question! Shit is the way!"

"Easy does it, hoss," I soothed him. "Start at the beginning."

And so he told me his story, and what a story it was, a real lol-lapalooza, and at the end of the story he said: "I have an appointment with a reporter from *Telerama*, the magazine. I'm going to tell her all. And they'll publicize it and after that I'm calling Christiane Amanpour from CNN and—"

"I wouldn't do that," I said. "It might be bad business for the home team."

"I must do it," he said. "I really must. People must know about this. I must tell the world."

"No," I said. "You won't. When the reporter gets to the hotel for your rendezvous, she will find the girl gone. And she will also find that you are missing. She will inquire as to your whereabouts, but she won't be able to locate you."

"Where will I be sent?" the young priest asked, his eyes as large as mutant Bermuda onions with fear. "To the retreat in New Mexico?"

"No," I said, shaking my head sadly. "Not there, not to America. Someplace worse, if that's possible, or far better . . . The choice is not mine, not yours."

I placed my arm around his shoulders fraternally and jabbed his windpipe with my knuckle, then lovingly dunked him in the water.

"Drink now, my brother," I said to the thrashing, splashing, bubble-making priest. "It's up to God where you go."

✠   ✠   ✠

"He needed to be alone for a minute. . . ." I told the old priest. "Solitude is a diet pill for the heavy heart."

"Did you find out anything?"

"Yes," I said. "He told me all he knew, which will set me in the right direction."

"And he is at peace now?"

"Oh yes," I said with a sigh. "You could definitely say that."

✧   ✧   ✧

The girl. I found her in the hotel lying on her bed, wearing a pair of Jackie Onassis sunglasses, her ass in the air, reading a current issue of *Marie-Claire*. And yes, she was beautiful, as hauntingly beautiful, as pale and mysterious and magnetic as everyone says, and as sweet, as innocent. And that ass. . . . Good Lord, but the good Lord had worked overtime on it.

"Are you ready, Rose?" I asked. "We must go to Paris."

"Paris," she said, like a brave patriot accepting the inevitable sentence of death. "Back to Paris."

"Yes, my dear, Paris. But first, if you don't mind, I think you should take a bath."

"That's what I came here for."

✧   ✧   ✧

Paris. Fabled Paris. The Las Vegas showgirl of world cities. The aging ageless stripper of Europe. A very classy old gal. A little beat up for sure. Bruised in body, battered in spirit. Hasn't had a good bath in years. Smells a bit after all the fun she's had—all the good times, all the hard times, all the sad sad songs. But still full of life and beauty. Still full of mystery and history and culture and wisdom. . . . Still crazy after all these years.

Ah, the stories she could tell if she was that kind of gal, a kiss-and-tell kind of gal, which she isn't—unless of course the money's right, and then she'll tell just about anything to just about anybody. But in this case, I'll have to do the telling, for this a story about what goes on beneath the skirts of Paris; and no classy gal, whatever her age, likes to talk in public about what goes on beneath her skirts—least of all what goes on in the privacy of her guts. It's up to a specialist to find out. . . .

So let us put a stethoscope up to the soft, undulating underbelly of Paris and listen. . . . No, not there! This isn't that kind of story. Higher. . . . Not there! That's her breast! Lower. Okay. . . . That grumbling you hear? It's all the stories bubbling in her guts. Yes, it's time to give that naughty old broad Paris a laxative, time to examine whatever it is that comes out, be it nuggets of gold or nuggets of shit. . . . What? You're in a hurry? Can't wait for the laxative to take effect? Okay, we'll give her an enema. Short and sweet. And hey, maybe if she gets all the crap out of her system, we'll even reward her with a friendly spanking. After that we'll worry about the bath.

✠　　✠　　✠

Our story begins, it really and truly and finally begins, in the sewers of Paris.

Let us peel away the spotted banana peel of the years to expose the mushy, overripe, regularity-inducing fruit of the matter.

Close-up: the sewers of Paris during the Second World War. The Resistance hiding in the sewers. Brave men and women fighting the Nazis with every last ounce of desperation and ingenuity in their patriotic French spirits. Yes, the sewers of Paris are the last bastion of democracy, the sloppy, soupy grave of martyrs.

Wide-angle shot from the Eiffel Tower (August 1944): What's happening? Like a giant anthill, the city is buzzing with activity and excitement! After the melancholy gray coma of the German occupation, Paris is waking up, taking on life and color! Yes, the Nazis have fled! Here come Uncle Sam and the gang! Hey hey, it's the Americans! Hale, hearty, milk-fed, corn-fat, beef-brawny Yanks riding Sherman tanks like white chargers to the rescue of Lady Paris lying flat on her back, her skirt up around her neck! The end of the war! Girls kissing soldiers! Soldiers guzzling wine! People cheering! Hugging! Songs in the air! Dancing in the streets! Champagne corks popping! Wine flowing golden and purple down chins! Grins splitting faces! Soldiers throwing chocolate bars and cigarettes to children of all ages! Citizens laughing and dancing and drinking and singing! Men shedding the shameful dead skin of defeat and being reborn! Women shedding their tired panties and rumpled stockings and fucking with joy once again! And again! And again! (To the eternal gratitude of the Yanks.) Jubilation!

But what is this? Not everyone is happy. Besides a whole generation of Frenchmen who will grow old muttering into their Calvados, never forgiving the women of their generation for gifting the Yanks with liberation rolls in the hay, not everyone is celebrating. Not everyone is drinking and dancing and screwing the night away. No sir, no ma'am. Beneath the streets of Paris, far from the ringing bells, far from the happy shouts of drunken grubby children—in the sewers to be exact—the war is not over. No indeed, for one band of brave patriots, stone-cold-sober sewer commandos led by a huge, brave man with a jagged, purple Frankenstein scar on his forehead, the war has just begun.

"The war is not over!" booms the enormous, pale man, his eyes glittering psychotically, the scar climbing down from his hairline pulsing like some malevolent blood-gorged worm.

"The war is not over!" his loyal followers squawk like demented parrots, adoration for the big man in their eyes.

And the man, known as the Prophet, smiles. He is wearing a burlap-bag jockstrap covered with rat fur, and despite the cool year-round sewer temperature of eleven degrees Celsius, and despite a complete absence of body fat, he never feels cold. He has no time for cold, no time for pain. The hot fever of purpose in his heart is enough to keep him warm.

Yes, when the Prophet speaks, his loyal commandos listen. They are in the large cave deep beneath the boulevard de la Madeleine, the chamber it took six agonizing months to chip out of the earth with picks and axes and shovels scavenged from soldiers and sewer workers. To gain access to the cave they have to swim a meter beneath the surface of the sewer, squeeze through a hole, wriggle up a three-meter-long air-lock passage before emerging under a pipe which pumps cold fresh water siphoned from the city drinking-water network. Once inside, they wash the sewer slime off their bodies, drink a bit, and, after drying off with burlap-bag towels (boy, that's refreshing, like a menthol cigarette in a Jacuzzi after a jump in the snow following sex with a Swedish nymphomaniac nurse in a sauna), they pass through a burlap curtain and sit down on the floor to listen to their fearless leader.

My goodness, it's an impressive place, large and airy, with plenty of relatively fresh oxygen coming in through holes drilled through the ceiling into a long-unused parking garage. There is a chimney for cooking (they use dried turds as fuel), candles for light (made of tallow from the bodies of dead Nazis and dead rats), and burlap-and-rat-fur blankets to sleep in. (Early in their exile beneath ground, the Prophet and his gang had stumbled upon an abandoned Jewish warehouse with a basement door open to the sewers, a warehouse full of burlap bags, enough burlap for a century. And the rats? The little bastards were an unlimited natural resource.)

"They might say we are free," the Prophet rants on, his eyes blazing in the candlelight. "They might say that life will improve, that there will bread for all, milk for the young. They might say that Herman the German is gone, nothing but a foul memory and the lingering odor of sauerkraut farts and beer piss . . . but those are empty promises. They lie!"

"They lie!" the disciples cry as one, their hair long and wild, their tattered clothing hanging loose on their fat-free frames, revealing flashes of flesh—a nipple here, a furry testicle there, a patch of uncoiffed pubic hair here and there.

"They call it a liberation up there, but it's really just a new form of slavery!" the Prophet cries. "An exchange of one master for another! The Germans might be gone, but they've been replaced by the Americans, nothing more than Nazis in sheep's clothing! The Nazi spirit has infected France! The oppressed has taken on the spirit of the oppressor! The bread and wine will be poisoned, the meat and milk will contain chemicals that will make you fat as prize hogs, as obedient as whipped dogs, as easily manipulated as puppets on a string! Ah, lamentations!

"Listen to me, children! I.G. Farben went to bed with Rockefeller—and Ford and Rothschild watched that obscene coupling like a pair of slobbering, perverted, global village idiots, playing with their shrunken juiceless genitals all the while—and the twisted fruit of that revolting union will grow up, in the fullness of time, to become the long-prophesied beast! The Corporate Devil incarnate! The real struggle, the battle for man's eternal soul, the real war has just begun!"

"The real war has just begun!" comes the echo.

"Heed my words, children: It's a Nazi world out there. The deals have been struck. The corporate bloodsucking Nazis are Satan's messengers! It's God versus Satan, as usual! But these are the last rounds of the fight, the final minutes of the game. The championship is at stake. God is counting on us! We, here in the sewers, we are God's warriors, the chosen, the last sane humans on the planet!"

Above ground, the head wound that the Prophet had received in defense of the Republic would have brought him a large, shiny medal with a pretty ribbon plus a good pension for life. Yes, on the outside, it would have guaranteed him a life of admiring women, free pastis at the corner café, and the best psychiatric care in France; but down in the sewers, in the moist, cool, fragrant darkness, slime-dripping spiderwebs on the walls and pipes, the echoes of scurrying rat feet on the walkways, the eternal river of shit and piss flowing on and on, it brought him only a vast existential despair.

And the Prophet said:

"From this day forward, there will be nothing but misery in the world, nothing but pain and strife and a gnashing of teeth, a tearing of hair, nothing but blood and tears, nothing but use-less monkey chatter, nothing but death and sorrow and pitiful pissing in the void, until that day, that special day, that mar-velous golden day of safety and deliverance which will signal the beginning of the end of the world, and that day will come, my children, that sanctified day will come when . . ."

The prophet paused for effect.

". . . When the Trillionth Shit passes into the sewers of Paris!"

"The Trillionth Shit!" cried the people, their hearts erupting like Krakatoas of joy, spewing the molten lava of hope. "The Trillionth Shit! The Trillionth Shit!"

"So, if within the next three years the population of Paris and her suburbs climbs to and remains at a steady ten million," the Prophet rattled on, now sounding like a government economist analyzing the latest census data, "and if each person shits two-point-two times a day—some shit more, some less—that's eight-billion-plus shits a year. . . . Now, in the near hundred years that the sewers of Paris have been in existence, there have been at all times an average of three million people shitting twice a day for a figure of two hundred and twenty billion. Now add all the tourist and visiting-businessman and relatives-from-out-of-town shits from this point on, say a million people each day shitting three times a day—after all, when in Paris, visitors do tend to overeat—factor in the Americans who eat twice as much as anyone else and shit up to six times a day, include the occa-sional Sumo wrestler from Japan who shits up to seventeen times a day, consider the fashion models who might not shit but once a week, and of course don't forget all the dogs and rats and alley cats and bums and horses shitting on the streets since the sewers were built, shit which usually gets washed into the sewers through the gutters, and I calculate that it will take a bit less than fifty-two years from this moment hence until the blessed day when the Trillionth Shit passes into the sewers of Paris! The beginning of the end of the world! The true liberation!"

He paused theatrically, waiting until everyone in the room had reached such a frenzy of curiosity that they'd have sliced off their favorite puppy dog's nose and swallowed it whole without salt and pepper and a beer chaser just to know the blessed date, and then he spoke matter-of-factly:

"The Trillionth Shit will come down the pipes on July 14, 1996, Bastille Day."

"Bastille Day!" came the response, and they cheered and hugged and kissed, just as joyous as the folks aboveground upon their false liberation.

Sure, one might find fault with his population figures, sure, one might quibble with his projections of human and animal and Sumo defecation capabilities, and sure, on the evidence available, even a good ultraliberal humanist might conclude that the man was a prime candidate for immediate sterilization if not doctor-assisted mercy killing—but, really, you've got to hand it to the man, he was cloaked in the mantle of greatness. He was a paranoid genius on the scale of a Richard Nixon; he was as captivating a speech-maker as JFK after a night of Scotch whiskey and Berlin hookers or Bill Clinton after ten or twelve McDonald's Happy Meals; and he was as good an organizer as Mao Zedong planning a Texas barbecue. A rare combination! How far might he have gone up above with the proper medication?

But, like any man of vision starting a new religion, the Prophet was not without his domestic complications. As the proud, healthy Yanks restored Paris to normality—as men and women emerged from the safety of the sewers, from the catacombs (that humongous underground city beneath the city, the caves and passageways that for centuries had sheltered revolutionaries and religionists, criminals and sweethearts and bums and just plain old rotting corpses), as all the secret heroes of war climbed out of the darkness blinking their eyes like befuddled starving bears after a prolonged winter's sleep—the Prophet's teenage lover Gloria, very pregnant, begged the big man to ease his anal-retentive restrictions against going outside, begged and begged with bucket after bucket of salty tears shed over a two-week period, begged and begged and begged to be allowed to exit the cave to have her baby in a proper hospital. But the Prophet was adamant.

"Woman," he said, stuffing his pipe with dried flaked rat-turds and puffing away, it is the Devil in you wheedling and cajoling! The Nazi Devil has stolen your brain and soul. No child of mine will be born out there in Naziville! Born in a Nazi hospital so that its forehead can be stamped with the three sixes in invisible Devil-piss ink. Tie the traitorous harlot up!"

And so his loyal band of followers, emotionally scarred by war and deprivation, hungry for meaning in their lives, held poor Gloria and smacked the sexy pregnant little wench over the head with a shovel, tied her up with ropes.

There was Remi and Claude and Henri, Georges and Maurice and Artur, and their mates, Sara and Marie and Martha, Maude and Eloise and Helene. Twelve of them. They called themselves the Merdistes, the Shit People, and they hung on the Prophet's every word like drowning sailors on rotten timber, never once questioning his sometimes questionable decisions. Yes, they loved him like loyal dogs. Followed him like loyal dogs. And like loyal submissive dogs paying homage to the Alpha dog, each and every one of the Merdistes gave him their ass to do with as he liked. And boy, did he like. He liked and he liked and he liked. Yes, regardless of gender, the Prophet liked his people's asses. One of his favorite sayings was, "An ass is an ass is an ass." A true democrat.

So Gloria, her hands tied, gave birth to a son, Jean. And that morning, while everyone slept, their rear ends sore as well-pounded veal cutlets from the Prophet's inexhaustible likes, Gloria bit through her ropes, grabbed her wee, sleeping, burlap-and-rat-fur-swaddled infant in its cradle fashioned from cleaned and dried and sculpted toilet paper, scurried through the hole, held her breath, pinched the child's nostrils shut, covered its mouth, and swam one-armed for freedom.

She was weak as a sick kitten from the recent ordeal of childbirth, thin as a bulimic bunny rabbit from eating nothing but stewed or flame-broiled rats, the occasional pigeon swept down the gutters, and mushrooms grown in the catacombs—yet valiantly she swam, clutching her infant in its toilet-paper cradle, the splashes echoing in the large sewer; valiantly she pulled herself and the child up to the thin, precarious walkway; and valiantly she ran. Pursued by the Prophet and the Merdistes, toilet paper and cigarette butts and assorted slime stuck to her hair and body, Gloria ran desperately through the dark, bare feet never slipping on the slick surface. But the Merdistes were gaining ground, so she kissed the baby, picked a glob of shit off his face, and lay the plaster-of-Paris basket in the flowing sewer water, then turned to fight.

Gloria punched and kicked, kicked and punched, arms and feet whirring fast as a masturbating adolescent's hand, invisible as lawn-mower blades, and Baby Jean floated off, moving with the shit and piss and soapsuds and toilet paper at the speed of one meter a second. It was eleven o'clock in the morning, prime shitting time in Paris, and the wide channel was crowded with shit and paper. And when the baby had disappeared into the dark, Gloria jumped into the sewer water and swam. Weeping in the muck, swallowing great mouthfuls of waste-water, coughing like a consumptive, she swam for freedom, stroking desperately.

And the Merdistes twirled their rock-ended ropes, the ropes they used to hunt rats with, twirled their ropes like lassos and flung them at her head. . . . Eloise swore forever after that she nailed the little bitch. . . .

One supposes that Gloria's intention, if she escaped, had been to exit the sewers, shake the shit out of her hair, hijack a taxi, pick the baby up at the end of the boulevard de la Madeleine sewer line, 7.1 kilometers distant, and then go on to live a normal life. Ah, but this was not to be, for the cradle, already starting to flake and melt apart in the acidic pissy water, was intercepted by a loyal Merdiste, Maurice, who just happened that day to be out on "ring patrol" with Henri and

Claude and Maude, checking the exits from as many of the ninety thousand Paris buildings as they could for wedding bands and other jewelry dropped down drains, which Maurice would then bravely take outside to a Jewish pawnbroker to sell, using the proceeds to buy delicacies such as grain and oranges, wrapping them in oilskin (this was before plastic bags) so they wouldn't get soaked on the swim back to the cave.

So Maurice returned the infant Jean to the Hall of Counters. And Gloria? Her fate remained unknown. Did she escape? Did she drown? The Merdistes never found her body . . . but it was possible that the sewer men found it, just another anonymous corpse bobbing with the rush-hour turds. She became known forever in Merdiste lore as "the harlot who ran like Jesse Owens" or "the whore who swam like Johnny Weismuller."

✢   ✢   ✢

Little Jean grew up in the sewers. It was a simple life, idyllic really, an old-fashioned life of prayer and work, sleeping by day in the Hall of Counters when the sewer men worked, swimming and climbing and hunting for rats by night, farming mushrooms in the catacombs.

There were rules to be followed—the sacred Five Commandments, chiseled into the stone walls, the letters inked in with shit.

1: Never go above. (This applied to everyone but Maurice.)
2: No smoking. (Methane and other gases from accumulated waste matter were highly combustible. Only the Prophet was allowed to smoke, and he confined himself to the Hall of Counters.)

3: No reading. (Except the Five Commandments. Whatever printed matter came in through the gutters—magazines, scraps of newspaper, agonizing love letters read in the rain and dropped in the streets—was forbidden to be touched.)

4: No hanky-panky. (Unless with the Prophet or in a union sanctioned by the Prophet—and even then, unless the Prophet gave permission for procreation, they were mandated to use the back door and required, upon penalty of a severe lashing with a rat-tooth-studded burlap whip, to wear at all times one of the limitless condoms the Merdistes plucked from the sewers and scoured with boiling water and hung to dry on the hearth like Christmas stockings.)

5: No speaking to strangers. (Not that a lot of strangers made it down to the sewers. Sure, there was the occasional tourist who wandered off from the tour (until the 1970s, when the government decided that for antiterrorist safety reasons tourist tours of the sewers were no longer viable), sure, there was the occasional lost bum, the occasional eccentric thrill seeker, and certainly there were the teams of hardworking sewer workers in their fishing boots—checking the pipes (the technical gallery, as the city's phone lines and water supplies were called), changing the pipes, gauging methane and other dangerous gas levels with newfangled meters, cutting blockages of plastic bags and plastic six-pack links and oversized panty shields at the ends of sewer lines, riding the sewer boat or hauling the wagons on rusted rails in order to clean the sewers and keep the shit flowing—but you could hear them from a long way off, you could see their lights.)

Paranoid and clever, strong and brave, the Merdistes maintained their privacy, their cherished anonymity.

Of course Maurice was in contact with the World, but Maurice would never—could never—tell anyone where the Merdistes lived. Late in the German occupation, while hunting rats, he'd been captured and tortured by the Nazis; but being the tough monkey from Le Havre that he was, he'd refused to reveal where the commando unit was lodged, so in a fit of poetic injustice the Hermans cut poor brave Maurice's tongue out. But as he lay there, blood geysering from his tongue stump, the Prophet and his boys came swooping in like John Wayne and the cavalry, slaughtering five Hermans in the rescue operation.

"Good candles," said the Prophet that day, after they had dragged the five German corpses up into the Hall of Counters, as he sharpened his rat-filleting knife on a whetstone. "These heathen Nazis will provide many good hours of light for prayer."

But just in case a sewer worker happened close, the Merdistes wore rat-body hats (dead rats stuffed with burlap) hooked to their ears, and if they heard or saw a sewer man coming—their eyes were as sharp as any nocturnal animal's—they would submerge beneath the waters, breathe through a straw (dried rat intestine) running out through the rat's mouth, and swim off with the current into the dark. . . .

The hats were called Gaspars. In fact, the rats were called Gaspar, a tradition borrowed from the sewer men. Henri had been a sewer man, and when he didn't emerge after the war, his coworkers assumed that he had been killed by the Germans in the sewers. Why, you can even see a plaque erected in his memory in the sewer-man locker room on the rue de ———.

✢   ✢   ✢

And so the years passed in a haze of shit and piss and rats and mushrooms. The Merdistes were swimmers, they were climbers, they were hunters and gatherers. And after their systems adjusted to the high-protein diet, they grew strong on a diet of Gaspar. Stewed Gaspar, baked Gaspar, flame-broiled Gaspar. Gaspar with mushrooms. Gaspar a l'orange. Cold Gaspar sandwiches. And each time they ate Gaspar, they thanked God for Gaspar, and they asked Gaspar's forgiveness for taking his life to sustain their lives. They drank no alcohol, no wine. They ate flat bread made of kosher grain bought from Jews, oranges from Palestine. And there was no disease to speak of. Their immune systems were incredibly strong. They brushed their teeth thrice daily with toothbrushes sporting rat-hair bristles, and they used pigeon quills for toothpicks. They had no cavities. And their slug-white skin, untouched by sun or soap, moistened by the mineral rich air of the sewers, was as soft and smooth as a baby's butt. The Oil of Olay people could have taken lessons.

✢   ✢   ✢

And so it came to pass that when Jean, son of the Prophet, came of age, age thirteen, that is—yes, there was a strong Judaic flavor to the Prophet's organization—he took to wife Danielle, the daughter of Maude and Maurice. . . . And Jean begot Samuel, and Samuel begat Pierre, and Pierre begat (drum roll and harp music, please) . . . Pierre begat Rose . . . sweet, sweet Rose, the rose of the sewers.

By the time Rose was born in 1977, the population of the Merdiste community had grown to near a hundred. And incredibly—given the slipperiness of the walkways, the hazards of flash floods after rainstorms, the possibility of Gaspar-bites getting infected (a good splashing of the Prophet's urine took care of that), and given the high rate of inbreeding and the vast amount of bacteria in the sewers—incredibly (like every word of this guaranteed-true story), not one Merdiste had died! Sure the Hall of Counters was a bit cramped and had to be expanded, and sure, the Merdistes had to make do with less grain and oranges—the sewer men had gotten more efficient at retrieving lost jewelry, having set up a special twenty-four-hour phone line—but sickness and death were unknown in the community.

Rose grew up, like her forebears, without ever seeing the light of day, without ever breathing the fresh, polluted air of Paris. And like all of the children born and raised down below, regardless of whatever recessive genes were snoozing in her DNA, her skin was white, whiter than white, and her eyes were pink, red almost in the dark. . . . But her ass . . . it grew lovelier and lovelier with the passing shit, blooming like a flower, filling out in the fullness of time into twin swollen globes of unsurpassed beauty. Muscular, powerful, yet incredibly feminine. Even the Prophet had to admit that it was special.

"This ass," announced the Prophet to his throng in 1989, some nine-hundred-or-so-billion shits into the wait, on the occasion of Rose's first menstrual period, as he stroked her delicate white orbs and drooled into his navel-long beard, shifting uncomfortably as the cold slobber dripped from his beard onto his lap, "this ass is off limits."

So he bound her ass and her sex with a chastity belt made from plastic bags and near-indestructible plastic six-pack links, he stopped her entrances, both front and rear, with champagne corks, and he ordained that when nature called she must eliminate waste in the presence of her great-grandmother Danielle—each and every time. . . . That became Danielle's duty, observing Rose's functions in a secluded corner of the rue de l'Arcade—undoing the intricate knots of her chastity belt, pulling the corks, handing her the toilet paper, driving off curious boys. And each shit had to be turned over to the Prophet, though every once in a while, when the mood struck him, the Prophet would personally collect her turds, wipe her special ass—not with the reconstituted toilet paper that everyone else in the community used, no, but with the oversized pink silk handkerchief from his collection of Nazi memorabilia, the one bearing the initials C.G. (Rumor had it that De Gaulle had dropped it on the street on a rainy day shortly after the war's end. It must have been the General's hanky! said the disciples. The volume of snot had been that copious!)

But what did the Prophet do with Rose's turds? After he put them in a plastic bag? That is a very good question, one which will be answered in about fifteen pages.

Sex for Rose was out of the question.

"She must remain a virgin," sayeth the Prophet, more than a smidgen of regret in his voice. "Both front and rear. And if anyone tampers with her purity they will be turned into a candle!"

So Rose remained a virgin, bearing her special status with complete humility and grace, perhaps even a touch of embarrassment.

While other girls wiggled their darling butts, swung open their back doors and willingly, yea joyfully, gave of their service-entrances to one and all (and of course to the lecherous old Prophet with his holy rod—it was considered the ultimate honor, and for an old man, the girls said, he could really deliver the goods), Rose remained pure as the driven snow. But just the sight of her dreamy peaches, bound by the tight chastity belt, swishing in the dark sewer tunnels, pipes dripping, slimy spiderwebs on the pipes, shit squishing underfoot, toilet paper and soapsuds and turds floating by, just a quick glance at lovely young Rose lying there on her burlap-and-rat-fur blanket (a quick glance was as much as one could bear), showered clean and fresh, her long black hair fanned out on a soft burlap pillow, her sweet cheeks twitching, releasing the periodic delicate rat-stew fart as she snoozed the day away, ah, it drove all the younger male Merdistes into a hormonal frenzy that could only be quenched by sliding on down the entrance tunnel to the cool darkness of the lonely sewers where they would yank their cranks furiously while imagining pulling the champagne corks out of Rose with twin loud POPS. . . .

Yes, the proud, Gaspar-hatted youths were sick with desire. Their right arms grew abnormally large and muscular from the repeated exercise, like the arms of tennis players—so much so that sometimes when a sweet little Merdiste chick bent over and offered rear-door entry, with the Prophet's blessing, the youth would sigh melancholically and say, "Not tonight, dear, I'm all Rosed out."

The girls started to resent Rose, so as a favor to her sisters and brothers and to the community as a whole she took to wandering off alone.

Ah, but she was a strong girl, a wonderful fighter, nimble on her feet, fast with her hands, as she proved time and time again—after all, she came from the Prophet's bloodlines—and each time some brave boy with tennis-player's arm attempted an assault on that ass, they got their ass kicked; but she never ratted on them; and she actually enjoyed her solitude, the long solitary swims and hikes around the underground city—it gave her an opportunity to observe the magnificent variety of life, and she realized that each neighborhood boasted turds of a different texture, a varied aroma. (The Prophet later explained this phenomena: "You see, Rose, Maurice has told me that up there Paris is changing, people are being flushed into the city from all over—Africa, Algeria, Asia, Italy, and Spain—coming here to join the Nazi community, and they all eat differently, they all shit differently. . . . Their shit might look and smell different but never forget that all shit is created equal, they are all Nazis.") She took great pleasure and pride in tending her own patch of mushrooms in a secluded part of the catacombs; she enjoyed playing with the Gaspars, teaching them to race, both on foot and in the water; she spoke with the Gaspars, she spoke with the spiders; she even liked the thrill of a violent rainstorm and she would ride the frothing surf to parts of the city she'd never seen before, discovering new tunnels, new places to perch and watch the wonderful world of shit pass by. . . .

One May day, after a particularly vicious rainstorm that gorged the sewers near to bursting, as Rose was couched high-up on a rusted pipe above the swollen torrents of spring, her Gaspar hat askew on her head, as she hummed the Merdeillaise (*"Allons enfants de-es égou-ou-outs, le jour de gloire arriverait . . ."*), dreaming of the time she'd be allowed to open her back door to the community as a whole, to the Prophet himself, Rose saw a terrified, soaked cat flow by chased by three Gaspars, and she was just about to jump in the water and rescue the poor kitty, when she saw . . . temptation itself, floating down the sewer in the form of a *Vogue* magazine, slick bright pages coated so that they were as clear and glossy as the day they were printed. She hesitated, after all she knew that reading was a sin, but being a curious lass and being so far away from home, she picked the magazine up, and feeling guilty but also experiencing a strange tingle deep in her bowels, she tucked it into her chastity belt, and for the first time in her fourteen years of life climbed the cold rusted rungs of a ladder leading to the street, put her shoulder to the eighty-kilo metal cover and lifted it a crack.

What was more exciting, her Gaspar-hatted head sticking out onto the street? (Fresh polluted air!? Cars!? Electric lights!? The occasional stylish French Nazi walking in the rainy midnight moonlight!?) Or the magazine? The magazine! Of course the magazine. As good old Gutenburg is purported to have said on his deathbed: "The printed page beats the shit out of real life."

The women! The clothing! The makeup! The styles! They took her breath away. She gasped with joy, her heart beat fast as a cornered Gaspar. And the men in the perfume adds! They were so different from male Merdistes, so handsome, so debonair . . . so clean!

The words in the magazine were meaningless (and if she didn't read them, she reasoned, she wouldn't be breaking the third commandment; if she didn't actually go all the way outside, she'd wouldn't be violating the first commandment) but the pictures were worth a thousand words. Her young heart rose to the bait, and she was hooked. Haute couture became her *raison d'être.*

She collected *Vogue* and *Elle* and *Marie-Claire, Biba* and *Cosmo and Dépêche-mode*—even looking at, before discarding, a few automotive monthlies and various film and TV magazines—and she absorbed the images, studying the styles and analyzing the stitchwork before stashing the sinful magazines behind an electrical pipe on the rue de l'Arcade. But eventually, after two years, the pictures were not enough; she took to actually peeking out the sewer holes, admiring and critiquing the fashions, recognizing outfits she'd seen in magazines months before.

"I can do better," she said to herself, red eyes gleaming beneath her Gaspar hat. "I know I can do better."

And so she did. In the dim remote cave where she grew her own mushrooms, she set about creating her own collection. From plastic bags, six-pack links, cellophane, newspaper scraps, tampons, panty shields, rat fur and burlap purloined from the Hall of Counters, she made skirts and pants and shirts and dresses, for both men and women. She stitched them together with needles fashioned from shaved-down rat bones, thread painstakingly created from braided cords of fine rat belly hair. And she didn't stop with clothing, she did jewelry too—necklaces of rat teeth, necklaces of cockroaches dipped in rat-tallow wax, the roach bodies strung together like strings of shiny brown pearls, spider brooches, or bracelets made of cigarette filters. . . . Anything that came flowing through the sewers was fair game for Rose. And the clothing was lovely. She had a sweet touch, a sense of whimsy. And not surprisingly, the ass was always featured prominently. She would model the styles for herself, perhaps a few of her pet Gaspars as audience: chastity belts, plastic culottes, flowing skirts made of stripped plastic bags (like Hawaiian grass skirts), hats made from condoms and tampons and panty shields, plastic bag–based pigeon-feather support brassieres featuring beer-bottle-cap nipple covers (they made Wonderbras look like your maiden aunt's jogging bra!), and always back to the chastity belts, chastity belts galore—her lovely bare butt framed enticingly, the curves accentuated by the plastic, but the anus always well protected with wine or champagne corks and maybe a stretched condom hanging like a cute, fat Gaspar tail. A perfect blend of safety and desire—yin and yang. Yes, Rose was a genius.

✛   ✛   ✛

Let us extricate our readerly noses from Rose's lovely ass for a moment—don't despair, we won't be gone long—and take a brief tour of a few other scenes happening on the underground circuit.

By the beginning of the 1990s four major groups had established themselves in the catacombs:

1) The white purity group known as the Célinéastes. Named after the famed splenetic novelist Céline, they hated everybody who wasn't pure white French—Africans, Asians, Arabs, Muslims, Jews, Eastern Europeans, even Italians— hated everyone, except Germans, with a democratic ferocity.

2) The heroin-dealing ring called the Héros—West Africans, Algerians, and tough whites from the suburbs.

3) Satan's Kids—Devil worshippers of all ages and races.

4) The Pride of France—a large mixed-race community of homeless people, many of them accordion players, licensed by the Mafia to beg on the subways.

Each group knew of the others, and they coexisted surprisingly well. Occasionally the Célinéastes and the Héros would have brief pitched gun battles or they would murder one another quietly with Rambo knives; occasionally Satan's Kids would grab a homeless child for use in one of their sacrifices; occasionally one of the Pride of France would beat his wife to death; but given the violence and confusion of the world above, life in the catacombs was relatively peaceful. The four groups shared a common desire: to keep the authorities from coming belowground.

All four groups had heard the rumors from some old bums, the rumors that had been floating about the dark underground for years like fireflies on a starless night, the rumors about the Merdistes. Like the horror stories adults tell children around campfires to raise the gooseflesh, they told stories about the Merdistes, the crazy Shit People who lived somewhere in the sewers, who tended mushrooms in remote secret caves, who hunted rats with rock-ended ropes, who had red eyes. One or two of the oldest bums had seen the Merdistes, or so they claimed, but their descriptions of the half-naked long-haired lunatics with rats riding on their heads were so outlandish, so ridiculous, that they were dismissed as the ravings of wine-addled maniacs.

So that was the state of the catacombs in the mid-nineties when Father Nicolas, the young, pale, Parisian priest we left some pages ago splashing peacefully in the bath at Lourdes, first started ministering to the various underground groups.

His primary mission—as ordered by the home team back in Rome—had been to tend the homeless flock on the streets of Paris. But the street homeless led him to the catacombs, where he met the Pride of France, who were like empty wine bottles waiting to be poured full of faith. So Father Nick took it upon himself to bring the Word to the catacombs, but in his wanderings below the earth's skin he found that each of the four major groups down there were as hungry for the true faith as . . . well, as the British are for beef.

Satan's Kids were ripe for the saving, as many of them had been raised in the Church before straying (a fair percentage of them had even written to Rome asking that their names be erased from the baptism ledgers); the drug-dealing Héros were highly superstitious and often had Christian mothers they supported with their illicit earnings, so they liked the idea of getting on God's good side; and the Aryan-brother Célinéastes were right there for the plucking, as they were of the fervent opinion that Jesus was a blue-eyed blonde dude, most likely a German, and they'd be damned if they'd let the other groups, those motley bums with their bare feet and beards and those goddamn mud-people drug-dealers and those evil fucking voodoo witches, worship their God without them there. . . .

Father Nick's meetings grew in size, and soon even hip Parisians who'd heard about his mission to the catacombs on Radio Nova, soon the cool cats and even a few daring churchgoers were coming too. He had only one rule: all guns and knives must be checked at the cave entrance. Yes, Father Nick was succeeding where the politicians and established branches of the Church had failed: he was uniting the downtrodden.

✚　✚　✚

It is said that there are no connections between the catacombs and the Metros and the sewers, but that is not exactly true. Of course there are connections. You need only know where to look.

Father Nicolas felt it his duty to check out the strange rumors he'd been hearing of a community of people living in the sewers. Yes, he thought, if these so-called Merdistes really do exist, they will need something to believe in.

One of the old bums showed him how to get into the sewers from the catacombs, wished him luck, bummed enough coins for some wine, and left the white-robed, innocent cleric to wander the sewers, flashlight in hand.

"Good day," said the priest in the dirty white robes to a young Asian fellow in the blue sewer, worker jumpsuit, as he stepped on a slick turd, almost slipping into the rushing sewer waters. "Are you a sewer worker? Do you know where I might find the Merdistes?"

The young Asian took one look at the long-nosed, fresh-faced priest and promptly hit him over the head with a heavy metal hook, then ran.

And the last thing Father Nick thought before passing out, his face cushioned on a large smelly turd, was: France is a great world democracy, and the underground of Paris is a microcosm, every race is represented. Too bad the Asians are so touchy. . . .

✣　✣　✣

Kaka Misumi, our young Japanese, had started coming to the sewers in 1987. Kaka was rich before he arrived, but after only two years mining the guts of Paris and investing the proceeds wisely, he was almost a billionaire. Yes, you might say that Kaka was a pioneer in his chosen field, an explorer in a brave new world— one part Marco Polo, one part Bill Gates. . . . But perhaps a bit of biographical information is in order.

As a teenager back in Japan, in the early eighties, Kaka made his first big score by selling his eleven-year-old sister's virginity to a Tokyo businessman. Following on the round heels of that morally questionable but financially lucrative transaction, he sold the man and the man's virgin-loving buddies all his sister's friends, and finally, when that particular crop of fresh plums had been harvested, he took to the subways, sweet-talking Japanese virgins to his lair by promising them McDonald's cheeseburgers and an introduction to his "good friend Michael Jackson."

But good things rarely last, as Kaka was soon to find out. The virgin business just happened to be traditional Yakuza turf, and the gangsters, after hearing about his success in their jurisdiction, warned Kaka in no uncertain terms—their terms were a friendly beating and a huge fine—to find a new way to skim a living.

I'm glad to be out of the business, Kaka thought, lying in

bed the next day nursing his injuries, his one unbroken arm slung across the pealike breasts of a secondhand virgin as another secondhand virgin showed him some of the gear-shifting tricks she'd learned from a Mitsubishi executive. Sure it's good money, but virgins have such a short shelf life. Even disposable razors can be used more than once before being thrown away. And a Japanese connoisseur of virgins can always tell the difference between a fresh virgin and a used virgin. (Kaka had found that out the hard way when he got the shit beat out of him by a Sony executive's bodyguard for trying to pass his then twelve-year-old sister off as a fresh plum.) There's a very specific vibe, he mused to himself, an electro-chemical vibe that can't be imitated. That's why the money is so good.

But where there's a yen there's a way, and Kaka liked the yen of the virgin biz—so after a great deal of soul-searching, he came up with the answer: he decided that his future lay in the underexplored world of virgin panties, virgin training bras, and virgin socks and shoes.

This time he checked with the Yakuza. . . . No, they said, you won't be poaching on our grounds, that's virgin territory. So Kaka plunged into his new profession with energy and enthu-siasm, hanging around the schoolyards and making friends with corrupt elementary-school gym teachers, paying the muscular brutes very good money to raid the virgins' lockers.

Kaka's customers were ecstatic with their new collectibles; but predictably, in only a matter of months, elementary-school principals' offices all over Tokyo were crowded with the angry parents of little girls who'd come home from school barefoot and with no underwear, so the gym teachers who still had jobs got together with Kaka and suggested a compromise: virgin pubic hair, virgin Kleenex, virgin tampons, virgin chewing gum—anything that virgins had used that they could safely scavenge from the toilet seats and locker-room trash cans of Tokyo's schools.

I think it's fairly obvious—given the shitty nature of this story—where Kaka was headed. In a short time, despite the success he was enjoying with his new menu, the connoisseurs grew jaded, they needed something more substantial to sink their teeth into, so Kaka took the next step, finally graduating to what would become his life work: virgin urine and virgin feces.

He paid the gym teachers to clog the toilets in the school bathrooms and he supplied them with jars; and the gym teachers, now a vast network of well-paid sneaky brutes, came through with the goods. A Japanese pervert—no no, Kaka always thought of them as aesthetes—a Japanese aesthete was willing to go up to five million yen for a good-sized virgin turd, two million for some watery virgin wee-wee; and for some of them—many of them— the smaller the turd, the better. And since each virgin was different, and each meal they ate was either different or digested in a different way, each turd was different. Each was unique, had a different shape and color and odor. And the supply was limitless! The aesthetes were ecstatic! Kaka was ecstatic! They say a sucker is born every minute—true; but for every sucker born, there are at least five virgins born! Yes, business was booming. Rock 'n' roll, Samurai style!

Two years. Two glorious years at the top of his chosen profession. Box seats at the Tokyo symphony, a luxury box at the ballpark. Power breakfasts with executives and government policy-makers. Kaka had became a man of wealth and taste, a man of respect. But then—ah fickle fate!—the bottom fell out of the Japanese virgin shit and piss market. The Japanese aesthetes grew weary of Japanese virgin shit and piss. It held no more surprises, no more mysteries. Yes, you could drink the pee and sniff or chew the turds, you could smear yourself before sitting on a virgin shoe and choking the chicken with a pair of virgin panties or training bra, but so what? The aesthetes grew as blasé and spoiled as junkies who need more and more dope to get off, they wanted something new, something exotic. . . .

So Kaka surveyed his customers, polling them for the item that would float their boats next, and one and all, to a man— even the three women on his list—they said: bring us the turds of little French virgins.

Why this was, the turdmaster had no idea, none whatsoever, but the customer is always right, so it was off to Paris for Kaka Misumi.

Ah, but the French gym teachers were not so easy to bribe. In fact, Kaka's very first effort in a Paris schoolyard resulted in a broken nose and a badly ruptured testicle that became infected and then gangrenous and finally had to be amputated; but that setback only strengthened his resolve, and as he lay there healing and scheming in his Paris hospital bed, he hit on a sure-fire method to guarantee his clients fresh virgin turds from France.

This is what he'd do. And all you mothers out there, warn your daughters to be on the lookout. . . . He'd stop a virgin in the street, a few blocks from her school—Kaka could smell an unplucked plum from a good ten meters (he'd never actually slept with one, they were too potentially lucrative)—and he would ask the little pouty-lipped little lovely if he might take her picture. Usually they said yes (ahh, Vanity: Daughters of the Republic, thine enemy is Vanity!), so he'd snap a picture, and as a reward he'd hand them some candy and a pack of Marlboro Lights.

Now, this candy was special. He made it himself, on a hotplate he snuck into his room at the Hôtel Splendid and later, after it opened, in his suite at the superchic Hôtel Costes, where he'd buy drinks for movie stars and hobnob with rock singers. He made the candy—really they looked like healthy, medium-sized poodle turds or Mounds bars—from milk chocolate, caramel, orange rinds, lots of nuts (Brazil nuts, peanuts, cashews, almonds, walnuts), and his secret ingredient, high-octane baby laxative. The candy was so delicious (next to it a Snickers bar tasted like shit), so indescribably delicious, that the virgins would shove it down their delicate throats, barely chewing, it tasted so good.

Kaka would follow them at a safe distance, sniffing in their wake like a happy dog at the first little virgin fartlets (the smell of freshly minted money!) puffing out of their tight little swinging cans, he'd see where they lived, go to the nearest sewer cover, pull off his stylish Issey Miyaki jumpsuit to reveal a copy of the Paris sewer-man uniform (only his was made of thin material so it could fit under his regular outfit)—he'd take a hook from his bag, open the sewer lid, and zip down the ladder in his waterproof boots, run up the sewer walkway to the building where the girl had entered and wait the few minutes or hours it took until she voided her bowels and flushed. The turds zipping down the chute were identifiable by the undigested nuts and often were accompanied by Marlboro light butts, and he'd scoop the precious nuggets up with his fishing net, put them in a jar with white rice-wine vinegar as preservative, and later, back in Japan—his steamer trunks full of row after row of plastic-bottled shit were never searched as he had diplomatic immunity granted by a high government official who shall go nameless here, one of his oldest and best customers—he'd attach the photos of the girls and sell their droppings (occasionally leaving in the Marlboro butt and toilet paper for seasoning) for obscene amounts of cash.

✛   ✛   ✛

The Merdistes had Kaka under surveillance for three years before the Prophet and a band of young Merdistes accosted him in the dark, lonely sewer beneath the boulevard St. Germain. The Prophet dismissed his commandos to stand guard.

Kaka took one look at the huge, long-haired, bearded old maniac in the loincloth and Gaspar hat, the hardy young warriors with the red eyes, chewing on pigeon-quill toothpicks, and he promptly dropped a load in his pants. Then he told all. . . .

"And the best thing about it," he concluded, "Is that a French virgin of eleven or twelve from a divorced family is good for sometimes as long as two years! All you need is candy and cigarettes."

"Yes," said the Prophet with a large, sigh, not even stopping Kaka from using his fishing net when a large, nutty turd flashed down the chute. "The French soul is easily bought. Candy and cigarettes. It is an old story, the same formula that the American Nazis used after the Herman occupation."

Kaka looked at the old man—the insane eyes, the Frankenstein scar, the wise long beard coming almost to his balls, the hair down past his ass—and he said:

"Please don't kill me, master. Many people back in Japan are counting on me."

"Kill you, my boy? Nonsense. Put that turd down and we'll talk business."

And in the ultimate sign of Merdiste friendship, the Prophet washed Kaka's rear end for him, and then he offered him a deal: in exchange for a heaping amount of gold, the Prophet would provide Kaka guaranteed French virgin shit—not that Nazi shit he was getting now, but genuine guaranteed hundred-percent virgin French shit.

Kaka thanked his ancestors for this stroke of good fortune—he'd already been kicked in his lonely remaining ball more than once by tough little French broads, the future ball-breakers of the Republic—and to seal the pact, the Prophet made Kaka an honorary Merdiste, inducting him into the family by bending him over and taking his back, door plum (what tight, tasty little buns! thought the Prophet) . . . and the young Japanese actually enjoyed it, though he did look a bit askance at the battered condom the Prophet pulled out of a plastic FNAC bag.

So that was what the Prophet was doing with Rose's shit. Trading with Kaka. Shit for gold. Rose's shit was financing the community, buying the kosher grain and oranges from

Palestine that the Merdistes treasured. And Kaka and the old man became close, like a father and son. Kaka brought a Polaroid camera to the Hall of Counters and took Rose's picture. He put Rose's picture on every jar of her shit he sold in Japan. And each time Kaka came to visit, he brought his French father sushi and his special candy bars, without the laxative. The sushi the Prophet could do without. To tell the truth the Prophet preferred Gaspar tartare, but the candy, yumm. . . . Yes, the Prophet was getting a sweet tooth in his old age. The back lower-left molar was even starting to ache.

+   +   +

The first time Felix the sewer man saw Rose was shortly after her sixteenth birthday, in 1994.

A ghost, he thought, crossing himself, she's a ghost. A ghost with red eyes and the finest ass on the planet.

Scared as he was, he chased that ass, but the ass disappeared beneath the sewer waters, and all he saw was a rat swimming away. (The famous Gaspar hat trick!) Felix had to pinch himself.

He told his team of sewer men what he'd seen—what he thought he'd seen—but they just laughed at him.

"Felix," they said, "you're fucking crazy, man. You've been sniffing too much methane. A ghost with a fine ass turned into a rat?"

But Felix had seen what he'd seen, and at night when he slept, he dreamed of the ghost. He saw the milky hemispheres of her corked ass, and he'd wake up in a puddle of his own lust.

Felix took to wandering off from the team, hanging near the

rue des Capucines sewer where he'd first seen the lovely appari-
tion, hanging there and hoping she'd come back.

I don't care if she is a ghost, he told himself, sitting in the
dark, in the peaceful dark with the cool, fragrant waters gurgling, I don't care if she's a shape-shifting demon from hell
who can change into a rat, I don't give a shit. I don't give a shit,
I'm in love.

He lost weight. He started drinking on the job. He wandered off alone more and more, putting his mates at risk. He
became a danger to the team. The sewer men had no choice
but to report him to their superiors. Felix was sent to a psychiatrist.

"Aha!" exclaimed the psychiatrist. "You say that the ghost is
white? And you yourself are brown, from a white father and a
black mother? I would say this is as definite case as I've ever seen
of a paternal grandmother fixation. Tell me Felix, did your
granny have a pretty behind?"

So Felix punched the little Freudian nerd in the nose, splat-
tering that sizable feature like a sledgehammer hitting an egg.

"Thank you," said Felix. "I feel better."

But Felix didn't feel better for long, though that was the last
he said to anyone about his ghost. He'd still wander off from
the team, a bottle of wine in his pocket, he'd still shirk his
duties, but that's the way it goes for the obsessed. And Felix was
truly obsessed. He didn't give a shit about his job. And so he
lost it. And in short succession he lost his friends, his apartment, and thirty pounds; and he didn't even go for the unem-
ployment benefits.

Down down down: Felix fell. He ended up living in the

catacombs—just one more depressed member of the Pride of France. His hair grew long and wild, like insane palm fronds. He shaved with broken glass, thinking: just one little slip of the razor and this misery is all over; but he held on—that one glimpse of Rose's ass sustained him through the dark days and nights. His eyes took on a haunted, ravaged look. He begged in the Metro. But that didn't stop him from visiting the sewers. No, he went to the familiar dark tunnels nightly, went with his methane meter in one jacket pocket and the sandwich and wine it took a whole day to beg the cash to buy in the other. His pants pockets were full of cigarette butts he'd collected off the station platform. And he'd walk and walk, checking gas levels and smoking when the level was low; and when he was too tired to walk any more, he'd eat his sandwich and drink his wine and he'd weep himself to sleep. Weep and weep and doze and dream. And the river of shit just kept right on flowing. Shit without end, amen.

And though Felix really did need new sneakers (those damned Nikes were falling apart!)—after buying his sandwich and wine and tithing to the Mafia for the right to beg in the Metro, and after giving a few centimes to Father Nick to help feed the homeless kids, there wasn't even so much as a franc to put aside. Yes, everything had gone to shit. . . .

And the river of shit flowed, flowed in his waking life and flowed in his dream life. He couldn't tell dream from reality anymore. It was all just so much shit. And one night—was it a dream? was it real?—Rose came to him, her red eyes glowing, wearing her plastic chastity belt, a cork in her butt, a pigeon-feather bra plumping her cleavage, a Gaspar hat with a condom tail on her head, and she touched his face with silk-soft fingers, stroking it ever so gently, saying:

"You're so beautiful. What's your name?"

"Felix," said the ruined sewer man. And then he said: "I love you," because in a dream, even on the first date, you can say any damn thing you want. "I love you!"

"I know," she said. "I've been watching you for a long time, I can feel your feeling. . . . Is this real?" she asked, stroking his brown face. "Your color?"

"I didn't get it on my yacht in Monaco."

"So lovely," she said seriously. "The blessed color of blessed shit."

      ✣   ✣   ✣

"Some dream," I told Felix. He'd already killed half the second bottle of wine. I'd gone through three lollipops.

"No shit," he said. "That was the beginning of the good times. I still thought I was dreaming. Living in a dream. By night I'd be with Rose and by day I'd sit here, right here on this seat, begging and drinking. This is my spot."

Ah, but I already knew that. That's how I'd found him, that's how I'd let him find me. The late Father Nick had clued me in.

"So you two became lovers?" I asked, though Rose had already told me all.

Tears came to Felix's eyes. I felt in my pocket, touching the priest collars I only wear on occasion, touching the two guns the Dispatcher had forbidden me to use—which reminded me, I hadn't called her, and I wouldn't, this was my show. . . . The old lollipop lady wanted messages in code. I'd give her code, the code of silence. She could suck on the silence. . . . I found a packet of tissues. Felix took them, nodded his thanks, and blew a soulful mucus blues.

"Sort of, Monsieur. . . . We kissed. Long kisses, more electric than any sex I'd ever had, and I'd hold that fabulous ass and stroke it and stroke it and it was as if my whole body was having a long continuous orgasm. And I'd say to myself: God, if this is a dream I don't ever want to wake up."

"But it wasn't a dream," I said.

"No, Monsieur, it wasn't. And when the time came that she asked me home with her to meet the family, I still thought I was dreaming, the weirdest fucking dream I'd ever had. The walls of that cave under the boulevard de la Madeleine were covered with carvings darkened by shit and cooking smoke—the Five Commandments were there, and a calendar so they could count the days until the Trillionth Shit, and some cave paintings of immortal moments in Merdiste history: battles with the Germans, the day old Maurice got his tongue cut out, the time the Prophet's chick Gloria ran off, the birth of Rose. And all the kids down there, these pale little red-eyed monkeys in burlap-and-rat-fur loincloths, they all touched my skin as if the pigment was gonna come off. The women fussed over me, stroked my hair, giggled, fed me some fried Gaspar, and God it was good, a happy, happy moment; but all the time the old Prophet was standing there in the candlelight and shadows, smoking his old pipe—it smelled like death eating a shit sandwich—and he had this ugly, angry look on his mug, him and all his old boys and girls, tough old birds, the disciples Maurice and Claude and

Henri and Maude—I forget all the names. They didn't dig me
one bit. So I asked the chief lunatic, 'You got a problem with me
and your great-great-granddaughter getting together?' And he
says yeah, but not because I was brown, like I was thinking, no,
but because I wasn't one of them. I was an outsider, a Nazi, he
called me. And after dinner the ugly bastard was gonna kill me,
but Rose begged for my life, said she'd go right ahead and fuck
one of the Merdistes and ruin his virgin-shit-to-Japan racket if
he didn't spare me—so the old buzzard just threw my ass out.
Rose and I were both crying. The Prophet ordered a couple of
young dudes to swim me away from the cave. Those boys swam
me and walked me for hours, all the way over to the avenue
Laumière in the 19th, before beating the crap out of me and
letting me go. Then I knew I wasn't dreaming.

"But Rose and I kept meeting, we'd meet in different spots,
prearranged—with old Danielle as a lookout—and it was beautiful. We never made love. She was a very religious chick, and I
can respect that. Our love was beautiful, it was pure. I know that
sounds like I'm making excuses for never getting to the prom-
ised land, but I mean it, it was a special kind of love. One built
on trust. She figured she could work on the Prophet and get
him to ease up on the Nazi shit and let me into the family. I
didn't even mind when old Danielle interrupted a kiss and
undid her chastity belt and pulled her cork so Rose could shit
in the plastic bag. I was that much in love.

"Rose was cool, Monsieur, and her fashions were something
else. She gave me private shows in the catacombs, just me and
the Gaspars in her mushroom cave, and I took her to the prayer
meetings down there too, hoping that Father Nick could maybe

convince her to convert so we could finally get it going on a sexual level. But she was strong in the Merdiste faith, deep into the shit. Of course all the dudes in the catacombs wanted a piece of that unparalleled ass, and the Célinéastes were pissed, me being brown and she being an Aryan goddess, so I had a few fights, but she kept coming to my rescue—she was a better fighter than me—and after kicking the shit out of a few of those horny racist boys, they all respected her and left us alone.

"Father Nick dug her spirit too. And when I told him how things were between me and the Prophet, he suggested he go have a little talk with the loony geezer. Rose didn't want to take him to the Hall of Counters. She figured they'd get into a theological debate and the Prophet would turn Father Nick into a candle. But finally she gave in. And when Father Nick met the Prophet, saw how peaceful and organized and really spiritual they were, despite all the anal sex, something clicked. . . . I don't know, maybe he'd been living underground too long, but he bought into the whole moronic rap about the Trillionth Shit like a country bumpkin getting sold the Eiffel Tower. He invited the Prophet to the catacombs, and the old Merdiste accepted, figuring that as long as they were approaching the time for the Trillionth Shit anyway, he might as well start planting the seeds for a worldwide revolution. And damned if the crazy old fucker didn't win over the whole fucking bunch of them—the Célinéastes, the Héros, the Pride of France, Satan's Kids. And why not? I mean, those people wouldn't be down there in the catacombs living like moles in a hole or grubs in a tree if they thought the world was any good. Am I right or am I right? They all thought the world was a stinking horrible bloodbath shit-storm already, so the Merdiste philosophy really caught on. And soon more and more people were coming. Those meetings were packed. And more and more of the people were from outside, good, God-fearing, churchgoing folks just aching for some substance in their empty lives."

Felix didn't have to tell me that. That's why attendance was down in Lourdes.

"But," Felix went on, "the old fuck still wanted Rose to stay cherry, so he ordered Father Nick to ban me. Father Nick was sad about it, but he did it—for the sake of the movement, he said; and the Prophet posted guards. I wasn't allowed in the cat-acombs or in the sewers anywhere near the boulevard de la Madeleine. Got my ass kicked every time I tried to get near her. So I cried and drank myself to sleep right here, right where we're sitting, and I wandered the distant sewers in the burlap suit Rose made for me. I'm still wearing it."

"It's a beautiful suit," I said, touching the filthy lapels. "Needs a serious cleaning, but really very beautiful."

"My Rose does good work." And then poor Felix broke down and wept. "I look for her, Monsieur. I wait in all the secret spots we had, but she never appears. I sit in the sewers and I wait. Or I sit here. I pay the accordion players to play *La Vie En Rose* and I hope. I dream. But it's all just shit. . . ."

I decided to fill in the blanks for him—not all the blanks, but enough so he could shake the shit off his spirit and feel like a man again, help me do what I had to do.

"Rose came looking for you. She scoured the sewers for you. No luck. Like ships passing in the night, you kept missing each other. And so she made the decision. She swallowed her fear of the world and she went up above. She ascended the cold iron rungs of the ladder, lifted the heavy cover and popped out of the bowels of Lady Paris into the light of day.

"Like a newborn babe she screamed at the brightness, there on the Place de la Madeleine. She saw the whizzing cars, the scurrying Parisians, and she was in a daze, so she backed up like a cornered Gaspar and her ass touched a glass window and she whirled and bingo: she was lost to the Merdistes. That was it, Felix. She looked into the glass window of the Baccarat crystal shop and it floored her, turned her knees to jelly. She'd lived her whole life thinking shit was pretty—shit, soft and full of color—and now she saw crystal—crystal, hard and clear and clean, reflecting the sun; and her heart was flooded with desire, a desire for material things, for bright, shiny, material things. Her innocent spirit was completely trashed, corrupted.

"She walked around that day looking in all the windows and she fell in love with everything—perfume, crystal, cosmetics, Oriental rugs, fine fabrics, clothes, shoes. And she smelled the cafés and the restaurants, the crêpes and omelets and escargots and all the other exotic bizarre cooking smells, and she began to drool, really drool. And she saw the happiness on the faces, the pure serene joy the people had out there in the light, and she embraced the World. 'Holy shit!' she said out loud. 'Where have I been my whole life?'"

"But how can you know all this, Monsieur?" Felix asked, astonished, perplexed. "How can you know? Are you making this up?"

"I know what I know, Felix. And if you listen to me, I can help you feel better. Maybe I can even get you back with Rose."

"Go on, then," he said. "I'll try anything."

And the hope shining in his eyes told me that he actually believed me. Poor sucker.

"So Rose wandered in a daze around Paris. Beautiful, half-naked Rose with the extraordinary ass and the red eyes wandering the streets, her feet bare and her heart open, and she completely forgot about you, Felix, I'm sad to say, and every guy on the street stared at her—at her face, at her breasts and long hair, at the way she was dressed (in a chastity belt, pigeon-feather bra, and Gaspar hat), and of course at her fabulous ass—and many whistled and called at her and tried every line in the book and even some new ones to pick her up. But she just ignored them. And finally, when she was almost back home, on the rue St. Honore, about to go home to the sewers, a man, an actor, an actor who had fashion savvy and savvy about asses, he got her to react.

"'Where did you get that outfit,' he asked politely.

"'This old thing?' she said. 'I made it myself.'

"And then she did a double take. She recognized him. From the TV and movie magazines. From scraps of newspaper. The former television host, Antoine De Caunes. And her heart did a somersault. He's so handsome, she thought. His eyes are so sensitive. And he's so clean!

"'You look hungry, Mademoiselle,' Antoine said. 'Hungry and lost. May I invite you to dinner? My hotel is here.'

"She looked at Antoine, then she looked at a sewer cover. Two worlds pulling at her heart . . . but it was no contest. The world of shit was lost to her. Really, she was smitten, with the crystal, with the things in shop windows, with Antoine—she'd never seen anyone so clean, and even if he was a poor deluded

Nazi—that's what she called everyone outside—he hadn't chosen
to be one. He'd been born that way. She felt sorry for him and
she let him take her arm, and into the beautiful Hôtel Costes
they walked. It was the same place Kaka Misumi stayed. Very *au
courant.* And they sat on red thrones, and Antoine introduced
her to Koko Bakonyi, one of the owners. (By the way, can you
imagine when Koko Bakonyi met Kaka Misumi? Koko meet
Kaka, Kaka meet Koko. . . .) And Koko gave them the best table
in the house, Antoine's regular table, and they dined that night
on shrimp and salmon and chicken and green beans and salad.
And wild strawberry tarts for dessert. They sat on the red thrones
and they drank champagne and wine and coffee—and during the
evening people came by to say hello to Antoine. Fabulous perfumed stars! There was Christophe Lambert, Emmanuelle
Seigneur, Catherine Deneuve, Gerard Depardieu, Isabelle Adjani,
Sharon Stone the American hanky-panky goddess, Naomi Camp-
bell, Helena Christianson—and Rose recognized them all from the
magazines. She was floored. And then, like a queen, in walked
blonde, fabulous Ophelie Winter! Rose had to pinch herself. Was
it a dream?

"And later, walking arm in arm on the Champs Elysee, they
ate ice cream, and Rose was drunk, drunk with wine, drunk
with the newness of things, drunk with the kindness in
Antoine's eyes—and she told him her life story. And of course
he thought she was insane, a pathological liar, demented but
brilliant, an escapee from some mental ward. But even so,
despite his misgivings about her sanity, that night, up in his
room at the Hôtel Costes, he put the moves on her. If anyone
could seduce her it was Antoine . . ."

Felix began to quiver with rage, his eyes grew violent.

"I'll find that bastard!" he cried.

I put an arm on his shoulder to calm him.

"Cool out, Felix. She nearly twisted the poor guy's pecker off."

Felix breathed a sigh of relief, scrounged a cigarette butt off the floor, lit it with his lighter. I looked at my watch. We really didn't have much time. The sewer men would be on duty in only a matter of hours. I moved into high gear, told it fast.

"But Antoine took it as a challenge. He decided that something that wild and fine with an ass that scrumptious was worth waiting for, worth working for. And maybe she actually did come from the sewers. Why not? So they slept together like brother and sister. They cuddled and huddled and kissed and petted like incestuous brother and sister, but they didn't go all the way. It was her first bed, and she slept like a rock. The next day Antoine bought her a pair of Jackie O sunglasses to protect her sensitive eyes from the light and he hired armed guards to take her back to the catacombs to get her collection. And he taught her about French culture, French history, French literature. She read Baudelaire and Rimbaud, Proust and Flaubert. He took her to the Louvre, to the Musée d'Orsay, to the Père Lachaise cemetery. He played music for her—reggae, blues, swing, bop, rock, country. It was like *My Fair Lady*, a Pygmalion experiment. And a few weeks later, after she'd gotten her collection in order and could quote Rimbaud and Apollinaire better than a Sorbonne professor, they hired the models, and Antoine invited everyone he knew in the world of fashion, in the media—everyone who was anyone in Paris—and Rose showed her clothes. These fabulous supermodels strutted down the runway in Rose's corked chastity belts, wearing pigeon-feather bras, plastic-bag Hawaiian skirts, Gaspar hats, condom hats, the whole kit and kaboodle, and the show was a magnificent success. How proud you would have been, Felix. Everybody in Paris—even Ophelie Winter and Mrs. Mitterand—started wearing Gaspar hats and pigeon-feather bras. It was all the rage, despite a public denunciation by Brigitte Bardot. Rose was in magazines, on the news; she was the featured guest on *Nulle Part Ailleurs*, Antoine's old show, and Philippe Gildas, the host, he was smitten. Antoine arranged for her to get a passport—even though she had no birth certificate and only one name—and he took her to London, put her on his MTV show *Eurotrash*. And when they went to Japan to show her clothes, there was a riot. Guys shoving jars of her own shit in her face to autograph. . . . Kaka Misumi, who hadn't run into her in the Hôtel Costes because he'd been in Japan selling a large lot of Rose's turds, he made an appointment to meet her there, in Tokyo—he tried to convince her to go home, or even to stay in Japan and shit in the bottles directly. But Rose would have none of it. She wore silk underwear now, diamond rings, velvet chastity belts. She laughed at Kaka. 'You think I want to live like an animal in cave and give up this? I don't need that shit anymore. Get lost, Kaka.' In three short months Rose had lost her innocence. She'd gone from shit to champagne, become the biggest new designer on the international scene. She made Gaultier look as old-fashioned as Gaultier had made Lacroix look when he first burst onto the scene. You'd see her on TV, in magazines, pictured arm-in-arm with Antoine, having her cheek kissed by celebrities and politicians—she even had tea now and then with

Ophelie Winter! But throughout all this worldly fame and fortune, like a good girl, and much to Antoine's chagrin, she retained her virginity."

"And all this time," Felix interrupted me with a sigh, "I'm looking for her in the sewers. "No wonder everybody was wearing Gaspar hats and chastity belts last spring."

"She's the perfect designer for the age of AIDS."

"But where is she now, Monsieur? I have to find her."

"We're getting to that," I told him. "You see, Felix, Rose had a problem. She couldn't digest French food properly. All the paté and caviar and sausage and pickles, the rabbit and chicken and potatoes, the steak and crêpes and fruit and tarts and bread and butter, all the rich cream sauces, the lamb and ham and Chinese food, the fresh milk and carrots and croque-monsieurs and ice cream and chocolate and cheese, plus all the strange food in Japan—everything she'd eaten for three months on the outside, it was all clogging up her insides, it had formed a solid concrete block in her guts. She hadn't taken a dump since she'd come up above. Her belly was swollen. Antoine thought she was pregnant and he felt betrayed, so he kicked her out and started dating a girl with less hang-ups, a supermodel. Koko Bakonyi gave her another room. She took an enema, but it didn't work, she took a laxative, but it was like trying to move a mountain with a shovel, like trying to break a rock with a feather. The condition grew painful, horrible. She canceled a show. She couldn't work, she couldn't create. She consulted the top gastrointestinal specialists in Paris—they all suggested an operation, but she didn't want that. She was in despair. . . . And then one day her limousine was stuck in a traffic jam on the boulevard de la Madeleine—it was right above the Hall of Counters—and she saw the street sign, the word Madeleine, at the exact same moment she farted, and the smell and the word merged in her mind and it was like an epiphany! As if the scales were lifted from her heart and mind and she was plunged into the lovely world of childhood memory. The whole happy world of her childhood came rushing back on the wings of her flatulence. She remembered everything. The love and camaraderie of life in the sewers, the smiling faces of her Merdiste family— Danielle and the Prophet, Jean and Maude and silent Maurice, Pierre and Samuel, all the horny boys and jealous girls, her cousins and half-brothers and sisters. And she remembered shitting in a plastic bag. The simple pleasure of shitting. And she remembered the good coarse food, the Gaspars, the oranges, the kosher flat bread. And she remembered the shit, the peaceful infinite river of shit flowing through the wet smelly dark of the sewers . . . the sewers, where life was safe and simple, where worries did not exist, where all her needs were taken care of. And Rose was filled with a longing, a deep, heartfelt longing for that gentle life she'd turned her ass on. She realized that the world was shit—what you and I would call shit—and that shit was her world. Yes, more than anything else in the world, more than anything else Rose wanted to be with her people again, to wait for the Trillionth Shit. 'Oh God!' she cried. 'How stupid I've been. I've forsaken my people! Forsaken my religion! In embracing the world I've forgotten about the shit!' So she hopped out of the limo and ran for the nearest sewer hole and she shucked her shoes and climbed down into the earth, home to the sewers. But you can't go home again, they say, and things were different there. The Prophet was sick, lying on his back with an abscessed tooth, the back lower-left molar—Kaka's candy be damned! And the Prophet took one look at Rose's swollen belly—Rose was weeping, begging his forgiveness—and his heart grew hard: he too thought she was pregnant. But Kaka, who was there to pick up a load of shit (which turned out to be no good, as the last homeless virgin—the Merdistes had long ago run out of their own virgins—a nine-year-old Bosnian refugee was no longer fresh, having just the day before given up both her front and rear plums to one of Satan's Kids), Kaka took one whiff of her farts and declared that Rose was still as fresh and virginal as the day she was born. But the Prophet was hurt, hurt and angry. He was convinced that Rose was pregnant and he felt that the honor should have been his, after all she was his great-great-granddaughter, so he expelled her, banished her. Rose, in tears, went to Father Nick in the catacombs for advice, for spiritual guidance. She told him how it happened, how she'd gotten in that condition—how she'd sinned, her pride, her gluttony, her embrace of the world, her love of, and rejection by, Antoine. And Father Nick knew that this was a spiritual crisis beyond his powers, so he decided to take her to Lourdes, for the waters. And that's where I met her. In Lourdes."

Felix was floored, speechless. I could see the life coming back into his face, the hope. Rose was alive and still a virgin!

I didn't tell him about how we'd taken the TGV, the speed train, first-class back to Paris. How she started telling me her life story. I didn't tell him how we'd gone to her room in Hôtel Costes, had some drinks, how she'd finished telling her story over champagne and caviar, and how good she felt after, how truly liberated—was it me or was it the bath at Lourdes kicking in?—and how she came to me then, naked, lovely, that glorious heavenly ass aching for love, despite the pain in her guts. No no, I didn't tell him that. He didn't need to hear that. I needed him on my side for what we were about to do. He didn't need to hear how I plunged through her rear door, exploring the loveliness of her back garden—how I plucked that Rose and tilled her rich soil, the mulchy, brown darkness, the rich, loamy, foaming sweetness, how I thought of rockets climbing, meteors rushing across night skies, sunsets and sunrise bleeding achingly sweet healing light across my damaged spirit, how I saw vast expanses of joy and future loveliness stretching before us. . . . How could I tell him that his girl and I had made love for hours? That she invited me in her front door. That we ended up face to face (for true love isn't about asses and genitals, no! It's about faces, it's all about faces! Faces and eyes and the exchange of hearts and souls)— no, he didn't need to hear that. Felix didn't need to hear that Rose and I had fallen in love.

"Yes, Father Nick stayed behind, and Rose took the holy water baths, and after we came back to Paris by train, she finally was able to go to the toilet."

It had been enormous. Massive. A three-foot-long shit, the hardness of concrete and the color of burnished gold. And it smelled, God how it had smelled. It was too big to flush. What had caused it finally to emerge from the safety of its lovely warm cave? Was it the bath at Lourdes, the lovemaking, or the confession?

"Rose came crying from the toilet," I told Felix. "Crying for joy, her belly flat, her eyes joyous, and she grabbed her suitcase and with absolutely no self-consciousness or revulsion she fished the monstrous shining shit out of the toilet, lifting it lovingly with her hands, and she stuffed it in her suitcase. . . . And then a knock came on the door. I opened it. A Japanese guy. Of course: it was Kaka Misumi.

"'I smelled something familiar,' he said. 'Is Rose—?'

"And then he saw it. Rose trying to close the suitcase on the big shit. His eyes popped wide. He pulled a gun, but Rose just whirled like Bruce Lee and kicked him in the head.

"You see, Felix, she wanted to make a peace offering to the Prophet.

"'I'm going home now,' she said then. I tried to follow her, Felix, but. . . ."

I showed him the ugly bruise on the back of my neck, showed it with shame.

"That's a girl who knows how to fight."

"That's my Rose," said Felix with pride.

"Kaka and I both came to consciousness at the same time.

"'She's still a virgin!' Kaka cried. 'And that shit she's got is priceless!'"

And I'd realized that to Kaka's unfoolable nose, Rose still was a virgin, for she had made love to me in complete innocence. With real love. And I was filled with great sense of peace. . . . I had been right all along. The secret guilt I'd been harboring over my past escapades disappeared like smoke in the mists of time. Sex was not a sin if it was entered into with love and an innocent heart.

"So now," I said to the ex-sewer man, a bit embarrassed, for in my all my years of work for the Big Kielbasa I'd never directly asked a citizen for assistance in a dangerous operation. "Now I need your help, Felix. Father Nick told much about the guts of Paris, he told me where to find you . . . and now that I've found you, now I need your help."

"Help for what?" He seemed mystified.

"To look for Rose."

"She's back with the Merdistes, Monsieur." He sighed. "That's her choice. She's a big girl."

"You have to take me to the Hall of Counters, Felix. We have to stop her."

"Stop her from what?"

"You know what day it is?"

"I'm a goddamn bum, Monsieur, the days are all the same."

"Felix, it's just past midnight—it's July 14, Bastille Day, 1996. . . ."

"The day of the Trillionth Shit," Felix said with wonder. "And you think . . . ?"

"The world isn't ready for it."

✜   ✜   ✜

It was dark underground, as black and lifeless as a dead planet in a dead solar system. But Felix knew his way. I had a penlight flash, but he ordered me to put it out.

"There may be guards," he whispered.

Occasionally he'd check his methane meter by a sliver of light beaming in from one of the little holes in the metal-covered snow grates in the middle of the streets, and when the meter showed the methane level was low, he'd light one of the butts he'd scrounged off the Metro station floor.

I must tell you, friends, I have been in some creepy places in my time—the cave in India where the Hindus worship a stalactite they think is Shiva's phallus, caverns in Burgundy where ancient Celts called on dark powers, I have been in slum basements in Newark, New Jersey, and Brussels where poor little children were boiled and eaten with apples in their mouth, like roast pigs—but nothing could beat the sewers of Paris that night for pure fear. There was a feeling, a cold creepy feeling, as if an unhappy corpse was stroking my spine. I crossed myself. I was there on God's business. My whole life had been one long preparation for this mission. The Merdistes thought they were God's chosen, but the captain of the other team had completely fooled their sorry innocent asses.

Yes, I am capable of fear. Just as I am capable of losing a fight, as Rose proved, or falling in love, as Rose proved, I am capable of that most basic of human emotions, fear. It's the thing I'd been running from my whole life, ever since that first priest whipped me back in my first orphanage. And now I was scared of fucking up. The home team was counting on me. If I lost the ball, it could be the beginning of the end.

God, I said to myself, give me strength. Let me win this one, and I'll never fuck up again. I'll get Rose out of there, fix the situation, and I'll quit the game. I'll hang up my collars and my guns like an old footballer hangs up his boots . . . I'll become a citizen, have a passel of kids with Rose. . . .

I felt clumsy, clumsy and stupid. Felix walked softly like a cat. I could feel the courage radiating from him. He held my hand as if I were a child, led me like a blind man. I had no idea where we were.

"Where are we?" I whispered when he stopped.

"No need to whisper," he said in a normal voice, as his methane meter bleeped like an excited bird, indicating dangerous levels of gas. "They're all up in the Hall of Counters. That's where the ceremony for the Trillionth Shit will be."

"Felix," I said. "I think I should tell you . . ."

"I know," he said. "You love her too."

"How do you know?"

"You are an actor, Monsieur, and a good one, but I, I am a sewer man. I've been watching shit my whole adult life and I can smell when something is good and when something is shit. And your story was good, very good, but there was one hole in it. You never once mentioned your reaction to Rose's beautiful ass. That was pure shit. The shit of omission. No man, even a priest, and I know that's what you are—I picked your pocket, Father, picked it five minutes into our talk and I found your collars—even a priest has a physical and emotional reaction to Rose. Father Nick used to go off alone and pound his pud after spending time with her. Even a gay man or straight woman or a Gaspar is affected. I swear, I've seen rats get hard-ons in her presence. She was made to be desired. So don't feel bad, and if it helps any, I forgive you."

"Thank you," I said. "You're a good and wise man."

"Father," he said. "I'm a sewer man. Proud of it too. And you've restored my confidence. Now, if you'll forgive my saying, let's fucking do it."

The water was cold, and yes, I felt toilet paper and shit float by, touching my face like an octopus gently sliding by in the sea. Felix took my hand and led me deep beneath the surface, into the hole. I wriggled in and followed him up the passage, and at the top of the tunnel we emerged wet and slimy under a dripping water pipe in front of a large burlap curtain. Felix turned on the spigot and we rinsed.

"You ready?" he whispered, handing me a burlap towel from a pile.

I nodded, dried off as best I could.

We went through the curtain and entered the Hall of Counters.

It was a huge, long room lit by many candles, the walls covered with writing and paintings, and it was packed. Packed with pale, long-haired Merdistes of all ages and sexes, red eyes gleaming under Gaspar hats; packed with shaven-headed Célinéastes; packed with ragged members of the Pride of France; packed with dark- and light-skinned Héros in hip-hop uniforms; and of course, scattered here and there, the most normal-looking folk in the room, like dentists and lawyers walking around a flea market on Saturday morning: Satan's Kids.

And in the center of the room lay the Prophet, reclining on a raised bed made of piled-up burlap bags, his scarred head on a burlap pillow, his beard and hair reaching the floor. The years had eaten away at his bulk, but he was still an impressive specimen. His eyes gleamed red, his scar pulsed, the hollows of cheeks and eye sockets made him look holy.

Next to him in a battered cradle (made of reconstituted toilet paper? Jean's legendary old cradle?) lay Rose's massive turd. The Trillionth Shit. It glistened and glittered like a wet otter in the moonlight, like a slick, huge, brown jewel, like a monstrous ridged brain. Sucking in light, giving off light, it seemed almost to breathe, to pulse. It contained every good and bad thing in France, in the world.

And the Prophet's voice boomed:

"We are here today," he said, "to celebrate the beginning of the end of the world: the Trillionth Shit!"

"The Trillionth Shit!" echoed the many. "The Trillionth Shit!"

"Yes, we have waited, and yes we have prayed, some of us for fifty-two years, some of us for less, but all of us here, we are all of one heart, one mind, one spirit. This is it. Can you smell it, children? The perfume of mankind's shame and hope? Can you smell it, children? The perfume of God's love? The Trillionth Shit!"

"Yes yes yes!" they cried.

"The perfume!" they wailed.

"The Trillionth Shit!" they cried.

And the Trillionth Shit sparkled malevolently—it seemed to smile.

"This is our signal, children, our beacon, our shining savior. It is time now, time to go forth and do battle with the Nazi forces of Satan! We will go outside now, out into the corrupt world! We will disrupt the Bastille Day ceremonies! We will cut the telephone lines and computer lines, we will flood the sewers! Paris will be paralyzed! Chaos and panic will reign and we will drive the Nazis into the sea! We have waited long enough!"

"We have waited long enough!" came the echo.

Felix stepped forward, into the light.

"Excuse me, pops," he said. "But you're wrong. You've miscalculated. This can't be the Trillionth Shit. The population of Paris and the suburbs didn't reach the ten million mark until the 1960s, but you said 1947! The Trillionth Shit won't be here till sometime in the next century. Sorry to shit in the punch bowl, folks, but it's just not time yet. That shit is an impostor!"

"Felix!" cried Rose, and she rushed across the room, barreled through the crowd, and embraced the sewer man, tears of joy rushing down her lovely face.

"Rose," he said, and his sigh was like a garden at sunset whispering a prayer of thanks. Thanks for the sun, thanks for the rain, thanks for the sweet sweet dream of life.

And right then, from somewhere in the crowd, came Kaka Misumi, gun in hand. He grabbed the cradle, lifted the heavy turd—kissed it and hugged it to his chest.

"This is going to Japan," he said. "Where it will be appreciated."

"Kaka," said the Prophet sadly. "My son. Why have you forsaken me?"

"Put a cork in it, Prophet."

I was watching this, friends, it was all playing out in front of my eyes like some curious play scripted by Samuel Beckett on a bad acid trip and then rewritten by William Burroughs. What, I wondered, was my role? And then I saw her. Edging toward the light, picking her way toward center stage, toward the Prophet and Kaka and the Trillionth Shit. The silver hair, the military fatigues. An unlit Brazilian cigar in her mouth.

The Dispatcher.

She too had a gun. And she put her gun against Kaka's head, grabbed the huge shit.

"Sorry, Chinaboy," she growled. "The shit goes to Rome, where it belongs."

And the Prophet looked up with big moist eyes.

"Gloria? he said. "Is that you, Gloria?"

And the crowd stirred.

"Gloria?" whispered the Merdistes.

"The harlot who ran like Jesse Owens?"

"The whore who swam like Johnny Weismuller?"

"Gloria?" I said.

"Hello, Gloria," said the Prophet. "You're back. Don't let the sewer cover hit your ass on the way out."

"Hello, Roland," said the Dispatcher. "Long time. The last time I saw you, you were trying to kill me."

"I'm sorry I didn't," said the Prophet with a sigh.

"And now, sucker," growled Gloria with an evil smirk, "now it's payback time."

She pointed her gun at the Prophet. A sick grin washed over her face, and I saw it. What she was, who she was, why she'd gotten the job in Rome. She was inhuman, a fucking monster, the proverbial dogshit on the white carpet—the Big Kielbasa had been completely fooled: she was the dark captain's little baby girl. The Trillionth Shit had been Satan's idea all along!

I walked through the crowd, weaving between the dealers and the homeless, the reformed racists and the Satanists—mute extras now, silent spectators in an old, old battle.

The Dispatcher was licking her lips around her cigar, ready to shoot, enjoying the moment.

"Don't shoot!" cried Felix, showing everybody his methane meter as he faked a cheeping noise, like an electronic bird. "If you shoot, old lady, the whole place goes up. The methane level is too high. That's one powerful piece of shit."

And then a middle-aged man ran to the circle of light and threw himself at the Dispatcher's feet.

"Mother," he cried. "It's me, Jean! Your son, Jean!"

"Get off my boots, snotnose. This," she said, indicating the Trillionth Shit, "this is my baby. My true child. Born of a virgin, the instrument of mankind's suicide."

It was time. Now, baby, or never.

I took the last lollipop from my pocket, bit it, creating a sharp shard of cherry-red candy, just as Gloria the Dispatcher had told me she'd done lo those many years ago in the concentration camp. I entered the circle from behind.

I put the lollipop to Gloria's neck, took her gun, put it in my pocket.

"One move, Gloria, and you're rat food."

"So you made it," she said, snarling. "You were supposed to call and give me reports in code. You forgot the code?"

"How could I forget the code? It's simple Latin. As in: *Fuckus offus*, Gloria."

"Listen. The big shit must go to Rome. It will live in the Vatican. From there the forces will be unleashed!"

"Shut up, Gloria," I said.

"I'll tell the Big Kielbasa!" she screamed. "If I don't come back to Rome he gets a letter, details of your sins. You'll end up in America."

"America, dead—I don't give a shit." And then I grabbed her short, silver hair, yanked her neck back. "Have a lollipop, bitch," I said, and I slashed.

It was a good cut, clean and deep, right across the jugular, and the blood spurted high into the air. It looked black in the candlelight. The Dispatcher clutched her throat, tried futilely to stitch the gaping wound with her fingers—but it was over. Except for the rattles and gurgles and spasms, the traditional dance of unhappy death. It was over.

I dropped her like a sack of shit.

"But on the whole I'd prefer America," I said, squatting like a weight lifter to grab the cradle.

Gloria's mouth moved. The cigar was stuck to her lips. She gave off a foul smell—all the nasty gases of her corrupt soul, the stored putridity of a long life of deceit and duplicity and death-dealing, a soul full of shit, a toxic spirit, it all escaped out of her cynical mouth and poisoned the air.

"Shit," she said, and died.

I picked up the cradle. The giant stinking turd was strapped in with a plastic six-pack link. Felix and Rose came then, they helped the Prophet to his feet.

"Let me go," he said. "I'm dying. Toothache led to abscess led to infection, and soon death. I should have laid off the candy."

"People!" I cried. "The Prophet miscalculated. This isn't the Trillionth Shit. This is just a regular old shit, a bit big, sure, maybe it belongs in a science museum or a circus or in an elephant's cage, but it's nothing special. Look at it: it's just shit. Shit is shit. Go back to your caves and wait—or better yet, go out into the world and look for jobs. And pray. But whatever you do, forget this shit."

There was grumbling, a real grumbling in the place, a mutter that grew into a buzz. It hadn't worked. Faith—even mis-founded faith, even faith built atop a fragile earthquake fault—faith doesn't die that easily. It was time for Plan Two.

I put the bloody lollipop to the Prophet's skinny chicken neck behind his beard and I walked him backward, one arm guiding him, the other holding the huge, smelly masterpiece of shit.

The people parted, cleared a path.

Felix tore down the burlap curtain.

And the people, magnetized by the shit, crowded us menacingly, grumbling and muttering. . . . And then, one and all, their jaws unhinged and they moaned as I dropped the big shit down the entrance tunnel. I heard a splash as it hit the water and was sucked into the sewer. And then nothing.

And then a mass cry of pain rang out—reverberating in the Hall of Counters—not unlike a herd of moose with giant, sharp, red-hot pokers up their asses.

Tears shot from the Prophet's eyes, wetting my hand.

"Don't cry, old man," I said. "It's not the end of the world. There'll always be another shit. Lots more shit. It's the one thing we'll never run out of. Shit and hope."

"There'll never be another shit like that. My life's work, down the drain."

And oh, my friends, my patient friends, you who read this, if ever anyone ever reads this, I felt the poor Prophet's anguish. He had really believed in that shit, poor deluded fellow. He'd invested long long years of suffering and faith in that shit. And all for nothing.

And then I knew what had to be done.

I whispered in his ear. And he smiled. The Prophet, the old mad Prophet with the beard down to his balls and the hair past his ass, the still-strong Prophet, smiled, smiled through his tears, smiled and nodded.

"Children," he said, his voice strong and sure. "Oh, loyal sheep of the shit, you must listen to this man. He is a messenger from God, he has saved us from the Nazi harlot Gloria who wanted to use the Holy Shit for evil purposes. He has done the right thing. The Trillionth Shit might be gone, but you have seen it, I have seen it! My life is complete. You must go now, into the world, and you must not cut the phone lines as planned, nor the computer lines, you must not flood the sewers, you must not foment hatred and strife, there is enough of that already—you must be peaceful! This must be a peaceful revolution! These are my last words. Kill the Nazis with love!"

And his loyal followers groaned as one. I could see the tears reflected off their candlelit faces.

"Rose." The old man reached for Rose. "Kaka." He reached for Kaka. "Support me, my children."

The Prophet put an arm around their waists. I was standing behind them and I didn't say anything when he worked a finger up Kaka's butt. And then his nimble fingers yanked the Moët et Chandon cork from Rose's ass and he inserted a long digit up there. For a second a shadow crossed his face. He knew! He knew she was no longer a fresh plum. And then he shrugged. His face broke like a sunburst of joy. He wasn't going to let anything piss on his parade.

"Goodbye my children!" he cried, and then he nodded his head and I slashed his throat with my American Express card. And as he stood there bleeding to death, smiling joyfully, his people cried. . . .

✤ ✤ ✤

It took a while for everyone to leave the Hall of Counters, but that gave Felix time to find the old sewer boat they used to use to clean the sewers and take tourists on tours, and it gave the people time, time to adjust to their grief. They stood there, lining both sides of the boulevard de la Madeleine sewer, watching the occasional small turd float by, discussing what they'd seen in whispers, coming to grips with it, many of the Héros and Célinéastes and Satan's Kids with flashlights. The Pride of France, of course, couldn't afford flashlights. Kaka Misumi wept inconsolably. He'd lost a father and a lover and a business partner in one credit-card transaction.

"What did you tell the Prophet?" Rose asked me. "What did you say that made him so happy?"

"I told him that the only way for his prophecy to live was for the shit to be gone, and for him to be gone. A religion doesn't function without sacrifice. Sacrifice plants the seeds of hope and faith in the heart, and his blood will water the hearts of his people, and their hope and faith will bloom."

Felix came then, rowing up in the sewer boat, a rickety old rowboat stained with decades of shit and piss. He'd gone up above and bought two cans of gasoline with money I'd given him.

We put the old dead Prophet in the boat.

And Felix, waving his methane meter, said to the people:

"Folks, the methane level is at an acceptable level."

I sloshed gasoline over the Prophet's smiling dead face, his poor thin body covered with rags. I sloshed gasoline over the boat.

"It's time," I said.

And as Felix lit his lighter and threw it in the boat, we three—

Rose, Felix and I—jumped into the water, submerging as the boat burst into flames and the great fireball filled the tunnel, consuming the poor Merdistes and all the catacomb dwellers, cleansing their sins with fire.

Felix had lied of course, the methane level was sky-high.

✦   ✦   ✦

The three of us waited in the Hall of Counters, empty now, empty save for Gloria's body. She was a nasty thing, evil, but still I was sorry. I never feel exactly good when I take a life, but still, hers was necessary (as close to a pleasure as it ever gets). And the Prophet and the Merdistes and Kaka and all the other mixed-up acolytes? Well, ideas die hard, even shitty ideas, and this one had to die. Had to be burned out of the hearts of men. There was no other way. Sometimes you have to do bad things to get good results.

✦   ✦   ✦

Rose and Felix and I left soon thereafter. The fire had done its work. The people were dead, the last of them floating in the stinking water, moving with the occasional turd and toilet paper at the speed of one meter per second, the smell of charred flesh and roasted shit still in the air. The pipes were damaged. The phones lines in the Madeleine neighborhood would be down for a few hours, the drinking water might not run until lunchtime. . . . But so what? The people would just have to suffer, drink Evian, and think for themselves for a few hours. But the important thing—and for this I smiled—the toilets were flushing. The early morning defecators of Paris were voiding their bowels. Yes, the shit was flowing. Shit without end, amen.

And as we walked down the sewer walkway beneath the boulevard de la Madeleine, tired and wet, I felt fulfilled. The dark captain was defeated. The team of light had won. He'd be back again, sure, he always makes comebacks, but the next time I'd be ready. I wouldn't be so scared and full of doubt. I had Rose and Felix to thank for that.

"Goodbye, Rose and Felix," I said. "And thanks for your help. If you're ever in Rome, give me a call."

"Goodbye," said Felix. "And thank you."

"Goodbye?" said Rose, and her eyes spoke volumes. In the aftermath of our lovely love, we'd planned to go off together, make a life. "I don't understand."

"Felix will explain," I said. "He's a fine man, Rose. You and me, well, we had something special, child, but my work calls, and where I'm going you can't come. . . . And Felix needs you, he loves you. . . . We'll always have Paris."

And a tear fell from her eye, plopped into the sewer.

"Goodbye," I said, patting her extraordinary ass for the last time. "And watch your ass."

✚   ✚   ✚

And so I left them there, Rose and Felix, left them to go back to my life. And as I walked down the long sewer beneath the boulevard de la Madeleine, 7.1 kilometers long, the longest sewer in Paris, my heart heavy with the loss of Rose but light with hope for the future of the planet, I ran into a man coming the other way.

An old man he was, very old. He wore a Gaspar hat and a burlap-
and-rat-fur jockstrap. His eyes glowed red.

"Hello, Maurice," I said. "Find anything good last night?
Any wedding rings?"

Maurice just grunted, poor old fellow. But the sliver of early
daylight shining through the snow-hole cover showed me
something. His arms were not empty. He held Jean's cradle,
and in the cradle: the Trillionth Shit.

"Ah," I said.

⁜   ⁜   ⁜

So I went back to Rome. I made my report. The Big Kielbasa was
happy in general, very happy how things had turned out. He likes it
when the home team wins. Of course he was disappointed in Gloria—
he'd had such faith in her, but then that just goes to show how fragile
a thing faith is. It just goes to show how sneaky the other team is.

So I'm in America now. New Mexico. Here for a little
purification. A small dose of celibacy never hurt anyone. At
least that's what I tell myself on those long, lonely nights when
I stand by the window watching the pederast priests kissing one
another out there in the mountain moonlight, as I listen to the
coyotes howl.

Hey, it could be worse. I could be dead. And then, who
knows where I'd be . . .

⁜   ⁜   ⁜

I got a postcard the other day from Paris, from gorgeous Lady

Paris. It was from Rose and Felix. They were happy, they said. Living in the Hôtel Costes. Married now and a baby on the way. Is it my baby or is it Felix's? It doesn't really matter. Not to them, not to me. Either way it was born out of love, out of face-to-face, loving sex, an exchange of hearts. They tried to get Maurice to come above, but he'd been underground too long. He lives alone now, they say, in the Hall of Counters, and he worships the Trillionth Shit by himself, sleeps with it, guards it with his life. They visit him now and then, bring him oranges from Palestine and kosher grain. The Shit is drying up, they report, shrinking, losing its luster. But, hey, that's life.

Rose is designing again, she has a show coming up. And Felix, well, Felix got his old job back. He is what he was born to be: a sewer man. . . .

And sometimes in the dark sewers, as the eternal river of shit and piss flows on and on, sometimes the sewer men see a phantom. His face is scarred, they say, as if he's been burned, and his hair is black and long. His features are decidedly Asian, they say, and they say he wanders the sewers with a fishing net . . . and legend has it that if you get too near, he metamorphoses into a rat and swims away.

I wonder . . . did Kaka Misumi survive the blast of flaming gas under the boulevard de la Madeleine? Perhaps. . . . But then again, perhaps what the sewer men see really is nothing but a ghost. I don't know. But whatever he is, each night before I sleep I get down on my knees and say a prayer. A prayer for the virgins. For all the virgins of France.

The Zillionth Star

THE RABBITS HUMPING ON THE balcony outside the motel room here in Hollywood are father and son. They belong to the heroin-addict couple in the next room. All they do is hump. The rabbits, that is. The junkies are beyond such simple pleasures. But the rabbits hump all the time. Empty-eyed humping. Hump hump hump. Except when eating or shitting or sleeping, they hump. And in the timeworn tradition of fathers and sons down through the ages, it's the father doing the fucking. . . .

And the son ain't exactly happy about it.

I'm not exactly sure where it is I write from—suffice it to say that I'm in Los Angeles, the city of the 99 cent burger, somewhere on the edge of the Hollywood Hills, to be inexact, on the second floor of a crumbling motel. It's nighttime here, and the Santa Ana winds sweep in from the desert, blowing hot and dry and continual, leaching the skin and filling the nostrils with the dusty crud of dried lizardshit and the faint, clean scent of baked bones. Down on the street, cut-rate hookers with phony melon breasts and hopeless crackheads as thin as bulimic wisps of smoke screech their joyless laughter to the Hamburger City moon like starving seagulls in search of scraps, their cheekbones as sharp as machetes in the glare of headlights; while high above, the dead fingers of parched palm trees scratch and rattle against the hazy yellow sky. If you imagine hard enough, the traffic sounds almost like surf pounding on a lonely beach; but it takes no imagination to see that the moon is pocked and ravaged and haunted, as if chewed upon by a syphilitic demon of unbearable gloom.

Nothing to do but wait. Wait for the dawn. Deflect the twisted energy of this twisted city and wait. Wait and pray. Here in L.A. This city of lost and demented souls—a city of dreams and burgers, silicon breasts and false hopes, lost faith and fractured fantasies. Dreams melt away like dogshit in the rain, but the breasts live on. Open a Hamburger City woman's grave in a thousand years and all ye shall find is dust and breasts. Dust and breasts. The future is nothing but dust and breasts.

The present is nothing but burgers and coffee, nothing but burgers and coffee and pen and paper. I need coffee to stir my brain, an organ grown sluggish with the carbon monoxide of passing cars, an organ seared by the heat, an organ hypnotized by the daytime parade of passing breasts. I need burgers to dull the edge, to shut out the frightening clarity. . . . Is that possible . . . ? I need to write this now, tonight, for tomorrow I must bring this tale to a conclusion. I must make my move, I must take the baby home. I must provide a graceful ending to this story.

I have everything I need, here in this room, this rented room . . . Burgers, coffee, memories, and a plan.

The baby sleeps peacefully.

I wait for the dawn.

Outside the window, by the light of the syphilitic moon, the rabbits are humping.

✣ ✣ ✣

It all started some months ago, back in Rome, with a book—a pamphlet really—the writing in Latin, the parchment yellow and delicate, smelling faintly of dust and roses. . . .

I sat on the edge of the Big Kielbasa's bed; the Big K sat in the gold-brocaded chair nearby, his ever-thinning frame wrapped in his favorite ratty old bathrobe. An NBA game blared from the jumbo television—African-American pituitary cases in short pants leaping and loping like turbocharged leopards. The Big K watched the game with interest, all the while massaging his aching neck. He had spent most of the overlong working day toiling under the weight of his high hat.

I took a huge bite of the burger I'd bought at the new Quick Burger on the Via Veneto and picked up the ancient pamphlet lying on the bed.

"That smells good," said the Big K, his nostrils quivering at the juice-oozing bun-wrapped meat, the layers of onion and tomato and lettuce and cheese glistening bright in the flickering shadows of the TV, a few chopped pickles shining like perfect iridescent emeralds. And far, far away the soft, soft sounds of traffic in the soft Roman night.

"What do you call it?" he asked.

"A cheeseburger," I said.

"Ah yes, I have seen them advertised."

"Have a bite, please." I held it out to him.

"Is it healthy?" he asked, regarding the fragrant offering with the yin and yang of suspicion and desire, taking it as if it were a live hand grenade. "I have been fasting lately."

"Perhaps a bit high in the cholesterol department," I said, as the leader of two billion faithful bowed his snow-thatched head, closed his eyes, and muttered a prayer of grace. "But it won't kill you."

And then he opened wide his pearly whites and. . . .

"Ahhhhh," he said, a look of sheer bliss eclipsing all health concerns, chewing slowly, savoring the perfect combination of tastes. "It's heavenly."

And so, as the Big K devoured my burger, I devoured the pamphlet. I read and he chewed. He chewed and I read. Rarely have I heard anyone enjoy a burger as much as the Big Kielbasa enjoyed that burger: he sighed, he moaned, he burped, he sipped red wine occasionally—just little sips. He was completely enthralled.

"A revelation!" he cried, his mouth brimming with bread and beef, ketchup dribbling down his chin, a bit of pickle falling to the floor.

And certainly, it was a moment of world-historical importance —the Pontiff's first cheeseburger—but I was far too deeply immersed in my reading to properly savor his bliss, for the author of the pamphlet was someone whom I have admired across the abyss of centuries, someone whose ideas and spirit echo in my heart with the sincerity and purity of mother love. . . . The author was none other than St. Francis of Assisi.

And the title of the short work: *How to Converse with our Brothers and Sisters in the Forest.*

It took only four pages—the script an elegant arthritic spider crawl of tortured Latin across the page—four simple pages for me to reach the conclusion that dear sweet St. Francis was insane. . . .

According to the old monk, all that was required was a simple two-month regime of fasting, celibacy, cold-water baths, and silent meditation, and then voila! Instant inter-species communication.

I remember saying to myself: these are the ravings of a lunatic—a lonely, insane, Christ-crazed, Madonna-sotted, hallucinating lunatic. Poor, poor fellow, I thought, as the Big Kielbasa loudly sucked bits of pickle and onion out of his teeth, you invested far too many late nights reading scripture by the dim glow of sputtering candlelight, too many bitter-cold solitary winters scrounging for nuts in the forest, too many long, hot summers broiling your beatific bald head in the brutal Italian sun. . . . Altogether too much red wine and too little brown bread. . . . Talk with the animals, indeed! The man had needed help, I reasoned, professional help. The kind of care not readily available back in old Pope Innocent's Italy, . . . Why, were he alive and penning such madness today, I'd have considered it my sacred duty to shuffle him off to a friendly mental hospital high in the Alps, I'd have placed him in the competent hands of a caring, compassionate Italian-Swiss psychiatrist who undoubtedly would prescribe laughter, dancing, and vitamin C, ping-pong, water sports, group therapy—maybe even strong antipsychotic drugs to break the cycle of delusion. . . . I'd have bought him a hat—any kind of hat—to shield his bald-spot from the noonday sun. . . . I'd have visited him on Saturdays, bringing him *Playboy* magazines and crossword puzzles, cigarettes and candy bars, I'd have dragged him—kicking and screaming if necessary—to a football match or a prize fight or a bicycle race—anything to let him know that he was not alone in this mad, strange, often-bitter-but-never-boring adventure we call life, that suffering was all well and good, but that life— mysterious, wonderful, terrible, unpredictable life—that life could be fun. . . . I'd have told him jokes, sent him satiric cartoons from the newspaper, made funny faces so that he'd laugh laugh laugh until his sanctified sides split and the tears flowed down his gaunt exhausted God-ravaged face. . . . And I wouldn't have stopped with humor—no sir! I'd have arranged that each Sunday, like it or not, he be bundled in a blanket and packed into the pas- senger seat of a Lamborghini Testarossa convertible for a long, therapeutic drive in the fresh mountain air, some John Coltrane blasting on the stereo, the wind whipping through his curious fringe of hair, a picnic basket stuffed with caviar, champagne, and cheeseburgers in the trunk, a gorgeous, giggling, prepaid, Scan- dinavian sex goddess behind the wheel. . . .

Poor, sweet, utterly mad St. Francis: my heart went out to him.

"What do you think?" the Big K asked as I finished the pamphlet.

"To each his own," I said, pulling a second burger from my pocket, unwrapping it. And then, in order to get the Big K off and running on another subject (so that I might eat in peace without having my new cheeseburger poached), I added:

"So what have you been up to lately?"

"Not much," he answered with a sigh. "Thinking about death."

Bingo! I'd hit the right button.

I took a huge bite—ah the deep beef flavor!—as my boss

picked up a broken ping-pong paddle from the bedside table. The paddle was split down the middle. He frowned and sighed again, stood up. His knees made two quick cracks, like the reports of a .22 caliber handgun. . . .

"Every day," he mused, pacing slowly, staring at his ping-pong paddle, "every single blessed day I contemplate just how much longer I have before I go home to God. . . ."

He stopped pacing and loosed the longest saddest sigh I'd ever heard in all my years of gauging the sadness of sighs.

"My mind is still good," he went on, turning his melancholy brown eyes on me. "It's just this body, . . . Old age is a drowning pool of frustration, . . . I mean, I cannot even make my backhand spin smash anymore."

He swiped the air feebly with his cracked paddle. A slow-motion shadow of his once graceful, formidable form.

"Do you know just how galling that is?" His voice broke. "Why, just last week I destroyed this paddle in a fit of foolish anger and now . . . why am I telling you this?"

I let that one go. He knew why: he needed some relief. Needed to flush the system. That's what I was there for. Even the head honcho of the largest ecumenical corporation on the planet needs to let his hair down now and then and sing his blues out loud to another warm body. Preferably human. Otherwise we'd all end up like St. Francis, wandering in the woods, chattering at chipmunks.

"So what's really on your mind?" I asked, taking another bite. "Aside from death."

"It's all about death. . . . Persecution of Christians in China, slaughter of the innocents in the Sudan—all over the world, death, death, death. These are the End Times, my son. . . ."

"You're in a cheerful mood today," I said.

"No, I am not," he said, too far gone in his blues to recognize irony. "Today, what's on my mind are those pederast priests in America." His brow furrowed with wrinkled waves of worry. "They infest the body of the Church like maggots in a virgin's corpse. . . . I've been trying to figure out a clean solution, but I cannot, tormented as I am by my impending death. . . . And you know, when I look beyond death, it's not the wonderful mystery of going home to God—no! All I can think is: Do I buy a new ping-pong paddle or do I just tape this broken one together?"

He stood there in the center of the room, completely baffled, swatting the air with his busted paddle, as if engaged in a private war against a swarm of invisible demons.

"With all due respect, sir," I said (with all due respect). "I think you can afford another paddle."

"Oh you think so, do you?" His eyes flashed dark anger. "Well that's where you're mistaken. The Church is going broke."

"Ahh," I said, my face betraying no surprise, though the news was certainly new, if not preposterous, to me. "And what are we doing about it?"

"Selling certain Church treasures," he said sadly, putting his paddle down and going for his favorite toothpick—the long ivory toothpick he kept in a velvet case on his bedside table. He dug into a back molar as Patrick Ewing of the New York team delivered a monster dunk to the roar of the crowd.

"Good shot," he said gloomily, spitting a minuscule bit of beef onto the carpet.

"So what can I do?" I asked. "How can I help the fiscal belt-tightening?"

"You can go to New Mexico," he said. "To the retreat for pederast priests. . . . And you can take some personal responsibility. Get in shape, my son, lose the gut, go back to basics. . . . Get in touch with God. Use the St. Francis Codex as a sort of general guide to weight loss and spiritual health. . . . And after a few months, please solve the problem of the pederasts—you have carte blanche. But take your time, get healthy first. . . ."

"And that's all?" I asked, catching the Big K's eye and holding it. The old man wavered.

"That's all?" I asked again.

"Yes. . . ." the Big K said in a tiny melancholy whisper.

And oh what a "yes" that was. A "yes" that said "no." A "yes" that said "I fucked up." A "yes" that said "guilt," "fear," "self-pity," "despair." That "yes" was a crack in the Moral Universe, a black hole I did not want to crawl through.

"Now leave me," he said, his voice cracking. "I need to watch my game."

And then he began to cry.

I put my arm around his quaking shoulders. He was registering a 9.8 on the Richter scale of self-pity.

"There there," I soothed him. "I'll fix things. I promise I will. I'll take care of the pederasts."

"Yes," he said, sniffling. "I know you will. It's not the pederasts. . . ."

"So what's the matter?" I urged. "You know you can tell me."

"If I tell you, you'll judge me mad."

"No no," I said. "I am incapable of judgment."

"I know. . . ." Fresh tears dribbled from his eyes.

"Tell me. . . ."

"It's just that I. . . ."

Here it comes, I thought, here comes the confession. . . .

"It's my ping-pong paddle!" he wailed.

"Shhh," I said. "Shhh."

I held him then. Held his heaving shoulders. Broad still—but oh (how times whittles us all down) so very bony and brittle. And through his body I could feel his troubled spirit—he was holding out on me. For sure, the Big Kielbasa was holding out.

He snuffled and sniffled. I got up to leave.

"One more thing," he said as I reached for the door.

"Yes, Father," I said, turning and waiting for the truth.

"Tell me," he said, letting loose with a loud, gaseous, oniony burp, smiling through the last of his tears. "Tell me, my son, tell me where I can get more of these cheeseburgers."

✝   ✝   ✝

As I strolled away from the retreat for pederast priests, burning so very merrily in the distance, the smell of roasting pederast flesh wafting on the crisp night breeze, a small, dark figure with a blaze of white on his neck emerged from the night. I recognized him from the home office back in Rome. . . .

The junior agent approached me, his long face split by a wolfish grin, and asked:

"What are you doing here, Father?"

"I might ask you the same," I said.

He looked at me long and hard. It was not a friendly look.

"Have you ever known anyone, Father," he said, "anyone you hated completely from the very first moment you met them?"

"No," I said. "I have met people I immediately feared or distrusted." You, for instance, I might have added. "That is quite a healthy emotion for an agent. But out-and-out hatred? Never."

"Well, I have." He nodding his head sadly. "It's as if I can smell a threat even before the threatening impulse has crystallized in the enemy's mind. . . . The hair stands up on the back of my neck, I feel a growl way down deep in my chest—oh, it's very primitive: I want to tear the bastard's throat out. . . . I know it's unchristian of me, but there it is. That's the way I felt about the baby."

"What baby?" I asked.

"What baby? Do you think I'm stupid? Why would you be here out in the middle of West Bumfuck if not to make sure I took care of the baby?"

I indicated the burning retreat crackling away in the distance.

"That," I said, "is why I am here. The pederasty has gotten out of hand. A message needed to be sent. The Big K told me to handle it."

"I don't believe you," the junior agent said as we climbed a rocky butte side by side.

"Really," I said. "I'm in the dark about this baby. What baby are we talking about?"

And then I smelled it—another fire. Yes, the smell of burning flesh, the tragic subatomic vibration of souls in agony, but something else as well: plastic. The retreat for pederast priests had been constructed entirely of wood and adobe, it had been a very holistic place—no computers, no plastic. . . . This was another fire I was smelling.

"Do you smell that?" I asked. "Are you having a little fire too? How coincidental."

"Don't play games," said the junior agent angrily as we reached the top of the butte and looked into another valley, looked at a huge home burning, burning. "You set your fire to cover up my fire."

"And why did you set your fire?" I asked.

"Please," he said with a laugh. "Don't play dumb with me. I've heard about you, Father. Your ability to milk a confession is legendary. . . . You would have been very valuable back in the Inquisition."

A zillion twinkling stars stretched above the New Mexico landscape like a safe, sweet blanket of eternity protecting us from the cold night of the spirit. The craggy, black mountains stood like ancient, knowing sentinels—silent, yes, but in the silence I could hear soft rumblings, vague grumblings, tired whispers, and sad, ironic laughter. The mountains were talking, talking about us.

"Ridiculous creatures of flesh and breath," they seemed to say, groaning with exasperation like the audience at a bad, boring, silly play, the message passing from rock to rock, from peak to peak, couched in the bellies of clouds, in the swirl of winds, in the flapping of birds' wings. "When will you ever learn to let good enough alone?"

Yes, the mountains everywhere were trembling with collective sadness and anger at Mankind's futile, slapstick attempts to cloak the planet in the suffocating garments of Order; and when the heavy cloak of Science became too painful to bear, too painful to wear, Mother Earth's thick yet oh-so-soft skin would quiver and split and rip wide open, and all the sad tragic laughter she'd been holding onto for the brief experiment of the human drama would spill forth—irony turned to ire—spill forth in the form of earthquake and famine, plague and pestilence and disaster: tidal wave after tidal wave of sad, angry laughter would flood the unhappy land, cleansing the stench of humankind from the nostrils of God.

Well, it's my job to help minimize the ridiculousness, to do my small part to insure that the mountains and seas and skies do not explode with laughter—to check the grumbling at an acceptable level, to nip the problems in the bud, to hamstring the farce before it runs into Molière country. Otherwise Mother Earth would die laughing; and the stars, already dead, long dead, the stars would twinkle on. Twinkle, twinkle little star. Dead stars shining on a dead planet.

"I think," I said, looking down at my youthful companion as we sat atop the butte, next to a fresh mountain spring, equidistant from the burning retreat and the mysterious burning mansion. "I think it sounds a bit like you let your emotions get in the way of your work. If I might speak candidly, as your senior agent, you've got to get a grip on that."

"You really think so?" he asked with a sneer.

"Absolutely. Worse than being unchristian, taking a life out of emotion is unprofessional. I've had my share of bloopers—we all have. . . . And look, if someone really deserves it, that's another story—but speaking from long experience, you can't

serve God if you decide to knock off every Tom, Dick, or Harry
you don't like the looks of. Even if those are your orders. What
kind of world would that be?"

The junior agent showed me his teeth. . . .

"I sense hostility in you," he said from deep in his throat. I
could feel him tensing, muscles vibrating and singing like a
power line in a strong wind. He was close to going for me.

"Look," I soothed him, "it doesn't have to be this way."

"It does!" he barked. "You're jealous of me! I got the baby
job and you didn't! You're old, you're washed up, you're history! I'm the new top dog!"

"Every dog has his day," I said with a smile. "Now, tell me
about the baby. And that's an order. I am still your superior
officer."

"Not for long," he said, grinning malevolently, almost panting
with desire for my blood: he was close to going for my throat.

"Tell me the story," I said with a sigh as the twin fires raged
on. "Tell me the story and then we'll figure out the ending."

✧   ✧   ✧

But before I relate the story that the junior agent told me that
night in the high desert, and before I tell you about the fires and
what happened after that, before I tell you about this baby he kept
referring to—and I promise you, I will get to the baby—before any
of that—I might do well to bring you up to speed as to what I had
done so far in New Mexico.

The retreat—run by a cadre of supposedly reformed pederast
priests—had been informed by the home office in Rome that I'd

been remanded to their care for gross dereliction of duty, i.e., for treating my sacred vows like a doormat.

The chief "ex"-pederast had objected.

"His sin is small potatoes," he complained over the phone as I stood there waiting to be admitted. "And nothing in his file indicates any interest in underage romance. He does not qualify for treatment."

"Sin is sin," I heard the Big Kielbasa say long-distance from Rome. "And until we've built a facility for more conventional sinners, he's yours. And make sure he follows his diet. Now, goodbye. This call is expensive." Click.

It was true—I had gotten fat. And I suppose, given the rules of priestly protocol, I had sinned. There was Maritza in the case of the Millionth Passenger, Birgitta in the Billionth Burger and Rose in the Trillionth Shit. Apparently the late unlamented Dispatcher—the former head of the security-intelligence division at the Vatican—had had me followed the past year or two, so there was documented proof of my transgressions. (The Dispatcher is dead now—Grade-A hell meat, if you will—I erased her myself in the sewers of Paris, dispatched her back to her proper home, the innermost circle at Dante's Disneyland . . . but that, I'm afraid, is another story.) But back to the question of sexual shenanigans. . . . Of course Church officials would prefer that we priests remain chaste, but boys will be boys, and folks are willing to accept a bit of clerical hanky-panky now and then—if only to prove that sin is universal—but for the sake of my cover story, the Big K had pronounced that, like Luciano Pavarotti doing squat thrusts wearing Kate Moss's panties, I had stretched the fabric of his patience beyond the point of no return.

I was there in New Mexico for two months before I decided to do anything about the pederasts. Why did I wait so long? Well, it seems that the high desert mountains were exerting a profound influence on me. Aside from beginning the long and arduous task of documenting my past cases in writing, I was hiking many kilometers each day—avoiding the very rare backpackers and houses—swimming in the icy Rio Grande, eating very little, rice and beans mostly, meditating continually, and having absolutely no contact with the female of the species—purifying my body and emptying my mind, scrubbing my spirit clean. Good god, I had even given up cheeseburgers! And to top it all off, I'd taken a vow of silence (initially because it seemed the best way to avoid verbal participation in the group therapy sessions, but later because it felt good, it really and truly felt good. St. Francis had been right: there is peace in silence, a clarity of thought and spirit, a sharpening of the senses that even copious amounts of red wine and the finest foie gras and burgers cannot deliver). I was, it would seem, getting in great shape. Which was good. There was serious work ahead. For a plumber of souls there is really no such thing as a vacation.

I had hoped at first, perhaps naively, that the pederasts would be similarly inspired by the setting. But when I looked at all those poor, twisted, American priests jabbering away day after day in the group treatment sessions, and after I'd digested their never-ending, never-changing confessions of lust for young flesh, their trembling, gleaming-eyed, almost-drooling recountings of spiritual and physical rapes of boys and girls too young to make choices, too small and weak to fight back, when I saw how their eyes danced and their crotches swelled, how

their Adam's apples bobbed up and down like fleshy yo-yos of
desire as they swallowed mouthful after mouthful of lust-spiced
saliva, I realized that they needed a different kind of treatment.

I killed the first one with a chicken bone. Hardly artistic—
decidedly slow and certainly not registering very high on the
compassion meter—it was, however, foolproof and very simple
to make appear an accident. I'd snatched the chicken breast
from the kitchen and brought it into Father ———'s room after
lights-out. As I sat there nibbling the chicken down to bare
bones and watching the old scalawag snore, saving the chicken
skin and a chunk of meat for later, and as I listened to the two
priests in the next room grunting away and making the bed-
springs sing in time to a Barbra Streisand CD playing *The Way We
Were*, I was struck with the righteousness of my decision. If I
didn't take action, these fellows would feign penitence, they
would weep crocodile tears of false remorse, and after a certain
amount of time, they'd be sent back out in the world to sin
again. Sent out there with a pat on the back, the slate wiped
clean, sent back out to rob some other young soul of its purity.
Call me old-fashioned, but when you get right down to cases I
just don't approve of adults screwing children. . . . So I shoved
the chicken bones down his throat, I sat on his chest, I clamped
his nose and mouth shut, feeling his gray bristles tickle my
palm, I pinned his poor, sweaty head to the pillow with an
elbow to the neck—standard moves from the opening chapter of
the Book of Termination—and yes, he gurgled, sure, he struggled and thrashed and turned pink, then purple, then blue—
but soon enough he was breathless and peaceful and pale, no
more wind in his sails, and there was one less chicken-hawk

priest in the world. And as I greased his hands and mouth with chicken skin and rubbed his teeth and gums with meat so that there would be no forensic doubt, I remembered what my first instructor back in the academy had told me: "Do it with love, my boy, terminate with extreme Christianity." So I kissed his forehead and said a prayer for his eternal soul.

✝   ✝   ✝

But as usual, I have digressed. The time is limited. The night is flying by as fast as the cars out there in the haunted Hamburger City night. I must get this story down, the story of the junior agent—what led him to New Mexico . . . and how cold, clean, pure hatred can sometimes be part of a greater plan. . . .

✝   ✝   ✝

First stop: Scotland. . . . Scotland the green. Scotland the lovely. But for our purposes, Scotland the green and lovely is outside the window. . . .

We are within the spotless, gleaming confines of the Jolson Institute for Accelerated Genetic Research. A seemingly soulless place, a spiritually cold place, a place where germs fear to tread. Disinfectants only fantasized about by Howard Hughes are used here liberally. You might well have heard about the institute—it's been in the news lately. That's where they performed the "first successful" cloning experiment, where just last year a sheep named Rosalind "donated" a cell from her mammary gland, had it injected into another (nameless) sheep's (DNA-emptied) cell and then implanted in another sheep's womb. . . . And the result was Dolly, the "first ever successfully cloned mammal."

But what you likely do not know, what no one outside the know knows, is that Dolly was not the first of her kind. No, that honor belonged to Baby, the clone of Mary.

"The symbolism is not unintentional," said Dr. Reggie McNaughton, known in scientific circles as the Clonemaster, as he addressed his staff that fateful day eighteen years ago when Baby came into the world. "The lamb is symbol of the Son of Man—gentle, kind, helpless—and she will in time grow into a sheep—and what is a sheep if not the universal symbol of Christian humility? The symbol of meekness and mildness and non-combative complacency. Yes, Baby is a potent metaphor. Once the Western World accepts a cloned sheep, then we can get on to the real business of cloning human beings."

The Clonemaster is logical, the Clonemaster is pragmatic, the Clonemaster answers to no one—or so he thinks—not to God, not to Man—he answers to Progress. But the Clonemaster is enough of a realist to know that in the early 1980s Progress is still a slave to Prejudice—the world is not yet ready for a cloned sheep, let alone a cloned human being. Progress must sit on its sizable ass and wait for the furor about *invitro* fertilization to die down. Artificial births must become as normal as runny noses for children or runny eggs for breakfast.

And as dearly as the Clonemaster desires to clone a human being, he cannot: he has yet to figure out the science. And to figure out the science he needs a critical cash transfusion—the Institute's endowment is hemorrhaging. . . .

Ah, the things we do for money, thinks the Clonemaster,

picking up the phone to call a colleague in Moscow. One minute you have a soul rich with integrity but nary a pot to piss in, the next you have a pot full of piss and a bankrupt soul.

So the Clonemaster dumps his integrity like a bad habit, he dumps the Western world and all its Judeo-Christian ethical prejudices, and he enters into negotiation with the Soviets. . . . But then along comes Gorby, and the Iron Curtain crashes. . . . And when the dust of *perestroika* has settled, all roads point to Cuba.

So it's off to Havana! Off to Havana for the Clonemaster and Baby and Mary. Fidel sends a rickety old jet for them. Baby sneezes at the reek of cigars left over from Fidel's last secret trip to Las Vegas to see Sammy Davis Junior (Ah, those were the days—Sammy still alive, singing and dancing, Fidel still smoking cigars), but all in all, it is an unremarkable journey.

In Havana, housed on a sweltering, squalid animal farm so very different from the cool, clean confines of the Jolson Institute in Scotland, Baby sweats. Her wool is hot, she develops asthma from the humidity and strain, she is lonely. The Clonemaster—the only father she has ever known—is already hard at work in his new scientific sugar daddy Fidel's ill-equipped lab, and poor little Baby has not seen her genesake Mary for days, not since the elder sheep was invited to Fidel's compound for a state banquet honoring some visiting Chinese dignitaries. . . . The Chinese ended up going back home, each with a box of cigars for Chairman Deng, each with fond memories of Havana hookers and Fidel's roast mutton. . . .

Baby grows lonely—can a little lamb cry? Oh yes, yes, when a little lamb cries it will break your heart. Baby cries and cries, she cries so long and hard and plaintively that the goats and milk-cows on the farm refuse to give milk. . . . So Fidel has her transferred to an air-conditioned apartment with a view of Havana Harbor, and there she grows strong on a diet of black-bean soup and Marxist rhetoric.

✢ ✢ ✢

Let us leave Baby alone in her penthouse listening to the radio under a poster of Che Guevara, and let us leave the Clonemaster fiddling with his beakers and chemicals in his crummy little Cuban lab, and let us jump north by northwest to cowboy country, to the high desert mountains of New Mexico, to the magnificent sprawling estate of Gill Bates.

Gill Bates—famous, brilliant Gill Bates, bachelor King Midas of the computer revolution—Gill Bates is well on his way to passing the Sultan of Brunei and becoming the richest man on the planet. But money isn't everything. . . . No, Gill Bates has a problem. . . . Gill Bates likes little boys. More than just liking little boys, Gill Bates loves little boys. In the Classical Greek sense of the phrase: Gill Bates loves little boys. (We're talking Socrates here, not Plato.)

But that is not Gill Bates' problem, loving little boys. No, Gill Bates' problem is getting enough little boys to satisfy his love. A love like Gill Bates' love knows no limit. . . .

But Gill Bates is not alone in his love for little boys. Gill Bates has friends who share his love, a whole network of friends around the world (the Man/Boy Love Network they call themselves), men of wealth and taste and power—rock stars, movie stars, corporation chiefs, bank presidents—all of whom share this love for little boys, who actually share their little boys, who pass little boys around the globe with the stealth and precision of the Brazilian national football team passing the ball.

People say that Romance is dead, thinks Gill Bates. People say that Romance is stone-cold dead, lying somewhere by the side of the road, raped and raw, clothing shredded, anus ripped wide to the prying eyes of the man in the moon and passing motorists, bleeding her last sweet drops of romantic red into a dark dirty ditch . . . but Gill Bates disagrees. Romance, he knows, is alive and well, giddy as a prepubescent boy dancing the night away. Long live Romance! thinks Gill Bates. Dance, baby, dance!

Yes, indeed, when it comes to Romance, Gill Bates is like a hunting hyena: nose to the four winds, he's always sniffing for the spoor of fresh love. Ah, the innocent doe eyes, the delicate smell of pee in the pants, the gentle curve of little-boy buttocks, the skin smooth as clarified butter, white as a porcelain toilet bowl—Gill Bates is a connoisseur. So when he reads in the *New York Times* that the Vatican is starting to crack down on the age-old tradition of priests giving little boys special personal instruction, Gill Bates has a very Romantic idea: he donates an old adobe hunting lodge on his land to the Church and specifies that it must be used as a retreat for pederast priests. The Big Kielbasa is pleased with the gift. He figures that therapy, along with prayer, will cure the pederast priests.

Wrong. The retreat is a dismal failure. A failure for the Church (not one single pederast priest actually gives up his love for little boys) and a failure for Gill Bates (not one single pederast priest actually gives up the address or telephone number of any of their little boys—they selfishly hold onto their protégés until the boys are well past the age of pubic hair—certainly not in the Christian spirit of sharing, thinks Gill Bates. . . . And to Gill Bates, Romance with a boy with pubic hair is as distasteful as eating a mushy banana). . . . And the Man/Boy Love Network—what started out as a grand organization of goodwill among men who love boys—the network is flawed as well, too much like a small-town public library: the little boys come to Gill Bates as rumpled and smudged and torn as popular bestsellers. No, Gill Bates wants what every grown tycoon who loves little boys wants: his very own lifetime supply of little boys, each and every one of them as fresh as a daisy, as innocent as a nursery rhyme.

Enter Fidel Castro. Fidel needs money. The corporation known as the Revolution is going broke. Fidel is searching for new avenues of revenue. Surely the cloning of farm animals for meat has helped, but the United States embargo is keeping the Cuban sheep—as well as Cuban goats and beef cattle—down on the farm. Fidel is beside himself with worry. He has implored the Clonemaster to find a way to clone humans—that's where the real money is. Fidel dreams of licensing the cloning technique to other nations, he dreams of cloning himself a baseball team from the best Cuban players, players who he is sure will soon be defecting to the greener pastures of the U.S.—a baseball team that can beat the Americans at their own game!—oh how Fidel loves baseball!—but so far the Clonemaster is stumped. He needs more equipment and more time.

Enter Gill Bates, always on the lookout for new Romantic entanglements.

Fidel needs money; Gill Bates has money. Gill Bates needs little boys; Fidel has an overabundance of little boys—young male street urchins running wild on the streets of Havana and clogging the jails. Fidel has the little boys; Gill Bates has the big money. A marriage made in a moral vacuum.

So Fidel trades Gill Bates little Cuban boys for lots of American money. The arrangement works—oh sure, some of the boys have been tampered with prior to delivery (Gill Bates has an unerring nose for damaged goods), and these Gill Bates returns to Fidel, marked DEFECTIVE—but essentially the arrangement works . . . it works until . . . until the little boys grow into bigger boys, at which point Gill Bates ships them back to Fidel. This is the last thing Fidel wants. More hungry, criminally inclined teenagers to tax the already overtaxed Cuban economy. So Gill Bates and Fidel reach a new accommodation: Fidel gets a ton of money and computer software, Gill Bates gets the Clonemaster.

Fidel's dreams of an All-Star baseball team—a team captained by a cloned Fidel Junior—are dashed on the rocks of economic necessity. . . . And so, with a heavy heart, Fidel bids *adios* to the Clonemaster.

America. The land of air-conditioned plenty. For the Clonemaster it is paradise. No more cheap Scottish bosses. No more broke Cubans with garlicky cigar breath berating him in unintelligible Spanish. Oh, it was a sad day when he said bye-bye to Baby, now a grown sheep with a bad case of black-bean flatulence, but working for Gill Bates is the big leagues! Unlimited money, not to mention more pizza and Coca-Cola—the breakfast, lunch, and dinner of scientific champions—more pizza and Coke than a devoted genius could ever hope stuff his face with! And the security is excellent. This is the first division! No more shady, vodka-swilling Soviet spies peeking in his lab, no more clumsy Marxist graduate students messing up his experiments—no! The Clonemaster is in the belly of the capitalist beast and he feels very safe indeed. The estate has high walls, many sophisticated alarm systems, armed guards, and vicious Doberman and Rottweiler dogs roving outside. It is the perfect setting for research and development. . . . And after only two short years with Gill Bates— a blip in the calendar of scientific time—with the highest of high-tech equipment available—no expense is spared—the Clonemaster finally—drum rolls, trumpets, dancing Disney elephants wearing tutus!—the Clonemaster—like that anonymous caveman so many eons ago starting the first fire! like Newton discovering gravity and applesauce! like Einstein squeezing $E=MC^2$ out of his fevered dreamy brain or Fermi chopping the atom in half! like Archimedes and Edison and Hawking!—Reggie McNaughton finally and triumphantly breaks through the ice of failure and emerges into the radiant sunshine of Scientific Glory!!!! The Clonemaster finally clones a human being!!!!!!

And it will come as no surprise to anyone that Gill Bates's first successful human clone is . . . Gill Bates.

Yes, like any good egomaniac of unquestionable wealth and questionable taste, Gill Bates clones himself. Oh, he has high hopes for that baby, All-American, apple-pie hopes. . . . But as the infant grows into a toddler, as the toddler grows into a little boy, Gill Bates realizes with a sinking heart: he is not attracted to Gill Junior—skinny, goofy, weak-eyed, freckled as a speckled bass and far too precociously brilliant than any toddler has any right to be (by the age of three he speaks Computerese,

Legalese, and Portuguese)—there are no sparks. Gill Bates weeps. For someone who so loves himself to end up not falling in love with himself—this is bitter medicine indeed.

So Gill Bates turns his attention to what he'd intended to do all along. He begins his breeding program. He lures talent scouts away from kiddie underwear catalogs and he sends these fast-talking heavy-breathing charmers on an international search for the prettiest little boys on the planet. His emissaries become quite skilled at putting these impoverished young fellows at their ease—plying them with candy, drugs, comic books, stuffed animals, "autographed" photos of Michael Jackson (or the occasional gift of cash or computer software for their mothers), before plunging their long needles into the soft boyflesh and extracting the necessary amount of juicy DNA needed for the cloning process.

In a short period of time Gill Bates's estate in the high desert is filling up with some very cute little male babies, all incubated in the DNA-scrubbed eggs and pink peasant wombs of poor, illegal immigrant girls imported specifically for this purpose from Mexico. . . .

But in the meantime, in between time, Gill Bates, incurable Romantic that he is, indoctrinates Gill Junior into the philosophical joys of Greek love. Or to put it another way: Gill Bates is humping his clone. The lack of attraction is no impediment. No indeed. Gill Bates humps and humps and humps and humps to the point that Gill Junior is a mess, a physical and psychological mess. Sore of body, sick of spirit, Gill Bates Junior is a very haunted and twisted little genius who fakes idiocy while wandering the mansion in between humpings. Gill

Junior wanders and watches, watches and wanders, watches the Clonemaster at work, watches the pregnant Mexican women in the basement growing large and plopping out clone babies with the ease and frequency of a stable of thoroughbred mares dropping foals. Gill Junior watches, a prisoner of hate, a prisoner of love . . . a prisoner of himself, so to speak. . . .

As Father Time leapfrogs through the forest of History, as the new little clones grow to the age of ripe pluckability, as Gill Bates's fortune grows larger and larger and the world gets smaller and smaller—the wired global village predicted by everyone from Nikola Tesla to Marshall McLuhan to Timothy Leary—as the information superhighway steamrolls into the brains and living rooms of people everywhere, as the demand for Rear Windows and his other programs rockets through the roof, Gill Bates, the founder of the modern religion of Computerism (a fine replacement, he thinks, for Catholicism and Buddhism and Communism, Computerism is the ultimate Imperialism, the penultimate ism), Gill Bates becomes bored with bits and bytes. The great unwashed—as spiritually malleable as wet clay, as intellectually docile as sheep—have been subdued by the Miracle of the Ones and Zeros, imprisoned in the Cage of Technology. . . . They're under his thumb. Give them the illusion of free will, he tells the Clonemaster, and they'll eat out of your hand, they'll eat whatever shit you feed them. Yes, it seems that Gill Bates has become bored with being the Avatar of Computerism. . . . And money, after a certain stage, money just clones itself. A bit like cancer cells replicating, Gill Bates muses to himself one day as he dandles a comely, blond, five-year-old Bosnian clone on his lap—his own personal laptop clone. Left alone, money grows and grows. Bits and bytes, ones and zeros, dollars and cents—these are not the things that should be consuming the time of the world's richest man—no! Gill Bates contemplates loftier goals—his place in history, his place in the Universe. Yes, Gill Bates yearns to belong to the ages. Actually, when you get right down to it, Gill Bates yearns to own the ages. . . .

And thus it is that Gill Bates catches the culture bug.

Paintings, sculpture, original manuscripts—his mansion begins filling up with these wonders. But more than being a reader, more than being an art guy, Gill Bates is a "thing guy." He likes "things"—personal things. Before the age of "personal computers," people had "personal things."

His first purchase in the field of *memento mori* is George Washington's false teeth. His second purchase is Alexander the Great's sandals. His third purchase is Leonard Da Vinci's undershorts. . . . And on and on he goes, collecting items associated with the great leaders and thinkers of the ages—Nietzsche's pillow, Rousseau's little black address book, Hitler's last toothbrush. . . . Oh, occasionally Gill Bates gets burned—Cleopatra's napkin, guaranteed by the agent to be from her last meal shared with Mark Antony, turns out after some costly tracing to be a modern Egyptian telephone operator named Khadija's snotty handkerchief. That'll teach me to mess with females, thinks Gill Bates. But all in all, Gill Bates's plan is working with the fascist precision of a factory-fresh Rolex watch.

⁜   ⁜   ⁜

I looked at the junior agent as he bent down to the mountain spring to drink. He was on all fours, his face in the water, his neck exposed. I could hear fire engines racing to both the burning retreat and the burning mansion in the distance—too late to save anything. It would be so easy, I thought. So easy to stop his clock right here and now and get on with the next phase of the operation. . . . But I had to make certain I knew it all.

✛   ✛   ✛

The logical next step for Gill Bates was the amalgamation of the breeding program and the culture program. Two for the price of one—Gill Bates wanted his cake and he wanted to eat it too. . . .

Let us skip all the thousands of failed attempts—the thousands of hairs the Clonemaster lost to stress and strain, the thousands of puzzled head-scratchings, the thousands of frustrated ass-scratchings, the thousands of pizzas and thousands of Cokes consumed in the name of scientific enquiry, the thousands and thousands of humpings Gill Bates administered to little boy clones as thousands and thousands and thousands of millions of dollars accrue in his bank account—fifty-eight billion and counting at last count—let us skip the stringy meat and stunted potatoes and mushy bananas of failure and let us arrive forthwith at the champagne and caviar and cheeseburgers of success.

It was a hot, clear afternoon. The Clonemaster had just finished yet another pizza. He'd spent the morning fine-tuning his newest revivifying compound. . . . Perhaps, he thought, as he scraped a microscopic pinpoint of gum blood from Adolf Hitler's toothbrush, perhaps this time. . . . He placed the Viennese dental detritus carefully in the compound . . . he waited with bated breath . . . he said a little prayer to the God of Science . . . and then . . . it fizzed! It fizzed! Like a chunk of meat dropped in a hot frying pan, it fizzed! No question, it fizzed! The Clonemaster had done it! He'd succeeded where others had failed! He'd woken up sleeping DNA!

At the very moment the Clonemaster is reaching his breakthrough, Gill Bates is attempting another kind of breakthrough.

"You're an idiot, boy," says Gill Bates, as he humps his miserable miniature genetic double, attempting to break through the boy's apparent stupidity. "You had so much promise, so much brilliance, but like Mozart all your best ideas came before your second set of teeth, and now your rosy gates are getting too large for my loving."

Gill Junior grits his second set of teeth and says nothing, but his brain is seething with hate.

"I'll tell you what, moron," says Gill Senior, sweating, out of breath. "When you reach puberty, I'm going to plant your ass in the backyard. That's right. At the first sign of a pubic hair, you're dead meat pushing up daisies. And then we'll try again. I'm gonna keep on cloning you until I get it right. Until I love you and you love me."

Gill Junior absorbs this fresh load of hate . . . and a seed of hope is planted in his fertile brain.

"Mr. Bates!" screams the Clonemaster, interrupting Gill Senior in mid-hump. "Mr. Bates! I've done it!"

So while Gill Bates Senior celebrates with the Clonemaster (yet more pizza and Coke), Gill Junior raids the Mexican mothers' drug cabinet and starts on a program of female hormones. Puberty, he thinks, I will deny thee. . . .

So as the years march by, one after another like an army of ants goose-stepping toward Bethlehem, as Gill Bates and the Clonemaster continue with the great work of replicating the foremost thinkers and leaders of world history (George Washington's false teeth are scraped and a crust of two-hundred-year-old dried saliva, rich in DNA, is placed in the revivifying compound—fizz; a pubic hair tweezed from Leonardo's undershorts, chock-full of Italianate genius—fizz; Rousseau's little black address book yields a blackened fingernail clipping—fizz; Alexander the Great's sandal produces some DNA-ripe sweat— fizz; some DNA from the left wisdom tooth of Peking Man (oh, Gill Bates could have bought a chunk of Lucy Leakey but he learned his lesson about girls with Cleopatra)—fizz; and on and on, fizzcetera fizzcetera), and while the original batch of pretty-boy clones reach the age of pubic hair and are planted in the backyard, Gill Junior remains as smooth and youthful as a baby seal, as bitter and lethal as arsenic, as brilliant and twisted as . . . Gill Bates. He wanders the mansion and watches. . . . He hacks into Gill Senior's personal files and learns with horror the scope and awful magnitude of Gill Bates's master plan, and as he absorbs his humpings, he formulates a plan of revenge. The hope for revenge is the only thing that helps him through the long, long nights as he listens to Gill Bates hopping from bed to bed, humping innocence in his zoo of historical greatness.

✞   ✞   ✞

"Listen," I said to the junior agent. "I'm fairly sure where this is going."

"Oh," he said, smiling, "I very much doubt it."

"May I hazard a guess?" I asked.

"Go ahead," he said with a weary sigh. "You'll never figure it out."

"It's worth a try. . . ." I said. "Gill Bates calls the Vatican."

The junior agent nodded, surprised.

"Yes, that's true."

✢ ✢ ✢

The Big K takes the call personally—after all, Gill Bates is by now the richest man on the planet, three times as rich as the Mormons or the nation of India, and as such he deserves a personal telephone audience. Plus, he's been generous to the Church—the Big K remembers the gift of the retreat. But when Gill Bates inquires about the availability of certain Church treasures, the Big K is insulted, very insulted. He hangs up the phone. But later, in the still of the night, alone with his torments, he decides to take Gill Bates up on his proposal.

✢ ✢ ✢

"He needed the money," I said. "The Church was falling on hard times."

The junior agent nodded. "Or so he claimed."

"So the Big K sold something to Gill Bates . . . something innocuous . . . like . . ."

"The Spear of Longinus," said the junior agent. "The spear the Roman soldiers used on Golgotha. Not so innocuous."

"Please," I said. "That old spear that was sitting in the

Vatican basement all those years gathering dust? If it was real, they would have it in a museum."

"Okay," said the junior agent. "You've got me there. The spear was a phony. But Gill Bates only found out later."

"Have you ever heard the saying, 'in for a dime in for a dollar?' It means, once you're hooked—like the Big K was hooked—you ain't swimming away. Gill Bates dangled more goodies and demanded something else, yes?"

"Yes," said the junior agent sadly

"And he got it, yes?"

"Yes."

"And he scraped the DNA from it, yes?"

"Yes."

"And this item . . ." I said, "this item was very near and dear to the heart of the Church, yes?"

"Yes."

"Not a phony, either, not like that dud spear. Not this time. True?"

"True." The junior agent was numb and dumb, as people often are when smacked in the face by the heavy hand of truth.

"If I said, my boy, that this item the Big K sold Gill Bates was the Shroud of Turin, rich with the blood of the Lamb, the original butchered Lamb, would you deny it?"

"No," said the junior agent with a huge exhalation of breath, a sigh for the ages. "You're right. The Big K sold Gill Bates the Shroud. He replaced it with a copy, but Gill Bates got the real thing."

"And so it came to pass," I said, "it came to pass, in the fullness of rotten history, that Gill Bates cloned the Son of Man."

"Yes," whispered the junior agent.

"And that," I said, "that is where you come in."

✠   ✠   ✠

Father Alonzo was a small, handsome fellow—one of the rising young stars in the security-intelligence division. Suave, with brown eyes behind dark glasses, a pale, pale skin, and a bold, prominent, Spaghetti-Western-star chin, he had the look of a glamorous cocaine trafficker or Mexican television soap-opera heartthrob.

A woman walking down the aisle on the airplane flying to New Mexico would take note of the dark glasses and the white cane with the red tip, she would perhaps stop to pat the German shepherd dog lying quietly at his feet—no cage in the cold cargo hold for this dog—and she would cluck sadly at the waste of a handsome man: the waste being twofold—one he is blind, two he is a priest. But a woman raised in the Faith would rejoice. He's perfect, she'd think. As a priest he is sensitive to my emotional needs and undoubtedly horny as an unmarried goat, and as a blind man he won't give a holy fuck what I look like in the morning . . . as long as I brush my teeth and wash under my arms. . . .

But Father Alonzo is impervious to the charms of women—he is that very common creature of the modern Church: a pederast priest. And Father Alonzo is not blind—he has twenty-twenty vision—the blindness is just part of his cover; and once the mission is complete, he and his loyal canine companion will walk across the desert and blend in with the other pederast priests at the retreat.

✣   ✣   ✣

"So," I went on. "When you arrived at the mansion, there is Gill Bates in all his nerdy glory, Gill Bates and someone you recognized. . . ." I paused, fishing for a name. I was sure Gill Bates had a partner. . . .

"After all," I prodded him, "the Shroud of Turin doesn't get delivered in the morning mail. There had to be a messenger."

"That is true," said the junior agent. "It was Sister Belinda."

Ah so, I said to myself, *a la* Charlie Chan, Sister Belinda. . . . A true knockout, originally from Brazil, with long blonde hair, a smooth *café crème* skin and the glorious eye-poking breasts of a Viking ship ornament or a California porn star. I remembered back to our hopeless attempt at love in the agent's sauna some years ago. She'd been cold as ice despite the Saharan heat, and my attempt to seduce her was reduced to a puddle of sweaty failure. . . . I salivate still, though, just thinking of her—the dramatic curves, the full, cushioned lips, the golden pubic hair shaved into a delicate heretical cross. . . . She was, without doubt, the best-looking nun ever recruited into the security-intelligence division. Sister Belinda made Marilyn Monroe look like Margaret Thatcher without makeup.

"Not your fault, Father," she'd said to me that long ago day in the sauna as my passion visibly wilted. "I'm afraid that I don't care for men, I'm just not built that way. . . ."

But despite my failure, I followed her career with interest. She was good, very good. Good at seduction, good at termination—a credit to her Faith. Which was why, a few years later, when the word got out that she'd quit the service, I'd been very surprised.

Perhaps, I figured, she's fallen in love, fallen in love with another woman, and maybe they're setting up housekeeping. . . . And then a most curious report filtered over the grapevine. . . . A priest visiting Chicago had spotted her lap-dancing in a Cicero, Illinois, strip club, and I thought: how ironic, Sister Belinda is supporting her lady lover by dancing erotically for men. . . .

But I'd been wrong, as the junior agent explained. Sister Belinda's reasons for exiting the service were much more complicated and much less innocent than mere Sapphic synchronicity.

The Big K had sent Sister Belinda to New Mexico on his private jet, and after she delivered the Shroud, when Gill Bates gave her the royal tour of his mansion and she saw the cloning labs and she saw the zoo of historical greatness, she was very impressed. And then Gill Bates proudly let her in on what it was she had delivered—the Shroud of Turin—and they both had an idea. . . . So that very same day she called Rome and gave notice to the Big Kielbasa. Sure, she loved the Church, she told him, but she also had ambitions of her own, ambitions of a worldly nature.

"I want very much to be a movie star," she told the Big K. "And Gill Bates is just the fellow to make my dreams come true."

And to herself she thought: Gill Bates is perfect—rich enough to buy a movie studio and completely uninterested in my booty. I'll marry him, then I'll have a baby—a very special baby—the Baby of Babies!—and then I'll become a movie star and no one will ever wonder about my sexuality because I'll have a baby! I'll have all the lovers I want and so will Gill Bates, and no one will ever know! The baby will be our beard!

The Big K accepted her resignation with resignation—he

figured she'd been seduced by wealth—but he asked her to complete one last assignment. She accepted. After all, without the Church, she'd be back on the farm in Brazil where she grew up, which wouldn't be so bad, but it wasn't any mansion in New Mexico, it wasn't Gill Bates, it wasn't being the mother of the Son of Man. . . . So off she went to Cicero, Illinois, and with her healthy farm-girl looks she had no problem getting a job as an exotic dancer.

✢   ✢   ✢

"Now, listen," I said to the junior agent. "You see I've figured most of it out. Don't hold out on me. If I'm to fix things, you must tell me the truth."

"The truth?" the junior agent laughed. "You can't handle the truth."

"Go ahead," I said. "Try me."

"Very well," said the junior agent. "Prior to coming to America, I was invited to the Big Kielbasa's bedroom. The first time I'd ever been there. I really felt very honored."

"I'll bet you did," I said. "That's the way he works."

✢   ✢   ✢

The Big K popped a video into the VCR, and the TV screen fizzed to life.

"Regard, my son," he said to the junior agent. "The Salvation of Rome."

The video was clear, in color, the setting tropical, palm trees outside the windows, blue water shimmering in the distance. The room was large. NBA basketball posters on the walls. Five nuns sat there holding five babies. Five white nuns, five black babies.

"Guatemala," said the Big K.

"Correct me if I'm wrong," said the junior agent. "But those nuns seem . . . well, they all appear to have a special glow, almost as if. . . ."

"Yes," the Big K said. "The nuns are the mothers of the babies."

"But—"

"You see," the Big K sighed, "as we enter the new millennium, we can no longer rely solely on the generous personal offerings of the faithful, nor on our old investments. I have even liquidated the tobacco stocks. . . . In twenty years the Church will be flat broke. The future of the global economy, my son, is communications, information, and entertainment."

"Entertainment?" The junior agent was puzzled.

"Showbiz, my boy. Those five little black babies are the financial bedrock of the Church's future."

The junior agent was confused, very confused. The Big K tried to clarify things.

"Do the names Michael Jordan, Walt Frazier, Wilt Chamberlain, Bill Russell, and Doctor J mean anything to you?"

The junior agent shook his head.

"American basketball players," the Big K explained. "The greatest. All of them Hall of Fame players."

"Sir," the junior agent said, groping to make sense. "What is the connection between the babies and the men you mentioned? Are they the ballplayer's illegitimate children put up for adoption? Or perhaps the sisters are former basketball groupies who found the Lord and took vows after they were already large with child?"

"Ah, my son," the Big K said with a heavy sigh. "If only it were that simple. This is a situation that defies all of the old definitions of legitimacy and illegitimacy. . . . "

The junior agent waited. Like all of us agents, he'd been trained to wait, to wait and listen, and if the Big K needed to get something off his chest—albcit even a demented Alzheimer's fantasy—the junior agent could wait, he could wait till they opened a hockey rink in hell, if need be.

"You see . . ." the Big K went on, "the babies are the ballplayers' clones."

The junior agent wanted to laugh. He wanted to tip his head back and roar with laughter.

"Go ahead," said Big Kielbasa. "Laugh."

The junior agent looked deep into the boss's eyes, searching for a lie, sniffing the air for the earnest stink of untruth, but the only thing he could smell was the sour old-man musk of incontinence and flaking skin. . . .

"You're serious," said the junior agent.

The Big K nodded, sadly.

"The technology exists, and I made a decision, a difficult decision, to get involved. . . . I posted Sister Belinda in a place, a club for indecent dancing outside of Chicago—a place frequented by basketball players, players both current and retired, and with her God-given gifts she had no problem isolating these lonely, talented, libidinous men and extracting the necessary DNA from their bodies. It took her two weeks to get it all.

The computer fellow Gill Bates provided the DNA-free eggs and the cloning technique, and after the NBA, DNA was injected into the eggs in his New Mexico lab, the eggs were flown to Guatemala and implanted in the nuns, who are all, by the way, good Italian girls. . . ."

"You mean. . . . ?" The junior agent's eyes opened wide.

"That's right," the Big K said with a nod. "Virgin births."

The junior agent paused, thinking: it's time to convene the College of Cardinals and impeach his crazy ass. . . .

"What I meant to say, Your Holiness, with all due respect, is that I'm not sure the ends justify the means."

"Desperate times require desperate measures." The Big K sighed. "This is Darwin Country, my boy, survival of the fittest. We are trying to save the Church. Perhaps the NBA clones started out as unholy, but now—baptized—they are, as our Hebraic brethren might say, kosher. Innocent souls, despite the complex manner of their births. And we have ten more being born in the next two weeks. And lest you think I'm gambling the future of our august organization on a bunch of babies, let me also tell you that Mr. Bates provided us six billion dollars in gold, a bountiful stock offering, and free Rear Windows 95 for all Church computers worldwide."

"And what," asked the junior agent, "did you give him in return?"

The Big K laughed and laughed, he laughed until he had to wipe a tear from his eye.

"The first part of the deal," he said, swallowing a final giggle, "was that I agreed to issue a papal bull recognizing clones as having eternal souls."

"Seems like a good deal for us," the junior agent said. "If the faithful approve."

"A good deal, my son, because I'll never make that announcement."

"A page straight out of Machiavelli and Al Capone," said the junior agent. "The old-fashioned double-cross."

"Call it what you like," said the Big Kielbasa with a sneer. "I call it a sound business decision. The faithful will never approve of clones. Never. And frankly, on a purely philosophical level, I don't either."

The little babies on the video went "goo-goo ga-ga." The white nuns suckled the infants' hungry little mouths with their basketball-sized breasts. The babies' eyes grazed the wall posters of their illustrious progenitors—and the junior agent saw it all. Or at least he thought he did.

"And what will you call your NBA franchise?"

The Big Kielbasa smiled.

"The Papal Bulls, of course. Can you imagine them in their uniforms—of course they'll all be priests—they'll be the greatest moneymakers and the most fabulous recruiters the Church has ever known! And the TV contract and merchandising windfall will be glorious! I might not live to see them play, but I'll be rooting for them from up in Heaven."

Or somewhere else, the junior agent thought to himself.

"But what if the ballplayers are as interested in . . . secular pleasures as their . . . as their, umm, fathers?"

"Who cares? Sin is the human condition. Slam-dunking a basketball is divine."

"So what," said the junior agent, "was the second part of your deal with the computer fellow?"

The Big Kielbasa sighed.

"In return for the NBA DNA and cash, I gave Gill Bates the Shroud of Turin. . . ."

"You did what?" The junior agent was shocked.

"I gave him the burial shroud of our Lord and I want it back. This is your mission. If you can't get it back, you must destroy it."

"I'll get it."

"It's not that simple. You see, Gill Bates has . . . well, he's married Sister Belinda . . . and it seems that she became pregnant and . . . and now he has asked me to send somebody, a priest . . . he wants the baby to be baptized. . . ."

"Let me get this straight," the junior agent bored in on the old man. "Shroud of Turin + cloning technique + pregnancy = baby. . . . Are you trying to tell me that Gill Bates cloned . . . ?"

"No names!" ordered the Big K.

"And you want . . ."

"I want my shroud back."

"That's it?"

The Big Kielbasa fixed the junior agent with hard, sure eyes.

"Don't be ridiculous. That's just the tip of the iceberg. I want you to go to New Mexico, my son, and I want you to terminate Gill Bates. I want you to terminate Belinda Bates. I want you to terminate anyone and everyone connected with Gill Bates and the cloning program. I want you to destroy all records of my ballplayers and all records of the cloning technique and then I want you and your partner to take the shroud and walk across the valley to the retreat for pederasts and from there you will return to Rome."

"And the baby?"

The Big K stared at the junior agent.

"Do I have to spell it out for you?"

"I'm afraid you do."

The Big Kielbasa sighed. "Terminate the baby," he said. "Terminate with extreme Christianity."

✢   ✢   ✢

When Father Alonzo and Max the German shepherd dog arrive at the mansion, supposedly to baptize the baby, Gill and Belinda Bates greet the blind priest enthusiastically.

"Welcome," says Gill Bates. "And if you'll excuse me, a young Asian lad is waiting for me in my study. He needs extra help learning the Rear Windows program."

So as Gill Bates heads off to tutor the pinheaded Peking Boy in the finer points of Computerese, the former Sister Belinda kneels down to pat the dog, smoothing the fur on his long canine face and planting a sweet, loud kiss on his cold, wet nose.

"Father Alonzo," she says. "May I show you and this beautiful doggy fellow here the dormitory."

The dormitory—what Gill Bates Junior thinks of as the zoo of historical greatness—is situated at the back of the mansion, the perimeter of which is guarded by roving patrols of Rottweilers and Dobermans. The windows are all barred. The security guards are in the basement, as they often are, having a midnight snack with the Mexican mothers.

As they enter the nursery, Father Alonzo's nose quivers at the smell of so much young, male innocence—the delicate odors of boy sweat and boy pee and boy dreams. The boys sleep peacefully. All except one. The eldest child in the room is awake. He is thin and goofy, he wears thick glasses. He sits in front of a computer terminal. . . .

"Hello, Gill Junior," says the former Sister Belinda in Portuguese. But Gill Junior doesn't answer. The former Sister Belinda points at her head and makes the universal circular cuckoo sign. But then she realizes that Father Alonzo cannot see, or so she thinks, and she laughs at herself.

"Now that," says Belinda, "over there is little George Washington. And that is young Fred Nietzsche—and can you imagine what wonderful miracles these children will be able to accomplish with a modern computer education? And that. . . . Oh, I'm sorry, Alonzo, you can't see them. But take my word, they look exactly like their genetic sources. . . ."

But Father Alonzo can see them, boy, oh boy, can he see ever see them—he sees them so well he has to wipe a string of drool off his chin.

At first Father Alonzo is disturbed by the clones, but later, deep in the night, as he tosses and turns in his bed, he realizes the morality issue is not so cut and dried. . . . If these young clones exist—regardless of how they came to be—if they exist, then they exist, and everything that exists comes from God, including the bad stuff, and if these boys exist, then they are souls, and souls need to baptized, and he is a priest, and once the souls are baptized, then what will stop them from sinning? And if they sin, then they'll need to be absolved of their sins, and didn't that little Adolf Hitler Junior have a lovely little well-formed rear end. . . ?

As the days pass, Father Alonzo is in such a fog of clerical lust (between baptizing all the little boys, including the former Sister Belinda's own baby (what a darling, peaceful little child, he thinks, dark like his mother), and the personal religious instruction he is giving the older boys (in one short week Father Alonzo sinned with (and forgave the sins of) George Washington Junior, Charles Darwin Junior (cloned from a piece of bone purchased from a London grave-robbing firm), Alexander the Great Junior, little Freddie Nietzsche, and blue-eyed Adolf Hitler Junior), he is in such a pederast paradise that he doesn't notice his canine companion sneaking off at night to visit the former Sister Belinda.

✝   ✝   ✝

"So you are not the storybook loyal dog," I said. "Going off to visit Belinda."

"You've read too much Jack London, my friend," said the junior agent Max, the blaze of white fur on his chest bright in the reflected firelight. "And undoubtedly, since we can communicate, too much St. Francis. When the Big Kielbasa had me up in his room and told me about the NBA clones and all, and when he showed me that damned pamphlet that taught you fellows how to talk to us so-called animals, I should have just grabbed it and chewed it to shreds, saved us all a lot of trouble. But to answer your question: no, I'm not the storybook loyal dog. I hated Father Alonzo. After three years of faking a fawning love for that idiot pederast priest, I was sick of the bastard. . . . 'Max, fetch my slippers, Max, fetch me a box of condoms.' Max this, Max that. Kicking me all the time and humping those poor little boys. He was a terrible agent. That's why the Big K gave the wet work to me."

"Alonzo knew nothing of your assignment? He was not your master?"

"He was there to baptize and provide cover. Only technically was he my master, but in matters of the heart, Belinda. . . ." The junior agent looked up at me with a wolfish grin, and his eyes went soft and dreamy. "Belinda was my mistress."

You see, I had been wrong about Belinda that time in the sauna. She was not a lesbian. She was just a simple Brazilian country girl who'd grown up on a farm and was fond of dogs. Fond? Very fond. Without getting into the details, it seemed that Sister Belinda was one of those rare people who enjoy the intimate company of animals. . . . And by the time Alonzo and Max showed up, she'd exhausted the supply of Rottweilers and Dobermans and was looking for a new lover.

"We had been making love," said the dog, "making love on a daily basis ever since I arrived. Usually when a girl grows up on a farm, she grows out of her love of animals, though of course there are stories in the animal kingdom about men and sheep being very happily married for life. . . . I had hoped that such might be my fate, that I might be able to save her from the Big K's edict. But you see, she didn't know—she couldn't know that I understood her when she talked—after all, she'd never read the St. Francis Codex—and that first night in bed, when she started rambling on about her movie career—how Gill Bates had bought a piece of a movie studio—about how she and Gill Bates would take me and the baby to Los Angeles—how the baby would be our beard—and with the baby as our beard, no one in Hollywood would know that she loved dogs or that Gill Bates loved little boys, and she would get me parts in films too, and I'd be the next Rin Tin Tin, and we could be lovers and movie stars, and life would be wonderful and eventually, after we retired from pictures, when the baby was grown, we'd rule the world. . . . When she told me all that, I knew she had to be silenced. . . ."

"So you terminated her," I said.

"Absolutely, Father. That was the assignment. I took no pleasure in it, after all, she was quite beautiful, but I did it. As insane as the Big Kielbasa's plan was, I had to follow it. I did everything he asked me to."

"You terminated everyone, including Father Alonzo?"

"That one was easy—I hated him. If you humans knew just how we felt about you, you would not keep dogs as pets. We'd be behind bars, like lions. Of course I killed him."

"That was when?"

"It was . . . it was tonight, last night, just hours ago. . . . I saw your fire and knew that it was time to do what I'd been sent to do. The local fire department would be busy at the retreat. . . ."

"And so you terminated the baby."

"Everyone is dead."

"Ah, Max," I said. "In the final analysis, you are loyal. Loyal to the Big Kielbasa."

The junior agent was silent, but I could feel him starting to get tense again.

"Calm down," I said. "I'm just trying to figure out why the Big K sent me here."

"To kill me, of course. To debrief me and kill me and bring the shroud back to Rome. Why do you think he made you read

the St. Francis Codex? So that we could have a little talk, you
and I, so you'd flush a confession out of me, and if I hadn't
done the job right, then you'd be right here to knock me off
and clean up after me."

He was on the money, of course. The Big K had used me.
He'd urged me to follow the St. Francis Codex, to take my
time with the pederasts, to hang around long enough to take
the junior agent's confession. . . . I'd been sent in as backup,
as an insurance policy. . . . But still, there was something
rotten in the state of New Mexico. The story felt wrong.

"Look," I said, soothing him. "I'm not going to kill you.
Why should I? You did your job. You killed the baby, and I
imagine, since Father Alonzo is not with you to be your porter,
you destroyed the shroud. Just tell me what really happened.
I've been at this game a long time and I know when people are
lying and when they're telling the truth, and you, my canine
friend, are walking a razor blade between the two. Watch out for
your feet, son, and tell me the truth."

"The baby is dead."

"I believe you."

"They're all dead."

"I don't doubt it. Just tell me how it happened. Tell it fast
and tell it clean."

"Okay," he said. "It was like this. . . . I was in the dormitory
yesterday, and Gill Bates Junior—you know, the twisted
clone?—he was changing his clothes. I heard him gasp. He'd
gotten his first pubic hair. That was his sign. . . . I knew it
because I'd heard him talking one day to his buddy, the little
Hitler boy. If Gill Bates found out that he'd sprouted, he'd

have him planted in the backyard. . . . By the way, if you're interested in anthropology, the backyard is quite fascinating."

"You didn't. . . ."

"No but the Rottweilers and Dobermans dug up clone bones and—"

"Get on with it."

"Okay. . . . So Gill Junior stole a gun from one of the guards. It was really very simple. Gill Bates Senior thought him a total moron, so he had access to the whole place. I was outside at the time, strolling the perimeter with the Rottweilers and Dobermans. I smelled your fire—and then I heard a gunshot: boom! And then another gunshot: boom! We dogs ran to the windows and watched as Gill Junior walked away from Gill Senior's dead body. Gill Bates was naked. He'd been tutoring Peking Boy again, and the poor little Chinese pinhead was dead too. And then: boom! boom! in the next room—we watched him shoot the Clonemaster and Belinda as they drank wine in the living room. And then he went to the basement, and I heard muffled shots as he took care of the Mexican women and the guards, and then he gathered all the computer files together and wrapped them in the shroud and he sprayed something, some kind of accelerant, and he lit a match."

"So you didn't start the fire."

"No, it was Gill Junior. I was locked outside. I ran around back to the dormitory and I looked through the window. The mansion was burning, but the flames hadn't reached the dorm room. . . . I watched through the bars as Gill Junior took a syringe. He must have loaded it with some chemicals from the Clonemaster's lab, and he squirted it into a big container of red beverage and then he filled all the babies' formula bottles. There were even extra bottles for the older clones. And then he woke up all the clones—they hadn't heard the gunshots—and he addressed them.

"'Listen, my unholy brothers,' said the little monster. 'You know what we are. Abominations! Gill Bates created us for his amusement, to hump us and to drain our brains, and when we're too old for humping, when our days of intellectual brilliance are over, he intended to plant us in the backyard and clone us again. Again and again! He was playing God, fucking history in the ass. Is that evil or is that evil?'

"'Evil!' they shouted as one.

"'But are we evil? Are we products of Nature or Nurture? If it's Nurture—then for sure we're rotten. We didn't ask to be fucked in the ass, but it happened, and it's made us bitter and angry—damaged goods. But if it's Nature, then only some of us are bad—those of us who come from bad genes.'

"'But are the genes bad?' asked little Charlie Darwin. 'Or was it just a bad environment imprinting our genesakes? I think I'll write a thesis. Does badness carry over from one generation to the next?'

"'Does it matter?' cried Gill Junior. 'I'm bad, I'm bad, I know I'm bad. . . . It's human nature to be bad. Look at history. And you, little Adolf . . . you can't claim to be good, now, can you?'

"'What did I ever do?' cried the little blue-eyed fellow. 'I've taken Father Alonzo's instructions and I've taken Father's humpings, but I didn't turn around and do it to anyone else. I'm not evil, I'm a victim!'

"'We're all victims,' said Gill Bates Junior. 'And we're all

damned—Nature and Nurture—a double whammy. I hate but I
want to love, I'm bad but I want to be good. I'm fucked, I tell
you! We're all fucked! But I'll be damned if I'm going to fuck
the world. . . . We have to die!'

"'But our futures are so bright!' cried little Humphrey
Bogart. 'I want to make movies!'

"'And I've never even been with a woman yet!' cried little
Jean-Jacques Rousseau. "I want a woman!"

"'I cannot tell a lie,' said little Georgie Washington. 'I want
a woman too.'

"'Oh Georgie, oh J.J.—don't you get it? I killed Father, I
killed Gill Bates!'

"'But that's like killing yourself!' said the sentimental little
Rousseau boy.

"'Like killing the creator,' said young Aldous Huxley. 'Like
killing God.'

"'How can anyone kill God?' asked little Freddie Nietzsche.
'God is dead.'

"'You're all screwy,' said little Humphrey Bogart, lighting a
cigarette.

"'Shit, Gill,' said little Charlie Darwin. 'Why don't you just
take over? I mean you're Gill Bates, the new Gill Bates, the Gill
Bates that ate the old Gill Bates.'

"'Charlie, Charlie, you could have been a philosopher,' said
Gill Junior sadly, as the flames ate through the wall. 'And all
you horny bastards, think about it, by the time you're old
enough to be with a woman, I'll be planting you in the back
yard. I'm Gill Bates! Don't you get it? And you, Humphrey, do
you really think I'd let you grow up to be a movie star again?

And Adolf, do you think it's possible for you to be a good guy this time? How can you know? How can any of us know? But we have a choice, maybe the only choice we ever had. We can end the speculation, end the vain repetition. Right here, right now. These bottles, full of delicious cherry Kool-Aid and a special chemical, these bottles will obliterate the need for an answer.'

"I watched from the doorway," said the junior agent. "I watched as little Freddie Nietzsche handed out the bottles. The elder boys held the bottles destined for the babies. Each of them took a baby.

"'It's your choice,' said Gill Junior.

"'I vote we do it,' said little Leo da Vinci. 'This is a fucked-up world from what I can see on television and the Internet, and I'm not feeling very creative this go-round. My asshole hurts. Father fucked us good!'

"'No shit!' cried Gill Junior.

"'I'm not afraid!' cried little Winston Churchill. 'The only thing to fear is fear itself! But what about the babies?'

"'They come with us!' yelled Gill Junior.

"'What about the baby?' asked Alexander the Great. 'The special baby? He hasn't been screwed by Father yet.'

"'He hasn't been screwed!?' screamed Gill Junior. 'What do you call getting crucified the last time? He got screwed by the real Big Daddy, he got fucked big-time, Alex, and if you ask me, he'll get it again!'

"'I don't think so,' said little Freddie Nietzsche. 'As I keep trying to tell you guys, God is dead.'

"'I vote he gets it!' cried little Adolf. 'He's a dirty Jew!'

"'So am I,' said Little Albert Einstein. 'But everything's relative.'

"'You'll get it too, science boy!' cried little Hitler as he grabbed the special baby from his cradle, grabbed him roughly. 'You'll get it too, for fucking with atoms!'

"The flames were in the room now, licking at the walls and sweeping across the floor. It was awful. The little boys gave the babies the bottles and everyone drank and instantly fell into convulsions. At least they died before the flames got them."

The junior agent wiped a tear from his eye with his front paw. He looked at me sideways, to see how I was taking it.

"Bullshit," I said.

And that was the moment the junior agent launched himself at my throat. I dropped down, caught him by the front legs and swung him to the ground, one hand around his powerful jaws and the other holding his jerking front legs together.

"Don't try to shit the plumber of souls," I said. "Or you'll end up getting flushed."

I let go his legs and pulled my gun, pointed it at his head, then loosened my grip on his mouth. He lay there, panting hard.

"Tell me where the baby is."

"I told you," said Max. "He's dead. Kill me if you like. It won't change history."

"Where is he?" I asked. "You stink of lies."

"Dead," he said. "Even if he'd survived the mass suicide and fire, I would have had to kill him. Orders are orders."

"You always do what you're told?"

"I'm a loyal dog."

"No such thing," I said. "You told me so yourself."

"I was lying."

"Not about that. Where's the baby?"

I screwed the gun into his ear.

"Tell me the truth or I'll shoot."

And then I saw the eyes, twenty pairs of eyes gleaming in the darkness. It was the Rottweilers and the Dobermans.

"Tell him," said a Rottweiler.

"We must tell him," said a Doberman.

"Kill him!" ordered the junior agent. "Kill him!"

"No," said a Rottweiler. There's been far too much of that lately."

"Okay," said the junior agent with a sigh. "All the boys and babies drank and fell moaning, and as the best minds of every human generation started writhing on to death, I noticed that little Hitler had not drunk and he hadn't let the baby drink either. He ran to the window, broke the glass and squeezed the baby through the bars. I took Him by the neck, and while Hitler drank, I did it, I tore the baby to shreds."

"So little Hitler saved the baby only for you to kill Him?"

"Yes," said the junior agent. "May God forgive me."

"I don't believe you," I said. "You have no blood on your paws, no conviction in your bark. You're still dissembling. And buddy, that's like trying to throw a lamb chop past a wolf."

"I tell you, the baby is dead. I hated the baby. There's been so much pain, so much blood shed in His name. I hated him."

"I don't think so," I said. "Maybe you hate what's been done in His name, but you don't hate the baby. I look into your eyes and I see goodness. Goodness and light. I see love. Now tell me, where is the baby?"

"Tell him," said a Rottweiler. "Tell him. You have to tell him. He's a human."

"No!" screamed the junior agent. "Are you a slave as well as an idiot? Humans are the ones who crucified Him before! Humans are the ones who made this mess!"

And then all of a sudden, the ground we stood on became lit with a strange, glorious radiance. I looked to the sky, we all looked to the sky, and there shining bright, right above us, equidistant from the smoldering retreat and the smoldering mansion, the twin bonfires of the profanities: a star. A brand new star.

"This way," said a Doberman.

"Don't do it!" screamed the junior agent.

But they led me, the levelheaded Rottweilers and Dobermans, they led me, under the bright, shining star they led me across the dark mountain path, and as we approached a cave, I saw ten coyotes and five eagles and three wolves and one white dove, and the coyotes and wolves started to howl, and the eagles started to squawk, and the dove started to coo, and I understood them, in all their varied languages, they were saying: "NO NO NO NO NO NO NO NO!" They were trembling with hatred and fear and hostility. . . . Once false move and they'd tear me to shreds.

"I come in peace," I said, putting down my gun.

"Let him pass," said the junior agent.

They let me pass then. And there in a cave, on a bed of eagle feathers, lay the baby, sleeping.

"What happened?" I asked the junior agent. "How was He saved?"

"It was little Adolf," said the junior agent. "He held his finger over the bottle and only pretended to give suck to the baby. Then and only then did Gill Bates Junior and the other clones drink. Adolf ran to the window and he managed to squeeze the baby through the bars. I took the baby by the scruff of His neck, like a puppy. The flames were licking at Adolf's legs, but he never cried out, and before Adolf let go of the baby, he kissed His feet.

"'The road to heaven,' said the little blue-eyed boy, drinking his hemlock, 'starts with one baby step.'"

I stared at the baby. He was a beautiful baby, a beautiful brown baby, a lovely shade of Middle-Eastern brown. He was radiant with peace and joy.

I picked him up. The animals held their breath.

"What will you do?" cooed the dove.

"I'm taking him home," I said. "I'm taking him home." And we walked into the desert.

       ✢   ✢   ✢

"And how was your trip to the New World?" asked the Big Kielbasa when I got back to Rome three weeks later.

"Very interesting," I said.

"You took care of the pederasts?" he asked, between bites of a cheeseburger. There were a number of burger wrappers on the bedside table. He'd obviously been frequenting the new Quick Burger on the Via Veneto. . . . He'd put on weight.

"You know I did."

"Ah yes, the fire. . . . And did you meet Father Alonzo?"

"As a matter of fact, no," I said. "But I met a young fellow, a junior agent named Max."

"Ahh, and where is Max now?" asked the Big K.

"He's in the desert," I said. "For good."

"Poor fellow," he said. "I thought him quite capable. Very loyal."

"More than loyal," I said. "He was faithful."

"And . . . and did he tell you what he was doing there. . . ?"

"I know about the baby."

"And where is the baby now?"

"The baby . . ." I said, "I took the baby home."

"Home? Home with the Father? You mean home in Heaven?"

"Home," I said, "home is where the heart is."

"I know it couldn't have been easy," he said with a sad smile.

"As they say," I said. "Everything is relative. . . . I brought you a gift."

I gave him a package.

"This is too small to be my shroud," he said, unwrapping the paper.

I'd bought it in Los Angeles. I'd gone all the way to Los Angeles, to Chinatown in Los Angeles, to get it for him.

He opened the box.

Inside: a brand-new ping-pong paddle, the finest Chinese ping-pong paddle money can buy.

His eyes lit up.

"How thoughtful of you."

"Enjoy it," I said.

"What about the shroud?" he asked.

"Ashes. . . ." I said. "By the way, have you heard from Guatemala lately?"

"You know about my basketball team?"

"Can't keep a secret from me."

"I see. . . . Well, apparently the phone lines in Guatemala are down."

"I know."

"You know?"

"I cut the lines myself. You see, sir," I said, "after I took the baby home, I made a little trip to Guatemala. And you know, I think that facility there would be a fine place to open a new retreat for pederast priests."

The Big Kielbasa looked confused. He stood there with his shiny new ping-pong paddle, his eyebrows screwed into twin question marks.

"I have another gift," I said.

I went to the door, opened it. I took the leash from the servant and led the sheep into the room. It was an old sheep, a very old sheep. She'd been in Cuba a long long time.

"Sir, I'd like you to meet Baby. The newest member of your flock. Baby, meet the boss."

"What is the meaning of this?" asked the Big K angrily.

Baby spoke then. She rattled off an analysis of Church doctrine from a Marxist point of view.

"What does she say?" cried the Big K. "All I hear is *baaah.*"

"Well then," I said. "You'll just have to give up the cheeseburgers and meditate, take a few cold baths. . . ."

"What did you do in Guatemala? Is my team okay?"

"Baaaah!" said Baby. "I'm hungry! Give me a cheeseburger!"

I wanted to tell him. Tell him how I'd taken the babies, the basketball babies. . . .

"Baaaah!" said Baby. "Who do I have to fuck to get some food around here?"

I wanted to tell him how I'd taken the babies and their Italian nun mothers, how I'd chartered a boat and how we'd sailed for Cuba. . . .

"*Baaaaaaaaaah!* Fidel knew how to treat a *señorita!*"

I wanted to tell him, tell him how Fidel had greeted us warmly, how Fidel and I had made the deal. One sheep for fifteen players.

"The babies are fine," I said. "And in about twenty years, expect the Cubans to be very good at basketball. Though, knowing Fidel, they might just end up a team of very tall baseball players."

"*Baaaah!*" said Baby as she let loose a humongous, ripping, black-bean fart. "Power to the proletariat!"

"I don't understand what she says!"

"You see, sir," I said, "I have always admired you. And I have always been loyal, but somewhere down the line you lost your bearings. I thought you were different from your predecessors, but it turns you're the same—you put the corporate needs of the Church ahead of everything else. You sold out to Gill Bates and the Death Machine. You traded the cosmic process for the magic of science—though, who knows, maybe that's how it was meant to be. . . . Forgive me for saying this, but you need to relearn humility, sir. And Baby is just the old girl to teach you."

The Big Kielbasa's face grew red with anger.

"I'll have your balls for dinner!"

"*Baaaah!*" said Baby. "I'll have black-bean soup!"

"No," I said to the Big K. "You won't stop me. I'm walking out of here, and if I die anytime soon, or if I disappear or if I call here and I don't get to speak to Baby, my case histories will be published. I have five copies with five lawyers. I won't bother to tell you where, but know this: a publisher in Milan is very interested. He also thinks we can get a movie deal from Disney— the animal angle. The man in Milan has only read an outline but. . . ."

"This is outrageous!" cried the Big Kielbasa.

"Isn't it," I said. "But I learned everything I know from a master. Goodbye."

I headed for the door.

"But why have you forsaken me?" he cried. "I have loved you like a son!"

And I walked out then, walked out on the Big K. Baby was *baah*ing, she was *baah*ing and farting, farting and *baah*ing, and Big K just stood there, stunned, confused, beaten, fanning the foul air with his brand-new ping-pong paddle.

So I left them there and I went on to my new life. And often I think about them, the Big K and Baby, and I wonder how they're getting on. Perhaps I'll call them soon. . . . But more than anything, more than anything else, as the old stars die and the new stars burn, as the planet spins and spins and spins and as human beings play out their mad petty personal dramas in these crazy crazy times of ours, more than any- thing, more than anything else, I think about the baby, the real baby. . . .

I'm so glad I took Him home. . . .

✢   ✢   ✢

The junior agent had chosen to stay in the high desert. He and the Rottweilers and Dobermans, all good creatures, uncorrupted by their time in the penitentiary of the modern world, had decided to stay in the wild, to stay with the coyotes and the wolves and the eagles and the dove. I wish them well. They are always in my prayers.

So as the fires died down and the New Mexico firefighters searched for bodies, I took the baby and walked across the desert. We came to a road and I put my thumb out. I did not know where I was going or what I would do. I put myself at the mercy of the winds.

A truck driver stopped for us, he drove us a ways, then he hailed another truck—and that's how we traveled across the arid land. And when we reached Los Angeles, the city of lost dreams and false breasts, the city of the 99 cent burger, I walked the streets. With the baby in my arms I walked the streets. And I saw firsthand, saw with utter clarity and deep sadness, the corruption of the world. The gleaming, speeding, poisonous cars, the false, milkless, showcase breasts, the mortgaged souls void of morality, the burger shops on every corner serving death to the dead. I heard the pigeons crying, the caged dogs sighing, the rats weeping—all lamenting for a world on its last legs, a world whose innocence had been sucked dry by the Death Machine. And I was very hungry, yea, and very depressed, and the voices of the animals were ripping my brain to shreds, so I bought a bag of burgers and I ate one, hoping the voices would stop. But the voices got louder—the voices of pigeons, the voices of sparrows, the voices of stray cats and leashed dogs and scavenging rats, the voices of scurrying lizards and cockroaches and ants, all crying "Save us! Save us! Save us!" And I bought the baby some formula and I bought myself

some coffee, and I found a motel, a crumbling motel somewhere on the edge of the Hollywood Hills, and I sat there and
I wrote, I wrote, I drank coffee and I ate burgers and I wrote,
and the rabbits on the balcony humped, they humped by the
light of the syphilitic moon, and the burgers did nothing to
shut the voices out of my head, and still I didn't know what
to do, what to do with the baby, and the son rabbit cried out,
"Please, Father, please don't hump me," and the father rabbit
cried, "I cannot help it, I cannot help it, I'm so lonely so very
lonely, it makes me feel alive," and then I walked out there in
the silvery Hamburger City dawn, out onto the balcony with
the baby, and the rabbits stopped humping and they looked
with wonder upon the radiant child, the glowing baby glowing
with goodness and sweetness and understanding and truth,
and the father disengaged from the son and they bowed their
heads and oh, I doubt that father will be humping his son
anytime soon.

And so I dressed in my collar and I took the baby and I went
down to the street and I called a taxi and the taxi came and it
drove us to the bus station and the cabdriver smiled at the baby
and he threw his pack of cigarettes out the window and said, "I
quit, no charge for the ride." And we took the bus, the bus to
Tijuana. Me and the baby and forty poor Mexicans going
home, and they crossed themselves and asked my blessing and
they looked at the baby, the dark, lovely, radiant baby and they
smiled. . . .

And in Mexico we walked, and everywhere we walked the
people crossed themselves. And as we walked by an American
factory, the smoke pouring hellishly into the air, we passed

poor mothers holding babies, babies with twisted limbs and huge deformed heads, and the fields in that town were fallow and gray and dead, caked with the sad crud of industrial waste, and the mothers with twisted babies were picking through mounds of garbage, hills of plastic and metal, the twisted shit of the twisted factory of the twisted nation of the twisted planet, and as we walked, the ground beneath us quaked and split, and fresh earth erupted from deep below the gray, dead, wasteland ash . . . and trees sprouted and the poor babies' limbs untwisted and their heads shrank and their features smoothed and the mothers fell to their knees weeping tears of thanks into the new fresh earth as orange trees and rose bushes and lime trees and fig trees and lush green bloomery greened the earth, as the sick land healed, as it healed, as it miraculously healed, . . .

And we walked south and south and south, we walked south until I heard a little voice inside that told me to go to the mountains, go to the mountains, so I took the mountain path and we walked and never once did the baby cry and my feet should have been weary and my arms should have been weary and my brain and heart and spirit should have been weary, but they were not, and in the sunset radiant sunset I saw a star, a very special star, the very same bright shining star I'd seen that night in the New Mexico mountains and I followed that star as the night grew black as other stars twinkled and I followed that star that new bright star, and finally as the rosebud dawn climbed over the rim of the Earth, we came upon a small poor shanty of a home, and a man and a woman dressed in the ancient rags of Poverty and Hope stood there, the woman washing her hands, and the man said welcome and he put down his hammer and I saw in the dawn that he had built a cradle, and the woman took the baby, she stroked His face, and the man smiled and the woman smiled and the baby smiled. . . .

The baby was home.